AF260947

Haunting Mysteries is Jason's second greatest accomplishment. He is looking forward to the future to do it all over again with more chilling stories.

Jason T. Goudie

HAUNTING MYSTERIES

AUSTIN MACAULEY PUBLISHERS™

LONDON • CAMBRIDGE • NEW YORK • SHARJAH

Copyright © Jason T. Goudie (2021)

All rights reserved. No part of this publication may be reproduced, distributed, or transmitted in any form or by any means, including photocopying, recording, or other electronic or mechanical methods, without the prior written permission of the publisher, except in the case of brief quotations embodied in critical reviews and certain other noncommercial uses permitted by copyright law. For permission requests, write to the publisher.

Any person who commits any unauthorized act in relation to this publication may be liable to criminal prosecution and civil claims for damages.

This is a work of fiction. Names, characters, businesses, places, events, locales, and incidents are either the products of the author's imagination or used in a fictitious manner. Any resemblance to actual persons, living or dead, or actual events is purely coincidental.

Ordering Information
Quantity sales: Special discounts are available on quantity purchases by corporations, associations, and others. For details, contact the publisher at the address below.

Publisher's Cataloging-in-Publication data
Goudie, Jason T.
Haunting Mysteries

ISBN 9781645754329 (Paperback)
ISBN 9781645754312 (Hardback)
ISBN 9781645754336 (ePub e-book)

Library of Congress Control Number: 2020919583

www.austinmacauley.com/us

First Published (2021)
Austin Macauley Publishers LLC
40 Wall Street, 33rd Floor, Suite 3302
New York, NY 10005
USA

mail-usa@austinmacauley.com
+1 (646) 5125767

I would like to acknowledge the hard work and dedication of Austin Macauley Publishers. I thank you so much for all you have done.

Chapter One
Eerie Awakening

In the middle of a chilly autumn night, Wayne Saunders stirred out of a sound sleep. Shivering, he voiced a grunt of surprise, coiled himself in the blankets, and tried to relax.

The blankets Wayne used this time of year were fleece and normally kept him warm. Even through the first few weeks of winter but without a little help from the heater, he would not have been so comfortable all the time. Nevertheless, that night felt different to him.

As the seconds turned into minutes, Wayne realized his attempt at comfort was futile. The cold temperature continued to nag at him. He glanced at the time. It was one o'clock. Fed-up, he threw off the covers and sat up. An abrupt gasp escaped his lips. It seemed as if dozens of ice cubes pressed against his entire body. He wrapped his arms around himself as his teeth chattered. It quickly reminded him of an early winter day when he was twelve.

He and seven of his friends – four male and three female – were at a park near the lake. It was one of their more frequent haunts. They were sitting at a picnic table playing a game called Truth or Dare. When it was Wayne's turn, they dared him to jump in the lake. There was no snow on the ground yet but it was cold that day. It was only six degrees below zero. With the wind, it felt more like minus fifteen. Nevertheless, he ran over to the lake and jumped in, but as he jumped, he remembered shouts of disapproval and shock. The water was freezing. It stung his body like a dozen knives. Wayne made it out almost on adrenalin alone, but the damage was done. He crumpled to the ground and shivered uncontrollably. His concerned friends rushed over to his side and threw their jackets on his to try to help raise his temperature. Luckily, two adults were nearby and saw what happened. One of the men rushed over while the other ran to a nearby house and called for help. The last thing Wayne remembered were the faint sounds of the sirens as they approached.

Curious, he looked at his bedroom window thinking he subconsciously opened it sometime earlier but the curtains were not moving. He then looked over to the thermostat beside the door. From where he sat, it was barely visible. He stood, walked over to it and turned on the light. His eyes widened. It was still set to seventy-five degrees, which was what he set it at that morning before he left for work. He kept the light on and turned away from the temperature gauge. His breath appeared from out of nowhere. For a brief moment, he watched in awe.

Slowly, he turned to look at his dresser mirror. At the angle Wayne stood, his reflection should have stared back at him. It did not. The mirror appeared fogged. He tilted his head in confusion and walked up to it. He slid his index finger across the glass and a clear line emerged.

Wayne turned away from the mirror and shook his head as if desperate to wake himself from a nightmare. He closed his eyes as he faced the mirror once more. Then slowly he opened them. What he saw next instilled him with fear. The words *'I am waiting, Wayne'* were written. He stared at the words in disbelief as he backed away. They were a horrifying reminder of what happened only two nights ago at 15 Birchcroft Drive. Not thinking of what was behind him, he tripped as his left heel tagged the foot of the bed.

On the floor, beside himself from what he had just witnessed, he looked at his closet. Wayne got to his feet and opened his closet door. Quickly, he dressed and made sure he had everything he needed then charged out the door. Wayne walked hastily down the hallway, passed the kitchen to his apartment door. He reached for the doorknob but hesitated. He glanced at the living-room window and wondered what the weather was like. Wasting no more time, Wayne rushed over to the window and flung open the curtains. All he saw was a thick fog. It was so dense that he was not able to see through it at all. He went to his hall closet, grabbed a three-season jacket, and went out the door to the elevator. His mind raced.

What the hell is going on, and why is this happening to me? When I went into that house two nights ago, that voice – who or whatever it was – said it would haunt me if I did not help it. At first, I thought it was some whacko playing a sick joke but this…this definitely proves otherwise.

Finally, the elevator door opened. Wayne stepped inside and repeatedly pressed the ground floor button. The seconds seemed like minutes as the door slowly closed. Vivid memories of what he saw and felt in that house plagued him as the elevator descended.

I thought shit like that happened only in movies, Wayne thought as he shook his head.

Arriving at the ground floor, the elevator stopped but the door did not open. Wayne stared at it impatiently as he waited.

Come on, dammit. Open up! Wayne thought.

The door remained closed.

Wayne wondered at the apparent irony of his situation. He was trying to escape a living nightmare while the elevator, thus far, succeeded in keeping him in it. He flung his arms in the air. The last thing he wanted to do was spend the night trapped in an elevator.

Remaining calm, he studied the control panel and quickly found the open button. He pressed his finger against it but nothing happened. Then he remembered the alarm button and held his finger on it for a few seconds, hoping someone would hear it. The bell rang throughout the building.

Nothing else I can do now but wait, he thought.

Wayne moved to the back of the elevator and sat down. As the minutes ticked by, his patience began to wear thin. He stood up and started pacing like an animal waiting for the right moment to escape its cage.

The lights blinked into darkness. Wayne halted his movements and stood still. He looked directly at the base of the door. There was not one hint of light. It made him wonder if the power was out in the whole building.

Great, he thought. *Now what am I going to do?*

Normally, Wayne was not afraid of the dark, but the past two days were slowly beginning to change that. Suddenly, he thought of the compartment that housed the emergency telephone. Just as he lifted his hands to feel around for it, the hair on the back of his neck rose, and something that felt like icy cold fingers touched his eyes. He gasped in panic and stiffened. Though he knew he was alone in the elevator, he sensed someone was behind him. He held his breath, as if waiting for a voice to say, 'guess who?'

"All right," Wayne said into the darkness. "You win. I will solve your mystery. Just please, let me out."

The cold sensation left his eyes and warmth returned to his skin. The lights blinked back on, but the door remained closed. He knew no one was going to be behind him, but he slowly turned to look anyway. As he suspected, he was alone. Without even thinking of the possibility of using the emergency telephone, Wayne lunged at the door with his arms stretched out. He battered the hard metal with the clefts of his fists in hopes that someone would hear him. The loud pounding echoed through the elevator. He stopped and nervously paced like a caged animal, but then suddenly the elevator door opened. He charged out of the elevator and out of the building until he reached the opposite side of the street. Turning, he looked back at his building and caught his breath. He was glad to breathe fresh air. Suddenly, he realized that there was no fog. He looked up, past the top of the high-rise, and found a star-filled sky that gleamed brightly.

How could a fog so thick just dissipate? he wondered.

Wayne looked both ways and then crossed the intersection at Fairview and Woodstock. He decided to walk to the nearest motel which he knew was on Woodstock Road. As he walked, he wondered how he would explain to Laura what just transpired. Not to mention what led up to it two nights ago. They were set to have a dinner date at eight o'clock later that same night.

They met fourteen years ago at a softball game during playoff season. The sun was shining bright with just a few clouds and a nice soothing breeze flowed through the air. The bleachers were full – except for one spot beside Wayne. The two teams had just finished practice when Wayne spotted Laura. She was looking for a seat and appeared to be alone. The two teams went to their respective benches and prepared to start the game. Laura was getting closer to the bleacher Wayne was sitting on. Being polite – just as if he knew her – he waved at her and indicated the empty seat beside him. She happily accepted and they had a great time. Ever since that day, they got together once in a while and had a few laughs. They went to more softball games and even tried to sit in the same seats they had when they met. Sometimes they succeeded when they arrived early enough. As it turned out, the more time they spent together as friends, the closer they became.

In a short time, Wayne arrived at the Silverwood Inn. He opened the door to the rental office and a small bell that hung on the door clinked its greeting. The office was small but tidy in appearance. A dark blue rug covered most of the tile wood flooring in front of the counter. Three different landscape paintings hung on three of the four white walls. The counter was white with a black top. Behind it was a cabinet attached to the wall.

That must be where they keep the keys, Wayne thought.

A man emerged from a door behind the counter. He was stout and slightly shorter than Wayne and appeared to be in his fifties. He was casually dressed in black slacks and a white shirt and had pepper-grey hair. The man smiled pleasantly and approached the counter.

"Hello," the man said. "How may I help you?"

"Do you have any rooms available?" Wayne asked.

"I sure do."

"Good," Wayne said. "I'll take one for the night and…actually, make that two nights."

"Very well," the man said. "That will be eighty dollars, please."

Wayne gave him the money. The man reached under the counter and picked up a key. He then turned and unlocked the cabinet behind the counter. He plucked a gold-colored key from it with a red tag numbered 7 and handed it to Wayne.

"Here we are," said the man. "Room number seven. When you walk out the door here, just go in by the entryway and head left."

"Thank you," Wayne said as he turned and walked out the door.

Shortly, he arrived at room number seven. He unlocked it, went inside, and closed the door behind him. Turning the light on, Wayne took a brief tour of the room. It was plain, but that was exactly what he expected it to be. There were four white walls, two end tables, a fair-sized closet with a wood panel finish, and a twenty-one-inch television set. Finding the bathroom, he turned on the light. He was both surprised and impressed to find it sparkling clean. His tour finished, he walked to the side of the bed and turned on the lamp. Then he turned off the other light by the main door. He got undressed, crawled into the bed and got under the covers. He reached over to turn the light off and he noticed the remote control for the television.

Oh, what the hell, he thought and scooped up the remote. *There must be something on that will take my mind off of things.*

Pressing the power button, he turned it on and went through the stations. He stopped when he found a documentary on ancient Egyptian civilizations. He loved any type of show that had to do with Egyptology. Whether it was about mummification, relics, historical pharaohs, or even fictional movies, he watched them all intently. During commercials, he thought about everything that transpired over the last two days. He wondered what he would do now that he agreed to help the ghost but came up with no solutions. Before the documentary was over, he drifted into a deep sleep.

Chapter Two
The Chilling Tale

During their candle-lit dinner at a classy restaurant called The Greek Palace, Wayne did his best to show Laura that nothing was troubling him. At first, it worked with talking about how their days went at their jobs, including the little funny things that happened. Nevertheless, she knew that something was up with him. She calmly put down her glass of Chardonnay white wine and frowned, but only a little.

"All right, Wayne," she began, "maybe, you should try telling me what's on your mind."

He tried hard to compose himself but with the look on her pretty face, it was obviously no use. "It's nothing really."

"Really?" Laura said with a knowing grin.

"Yeah," he said. "Just something strange that happened two nights ago, that's all." He paused as he took a rather large gulp of his wine.

Curiously, Laura leaned forward in her seat.

"Well?" she said.

"It was rather chilly that night during my walk. I thought it was just like any other night but with everything that happened, it was just so weird! Birchcroft Drive was usually lit up by at least fourteen street-lamps and most of the houses. Especially at eight thirty, as it was around that time. But on that night – and only on that street – not one house or street-lamp was lit up. There was nothing but complete darkness. Anyway, I walked into the darkness to make my way over to Orchard Drive. The Street seemed like a ghost town compared to the other streets I walked on that night. I thought maybe there was a power-outage, but there have been no storms of any kind within the last couple of weeks. I still do not know why, but I stopped in front of one house. It was an eerie feeling – as if something was just not right. Slowly, I turned to face the house. Only the gentle light from the moon outlined it and for a brief moment nothing happened." Wayne paused to take another sip of his drink before he continued. "Then from out of nowhere, a gust of wind picks up and rustles the leaves. I never took my eyes off the house though. Suddenly, the wind somehow hushed into silence, yet I still felt it and saw the leaves rustle about in the trees. It was creepy. The hair on the back of my neck began to rise. It felt as though someone's face was not even an inch behind mine. I shivered at the sensation, but never took my eyes off the house. Then it happened. One immediately after the other a light began shining in every room within my vision. As soon as one room lit up, the other light in the adjoining room went out. The odd thing was I saw no one: no one at all." Wayne paused again, though only briefly. "Then, before I knew it, as quickly as it had started, it stopped. Complete darkness returned to the house. I stood there for a moment. A few minutes later when I was able to move again, I approached the house. I remember walking as if in a trance. It was as if someone was calling to me. I tried stopping myself, but my courage got the better of me."

"All right," Laura said slowly, not seeming to believe my story. "So, what happened next?"

He began again. Staring off into space, recalling everything as it happened.

"I arrived at the front door only a minute later, but just as I reached for the handle I stopped. I looked both ways over my shoulders and behind me, to see if any lights had come on in any of the other houses. All was still dark and quiet. Frankly, I thought it was too quiet. At that point, I heard a rather loud click and the door very slowly creaked open. Before I moved any further, I waited for something to jump out at me."

"Now hang on just a minute," Laura said in a low voice. "Do you mean to tell me this door opened on its own, with no help at all from you?"

"Yes. That is what I am telling you," he replied.

"Did you go in?"

"Yes. My hand was still reaching for the doorknob – even though it was no longer there – and the door was now wide open. Still, I did not move a muscle. I called into the house, and of course, no reply came. I tried calling again, only this time much louder. Still no answer came. Slowly and with extreme caution, I walked into the house. It was very dark and I could not see a thing. I placed my hands in front of me so I would not bump into anything. One again I yelled 'hello' and the door suddenly slammed shut behind me. I must have jumped about three feet off the floor. I swung myself around, ready for a fight – but no attack ever came. For at least five minutes, I waited there in the dark, listening for any sign of movement or sound – but there were none."

"Is that all that happened?" Laura asked, taking him more seriously now.

"Oh no," Wayne replied with an uneasy chuckle. "There is a great deal more. Shall I continue?"

"Will it give me nightmares?" Laura asked with a side grin.

"Maybe," Wayne replied honestly. He knew she would have nightmares if he continued. On the outside, Laura appeared as though nothing bothered her, but deep down he knew it was only a front. "It does seem as if it would take a great deal to scare you."

Thoughtful, Laura was quiet for a moment. "Okay, I'll take my chances. Tell me everything."

Wayne continued, "Once my eyes became used to the dark, I began to look around. I found nothing on the main floor. No furniture, no dishes…no nothing. The house appeared to be empty. Nothing happened during all that time. No lights mysteriously came on, there were no weird sounds and still no one jumped out at me. I came to a set of stairs that led to the upper level. I began ascending them as quietly as I could; yet with each careful step I took, they creaked as if they were a hundred years old. About halfway up, I heard the unmistakable sound of someone breathing – but it sounded winded."

"Winded?" Laura repeated curiously, unsure as to what he meant.

"Yes. It was as if someone ran for a city block and stopped from being tired. I stopped dead in my tracks. I felt my heart pound in my chest. I slowly scanned my surroundings. I did that because the uncanny sound appeared to be coming from all directions. Of course, I could not see anyone."

"I bet you freaked," Laura said.

"Actually, I tried so hard to keep myself calm but yes, deep down I was scared stiff. I keened my ears to see if I could determine exactly where the breathing was coming from but then it suddenly stopped. Just then, though in a barely audible yet seemingly long whisper – I heard my name. It came from the top of the stairs. I quickly glared in that direction but still saw nothing. Then I heard the voice call my name again, in a slightly louder groan. My breath caught in my throat. Frustrated now and gaining some courage, I said, 'Who are you? How do you know my name? What do you want from me?' and I waited for an answer."

Listening intently, Laura was sitting on the edge of her seat, but a sudden thought occurred to her. In all the years that she knew Wayne, fear was a word she thought was unknown to his vocabulary. Before Wayne continued, she pointed it out to him.

"Wayne, I never knew you to be so afraid of anything. In fact, I remember a number of bullies you stood up to when you were younger. Back then, they were all bigger than you were. Now, you are twenty-nine years old, six feet tall and weigh – two hundred pounds? I on the other hand, am two years younger than you are. I am only five-foot-four and weigh one hundred and twenty pounds. I was afraid of almost everything. Even now as a grown woman, I would have run out that front door screaming." She paused briefly before adding, "I could only assume no answer came?"

"That's right. At first, I thought maybe I was not loud enough – but on the other hand, I wanted what or whoever was playing that sick game to hear me. Then I heard my name again; even louder that time as if from just inches away. Now I was much more scared than angry, but I have had enough of the games and I charged up those steps. When I got to the top a few seconds later, there was still nobody there. Anyway, I felt like a burglar in this house but it was too late. I was too involved now and—"

"You couldn't leave?" Laura interjected almost impatiently. She glanced at her watch. "I do not mean to interrupt your great story and I am not trying to cut you short. But if anything else unusual happened, can you sort of get to it a little faster?"

Laura did not mean to make it sound so harsh and hoped she did not offend him. She did not like where Wayne's story was going, and was not sure if she wanted to hear more.

"I am boring you," Wayne said with a gentle smile.

"Oh no, honey, it's not that. It is just that it is ten o'clock already, and my curfew is eleven. It has been a long day."

His eyes widened. "You have a curfew?"

Laura was worried about him, but she hid it well and laughed. "I have to work in the morning, silly."

"Oh, I see," Wayne said with a chuckle.

She looked at him with a smirk and giggled. "Get on with it, smart-ass."

"Okay, there were three bedrooms. I peeked into the first one, saw nothing, and then moved on to the next room. Again, I heard my name but this time, it sounded muffled. It seemed as though it came from the final bedroom at the end of the hall. Slowly, I walked toward it, but as I passed in front of the second bedroom, something caught my attention. It was a shadow of a human-like figure of a man or woman – I was not sure which – and without even thinking, I stormed into the room toward it. Once again, the door slammed shut loudly behind me. I cried out and spun myself around. There was nothing there. I remembered the reason why I went in that room in the first place and turned back to the window. The shadowy figure was gone. I thought I was losing my mind. I scratched my head as I scanned the room. Then I said, 'All right, who or whatever the hell you are…show yourself. I'm sick of playing this game.'"

"Did you get an answer this time?" she asked.

"Yes. I listened closely as the voice said, *'In this house you will find nothing but mystery. Stay away from the final bedroom. Evil lurks there.'* Believe me; I did not move a single damn inch! The hair on the back of my neck came up again. I was scared stiff now. My voice cracked as I said, 'Evil lurks there, huh? Then what the hell am I in here with?' and after that, there was nothing but silence." Wayne concluded rather quickly and returned to my wine.

Laura leaned back in her seat. Her graceful hands cupped her glass of wine. She was trying to read Wayne's thoughts by the expressions on his face. It did not always work, but most of the time it did. Normally she could tell if Wayne was playing a joke or fibbing, but not this time. To her, Wayne's story seemed a little too unbelievable. Deep down she hoped it was just a sick joke. In reality, she had a bad feeling it was not.

He would never be so mean to play a sick joke like this, would he? Laura wondered. *As far as I know, Wayne never lied to me before so why would he start now? It makes no sense. There must be more to this story. It just cannot end like that.*

Laura played her hunch. "You're not telling me everything, are you, Wayne?"

Wayne did his best to give her a look that said he had told her everything. To his dismay, she did not believe it.

Laura wagged her index finger at me in friendly warning.

"No way, Mister Storyteller," Laura said. "Spill it."

"B-but," he stammered.

"But my foot," she added, placing her glass gently on the table. "If you don't tell me the rest of what happened, I will go to this haunted house and find out for myself."

Wayne bowed his head in defeat. "Okay, okay." He took a deep breath before continuing, placing his glass on the table in front of hers. "The voice told me that I had been summoned there to solve several Mysteries. It also told me that if I fail, it will haunt me for the rest of my life."

"What?" Laura cried in a hushed whisper.

"Nevertheless, I tried to tell this…this thing – as terrified as I was – that I was not an investigator or paranormal researcher of any kind. Suddenly, the bedroom light clicked on. I cringed and quickly covered my eyes with my hands. At that point, I was not sure what to expect. When my eyes were used to the light, I reluctantly looked around the room from one wall to the next. When I was near the end of the third wall, something caught my peripheral vision and my eyes shot right to it." Wayne paused to take another sip of my wine.

"And, and?" Laura said, on the edge of her seat now. "Well, what happened?"

"In blood – or what looked like blood – was written what appeared to be a riddle."

"Sweet Jesus!" Laura whispered in shock. "How can you be sure it was blood though?"

"I'm pretty sure," Wayne replied, "because, it was written in dark red and each letter was dripping. I do not mean a few measly drops either. I mean dripping as if it was freshly painted. Every type of paint has a certain odor to it, but I detected none."

"One of the mysteries, I assume," she said as she rubbed her arms as if she were cold. "Creepy. What did it say?"

"It read, 'The heavenly gates lock at 4, recite the right verse, under a roof yet not under a floor, 3-15 before the 75th hour or face my curse.'"

Laura simply stared at Wayne. The look on her lovely face seemed as if she had seen the words in his eyes. She appeared about as spooked as he had been at that time. She spoke in a concerned whisper.

"You cannot go back to that house. I will not let you. If everything you are telling me here is true – and I believe it is – then there are powers in that place you should not be messing with! What if it tries to possess you?"

Wayne replied calmly. "Didn't you hear me say that it will haunt me forever if I fail?" Laura grew quiet for a moment before he added. "As for possession – that has not occurred in centuries. At least, not as far as I know."

Convinced that he would not back out of this situation, Laura relented. "Fine, then I am going with you whenever – wait a minute, if this happened a couple of days ago, then—"

"You think it would have begun to haunt me already?" Wayne said, completing her thought.

Laura nodded slowly.

"I'll let you in on a little secret. It has done exactly what it said it would do."

Laura placed her head in her hands and rubbed her temples. "How did I know you were going to say that?" she said in a slow exhaling breath. "What happened?"

"Last night I woke up to a freezing cold bedroom. It was about one-thirty in the morning. I swung my feet over the side of the bed and folded my arms across my chest. It was so cold that my teeth were chattering. I remembered turning on the heat before I went to bed because it was rather cold that night. Anyway, I got up and made my way over to the thermostat. I tried checking to see what it was set at but it was too dark to tell. Flicking on the light, I found it set exactly where I left it – at seventy-five degrees. Then I realized I could see my own breath. I looked at my bedroom mirror and it was fogged up as if the room were a sauna. I even ran my finger over it. Then I looked at the bedroom window and found a fog so thick that I couldn't see anything through it.

To top it all off – I clearly saw the words '*I am waiting, Wayne*' being written right in front of me. The hair on the back of my neck rose up again. I did not have to be a rocket scientist to know I was no longer alone in my own home. I did not sleep the rest of the night. Oh! And do you want to hear something else?" Before Laura could reply, he continued, "I threw on some clothes and went downstairs to go outside. When I walked through the front door, there was not one bit of fog."

"No fog?" Laura said curiously.

"None," Wayne replied, "and from what I saw, there was not a single cloud in the sky."

Laura was quiet for a moment before she replied with a look of shock on her face. "That is just plain disturbing. Come on," she added, quickly rising from her seat. "We're going to my place."

"I thought you said you had to work in the morning," he said, surprised.

"I do," she replied, "but I won't be going in."

Wayne stood after her and reached into his right front pocket to remove his wallet. He withdrew forty dollars to pay the delicious meal.

Chapter Three
A Night of Old Times

They were quiet in Laura's 1997 navy-blue Mazda sport during the drive to her home. The only sounds they heard were the tires occasionally driving over the long narrow cracks in the roads, the ticking of the turning signals and the jingling of the car keys when they ran over bumps. Wayne was looking out his window when Laura finally broke the silence.

"So, what happens now?" Laura asked curiously.

"Tomorrow, I go to Wilmot Rural Cemetery," Wayne replied.

"Why on Earth would you go to a cemetery?" Laura asked.

"What other place do you know that has the heavenly gates logo?" Wayne said. "Of course, I am only playing a hunch here but I know of only two cemeteries in Fredericton…Wilmot Rural and Heritage. And the Heritage has only wrought-iron gates."

"I am going with you," Laura said.

"No, you are not," Wayne said with a brief laugh. "I would much prefer if you were somewhere safe."

"Wayne, I said I was going with you," she argued.

He began to protest but Laura would not have it. She was determined not to let him do it alone.

"You will not talk me out of this. You and I are very close friends and I won't let you face this thing alone," she said firmly. "Besides, what kind of a friends would I be if I just let you go off and do something stupid like this?"

Wayne remained silent.

In a short time, they arrived at the apartment complex where she lived on Nethervue Street. The small red-bricked building was only three stories high. Most of the windows were dark but a few lights were still on. They walked into the building and got into the elevator. Stepping out on the second floor, they went down the hall until they reached apartment number three. Laura unlocked the door and they stepped inside. They removed their shoes at the door. Laura spoke.

"Don't be shy, go into the living room and make yourself at home. I will be right there."

"Okay," Wayne answered.

He headed to the living room. On his way, he noticed a beautiful oak grandmother clock in the hall and a painting of a large passenger-ship on the ocean.

Even for an administrative assistant in the government, that clock must have set her back a few months' pay, Wayne thought.

He walked into the living room and sat down in a navy-blue recliner. He found it very comfortable. He looked around the room. To his right was another recliner of the same color. In between the two chairs was a pine end table with an old-style lamp on it. It had a dark finish and brought a certain flattery to the lamp. In front of him was an oak wall-unit with a twenty-seven-inch television, a state-of-the-art stereo and a VCR. It even had three small potted plants on top. It was a very spacious living room.

As he waited for Laura to join him, Wayne could not help but think of the riddle that came to him at the house on Birchcroft. He thought about what it could possibly mean, and wondered if there were any more surprises waiting for him inside it.

Laura joined him a moment later, carrying a silver tray with two half-filled glasses and a bottle on it.

"What is this?" Wayne asked, quirking his left eyebrow.

Laura smiled gently. "Oh, it's just a little something from the kitchen to help us relax," she said as she handed him a glass while she kept the other. "I do apologize for taking so long. I had to call my boss to let him know I will not be in tomorrow."

"That's quite all right, my beautiful friend," he said.

"Aw, why thank you, handsome," Laura said, giggling. She sat in the other recliner and clinked Wayne's glass.

"I didn't know you had a bar in the kitchen."

"I don't," Laura replied, "but I keep my liquor in one of the lower cupboards."

They sipped from their glasses at the same time.

Wayne complimented the drink with a slow approving nod and then glanced at the bottle.

"Surprisingly good for brandy," he said.

"Oh, I'm sorry, Wayne. I did not know you were not too fond of brandy."

"No, no, that's fine, really. It normally doesn't agree with my system, but tonight it tastes just fine."

"Good," she replied. "Now, tell me. What do you think this riddle means?"

Wayne exhaled a thoughtful sigh.

"There must be something written, either inside a tomb or on a piece of paper that could be found somewhere on a body," he said.

"What do you mean?" Laura asked.

"In the riddle," Wayne explained, "it said, recite the right verse. So there must be something that I have to read, probably out loud."

"What do you think will happen after you read whatever it is that has to be read?"

Wayne grew quiet for a moment as he thought about this. He took another sip of the smooth brandy before he answered.

"I honestly have no clue, Laura. I guess we will just have to find out when that time comes."

They finished off their drinks and she refilled their glasses.

Wayne suddenly noticed that he felt more secure when he was around Laura. Now that he thought about it, he supposed he always did. He was always happier with her than with anyone else. She was indeed a very attractive woman. He cared about her a great deal. At times, he thought perhaps a little too much.

They sat there, sipping their drinks. They became very quiet and thoughtful. You could almost hear a pin drop from the silence. However, that silence was broken when the grandmother clock struck one in the morning. Wayne stood from his chair.

"And where do you think you are you going?" Laura asked in a curious yet concerned tone. "To the bathroom I hope."

"Actually," Wayne replied, "I really should be heading home."

Laura stood from her seat somewhat quickly and stood in front of him. "Not a chance in hell, buddy," she said calmly. "You're staying right with me here until all of this paranormal stuff is over."

"I appreciate your concern but I will only be in your way. Besides, if I stay, it may haunt me here and I do not want this thing getting to you too."

"Let it come then," Laura argued stubbornly. "I am not leaving you alone; not after everything I just heard. Now, let's sit down," she pushed him softly back into his seat, "talk about old times and have a few drinks."

Wayne could not help but grin. "I like when you're pushy, you know that?"

Laura laughed. "All too well. So, what do we talk about first?"

For the next two hours they talked, laughed and drank and before they knew it, it was three o'clock in the morning. They were both tired and knew that it was high time that they tried to get some sleep.

Laura stood and stretched. "Well," she said with a wide yawn. "I don't know about you, but I'm pooped."

Wayne nodded and followed her yawn with one of his own. "I know what you mean. I think I will turn in too. Sweet dreams Laura."

"You too," she said. "Is there anything I can get you before I go – a blanket or a pillow perhaps?"

He lay back on the couch and replied. "No thank you, I'm fine."

"Okay, try to get some sleep. Tomorrow is another day."

"I will," Wayne answered as he closed his eyes.

Laura smiled down at him and then left the room to go to bed. She was glad that he decided to stay, considering what he told her. She did not want him to be alone. If he had decided to leave, she knew that sleep would never come. She would be too worried and would only toss and turn through the night, wondering if he was okay. Softly, she closed her bedroom door and prepared herself for bed.

Before turning in, she sat at her vanity table and picked up a hairbrush. She looked in the mirror and began brushing her hair.

After all these years, Wayne Saunders, Laura thought, *I never knew I would be falling in love with you. At least I think I am. More and more, I look forward to seeing you and spending time with you.*

She stopped brushing and shifted her eyes to the bedroom door.

I just hope that one day you feel the same way about me. Her thought concluded.

She continued brushing for a moment before she stopped and got into bed. She turned off the light, rolled over onto her side and finally closed her eyes.

Chapter Four
Disrespectful Awakenings

Wayne was not sure if he was dreaming or if he was awake. Only his eyes were able to move as he attempted to get his bearings. It seemed clear that he was still in Laura's living room on her couch, but he was unable to move or utter a single sound. Above all, he could not breathe. It felt as if someone was sitting on his chest only there was no one there. He felt a strong presence…as if being watched. He began to panic and tried so hard to move without success. He felt paralyzed. He opened his mouth, wanting to cry out in terror, but still no sound came out. Desperate to breathe, he continued to fight, to bring some life back to his unmoving body. Finally, after what seemed like an eternity, he managed to force a loud growl. His body jerked into life again. Before he knew what happened, he bolted into a sitting position. He had broken out in a cold sweat and short of breath. He was also surprised to find himself on the floor. He wondered how he got there. Suddenly, the living room light popped on. Immediately, he gasped and cringed, covering his eyes quickly. A pair of gentle hands touched his shoulders.

"You're all right," Laura comforted calmly. "It's gone. It's all over now."

Wayne's breathing slowly returned to normal. Feeling her caring eyes on him, he looked up into them. She saw the fear in his.

"Hey, it's just you and I. We are all alone here. Please, snap out of it honey, you're scaring me," she said ever so calmly, sitting beside him on the floor.

Wayne replied in a quiet voice. "I couldn't move. I couldn't talk or breathe…"

Laura said softly. "Hey, it's okay. My gut told me that something was wrong out here. I am glad I checked."

"I just hope I know what I'm getting us into," Wayne said. "It would make me feel so much better if you just…stayed out of this."

Laura raised her eyebrows and shook her head slowly.

"Wayne, I already told you and I will tell you again. I am not leaving you alone to face this thing by yourself. We will face it together, like good friends should do." Laura paused a moment before she added. "Never have I seen you like this before. It worries me to pieces."

"If it's any consolation, I've never faced anything like this," Wayne replied. "I loved reading about ghosts in books and watching them on television. I never thought I would one day face one in real life."

"I see," Laura said. "Now I understand why you will not back out of this." She helped Wayne back onto the sofa. "Do you think you can fall back asleep?"

"To be honest with you, I don't think so."

Laura nodded understandingly. "Okay. Come on."

They stood from the floor and walked out of the living room.

"Where are we going?" Wayne asked.

"To my bedroom," Laura said. "Both of us need to get some sleep. We have a long day tomorrow."

Following her, Wayne said. "Won't it feel awkward with me lying beside you?"

"Not really," Laura replied. "Besides, we are not having sex. We are only keeping each other company. I trust you. Will you be okay with that?"

"Um…sure," Wayne said.

"Are you sure?"

"Of course," he added.

"Good," Laura said, smiling. "Now, go on. Get under the covers. I am just going to put on a more decent pair of pajamas."

She reached into her dresser drawer and pulled out another pair of pajamas, then stepped into the bathroom across the hall and softly closed the door behind her.

Wayne did as she instructed, even though he was fully dressed. He could not help but be a little shy considering he cared so much for her.

A moment later, Laura emerged from the bathroom, wearing a woolly baby blue pair of pajamas. She crawled into bed beside him and lay on her back.

"So," she said. "What time do you think we should get up at?"

"Well, I figure we should get an early start," Wayne said, "how about eight or nine O'clock?"

"You do plan on eating something before we go, right?" Laura said as she set the alarm, knowing of his bad habit of skipping breakfast.

"Maybe," Wayne said nonchalantly. "Right now, I can't even think of food. All I keep thinking about is that riddle. If 3-15 is actually a tomb, then how in the hell are we going to get in there?"

Wayne glanced at his friend. She lay on her back staring at the ceiling. On more than one occasion, Laura chastised him for not eating breakfast. Her words played back in his mind:

'Wayne, I swear to God, one of these days you're going to crash and burn. Stop being such a stubborn ass and take better care of yourself.'

Laura turned over onto her side to face me and slowly commented upon my thoughts. "You do realize, of course, that by forcing our way into someone's tomb, we will be breaking the law."

"I know," Wayne said quietly. "This is another reason why I want you to stay out of this."

They talked quietly for a little while longer, making plans for that morning. Eventually, they drifted into sleep with hopes of a successful day.

Chapter Five
The Journey Begins

The alarm clock sounded at nine o'clock a.m. Though Laura and Wayne were still quite groggy, she switched off the alarm and they got up. Out of common courtesy, Wayne let her use the bathroom first. After a very brief time, she came out and turned it over to him. When he emerged, he went to the kitchen and found Laura already busy preparing coffee. The bright morning sun streamed in through the sheer white curtain on the window. It lit up the room. He was surprised at how easily Laura could just get up in the morning and be so full of energy. Wayne on the other hand, was still slowly waking up.

Laura's back was toward him as she worked. He leaned against the kitchen's entryway and watched her with interest.

Picking up the two cups of freshly brewed coffee, she turned slowly and noticed him standing there. She smiled broadly.

"Good morning, sunshine," Laura said cheerfully, yet with an odd grin. "Slept well?"

"Morning," Wayne replied with notable curiosity. "Not bad, I think."

She sat at the kitchen table. "Come," she said. "Sit with me and have some coffee."

Almost cautiously, he sat at the table across from her. He rarely found her that happy first thing in the morning. At least, not until she was fully awake and had her third cup of coffee.

"You seem rather chipper this morning," Wayne commented.

"Uh huh." she hummed quickly in response.

Wayne grew thoughtful as he stared down into his steaming cup of coffee. He asked, "Did I do something last night that I should know about?"

"No not really," she replied. "Besides, you were in a pretty deep sleep."

Blushing and embarrassed, Wayne lowered his head toward the table. "I knew it," he whispered in shame. "I am so sorry."

Gently, Laura placed her hand over his. "It's okay. You only had your hand on my thigh."

"Oh, dear lord," Wayne said.

"I did not mind at all," Laura added gently.

"You didn't?" Wayne said, surprised.

Laura shook her head. "No. Actually it made me feel…not so lonely."

All Wayne could do was grin shyly. He had no idea his hands would travel and have a mind of their own.

"So," she said, bringing me back to reality. "What would you like for breakfast?"

"Oh, I don't know. What would you like to have?"

Thoughtful, Laura said, "How about something easy, like scrambled eggs, hash browns and toast?"

"Actually, that sounds pretty good," Wayne answered.

"Good. It is settled then," Laura said.

Laura finished off what remained of her coffee and began preparing their food. He watched as she worked, still impressed at how easy she made it seem and with so much energy.

"Is there anything I can do to help?" Wayne asked.

"No, I am fine," Laura replied as she turned to him and cracked an egg into a glass bowl with her right hand, "but thank you for asking. Would you like some more coffee?"

"Yes, please."

She refilled his cup and smiled at him.

"Thank you," Wayne said as he returned her smile.

"You're welcome," she said.

As he drank his coffee, the delicious aroma of scrambled eggs filled the kitchen. His stomach growled hungrily, yet quietly enough that Laura could not hear it. Back to the riddle his thoughts went. Questions ran through his head about the house on Birchcroft, and the spirit who resided inside it.

What could have happened to that man to make him seek justice so insistently? he wondered. *Was he murdered? Had other people tried to solve his mystery? Was the house his before he died?*

Before he could attempt to name several possible answers, Laura placed their breakfast on the table.

"That was quick," Wayne said.

"Not bad for a little cook eh," Laura said, but noticed an odd look on Wayne's face. "Are you all right? You seem a little distant."

He nodded. "Oh, yes, I'm fine. I was just thinking about that house and our invisible friend. Why he could be there – if the house actually belonged to him before he passed on – just stuff like that."

"Oh? Did you come up with any conclusions?" Laura asked.

"No," he answered. "Let's just enjoy our meal and I'll help you clean up after. Then we could get ready to head out – If you are still up to it that is."

"Don't you worry about me," Laura said with a small laugh. "I am about as ready as I will ever be. I do apologize for last night though. I should have taken you to get a change of clothes and some necessities. I could still take you if you want me to."

"Don't worry about it," Wayne replied. "Actually, all I want to do is head down to the cemetery and see if we can solve this thing."

They ate in silence. The occasional chirps and songs of birds echoed though the kitchen window. It set a nice relaxing mood.

Laura began clearing the dishes away and Wayne helped her. At first, she wanted to be a gracious hostess and do it all by herself but Wayne insisted that she let him help.

"It is the least I can do Laura," he said calmly yet stubbornly. "Let me show my appreciation for your generous hospitality by helping."

Smiling, she finally relented and handed him a dishtowel.

It did not take them long to get the dishes out of the way. Then one at a time they freshened up. Laura went first. When she was finished, she handed Wayne a new toothbrush and a clean towel.

"If you would like, there is some styling gel too. So, whenever you're ready, okay?"

"Okay. Thank you."

In no time at all, Wayne was finished and ready to go. Locking the door behind them, they walked down the hall to the elevator. Laura pressed the down button.

While they waited, Laura wondered if Wayne was actually ready to go to the cemetery and do whatever it was he had to do.

I hope he knows what he is doing, she thought.

The elevator door opened and they got in. They were quiet until they got to the ground floor and stepped out into the fresh air. They sun's brilliant rays made their eyes squint.

"Whoa," Wayne said in a husky voice as he hooded my eyes. "That's one bright sun."

"You're not kidding." Laura added as she shaded her eyes as well.

It was a gorgeous day with a faint breeze, which was a delightful change compared to the chilly nights they had been getting lately.

"Well," Laura began. "We could either take a long walk or a drive. Which would you prefer?"

Wayne could not help but chuckle at that. "With all due respect, of course, the graveyard has to be at least two miles away. I normally have no objection to a long healthy walk, but we may need all of the daylight time that we can get.”

“All right,” Laura agreed with a nod. “Let’s get going.”

Getting into Laura’s car, they backed out of the driveway and headed down the road toward Woodstock Road, which was the main highway to get the cemetery. They rolled down their windows because it was so warm in the car, but the soothing breeze quickly cooled them down. Wayne took a deep breath of the fresh air and smiled.

“Ah, what a beautiful day,” he said.

“Yes, it certainly is,” Laura replied and then added with a notable smirk, “and we’ll be spending it in a cemetery.”

“Look at the bright side,” Wayne said. “It could be night time with pouring rain.”

Laura laughed and shook her head. She tapped his left leg just above his knee. “Honey, you’re one of a kind. Don’t ever change how you are.”

“Don’t worry,” Wayne said. “I will probably be old and grey before I change.”

Laura concentrated on the road and turned onto Woodstock Road; yet as the cemetery drew closer, she felt a knot building in the pit of her stomach. She had never broken the law before and hoped she did not have to start now.

Looking out his window, Wayne felt a little nervous too. Normally, whenever he took a walk in a cemetery, it was to help him find inner peace – or to clear his mind. Wayne had a great respect for the dead and was never sacrilegious. He never sat on a headstone, stood on – or even walked over someone’s grave. Any cemetery was one of his favorite places to visit; he always believed it was one of the safest places in the world to be. Even at night, with or without a full moon. He had no idea what he and Laura were about to get into, but they would soon find out.

So much for being respectful, he thought.

“Well,” Laura said as she hung a left, turning into the entryway of the cemetery, “here we are. Which way do we go first?”

Wayne thought about it briefly. There was a narrow road to his right and one to his left.

“Well I am not really sure,” he replied. “The riddle is pretty vague. The heavenly gates lock at 4, recite the right verse, under a roof yet not under a floor, 3-15. A roof could be anything from that building right there,” he nodded to the cemetery office building, “to a mausoleum somewhere on these grounds. Now, not under a floor tells me whatever we are looking for is not underground. So, at least we know we do not have to dig anyone up.”

Wayne paused and looked toward his right.

"Let's try this way first. Maybe we can find something with the number 3 or15 on it."

"I imagine the numbers of many of the headstones and mausoleums are old. Maybe it would be better if we walked?" Laura said. "We can cover more ground that way."

Wayne agreed and Laura found a parking spot. They got out and started walking along the right path. Laura scanned the left side while Wayne searched the right, scanning every headstone they could see.

After an hour of searching, Wayne's patience was beginning to wear thin. He stopped in front of a fairly tall shiny marble obelisk headstone and turned to Laura.

"I am beginning to think we are going about this all wrong," he said.

"What do you mean?" Laura asked.

Wayne glanced at his watch. "An hour has already passed and nothing adds up. I do not know about you but even if it turns out we are looking for a mausoleum I have yet to see one."

"Maybe they are on the other side of the cemetery," Laura said.

"All right," Wayne said. "Let's cross over on this path."

They continued to search the headstones yet still found no sign of the numbers they looked for. As they arrived at the other side of the cemetery they looked left and right down the narrow roadways only to find no mausoleums.

"At this rate it could take hours to find what we're looking for," Wayne said.

"Okay, so what do you suggest?" Laura asked.

"Well, maybe someone in the office back there can help us."

Laura laughed.

"What?" Wayne said. "They might."

"And what would we say?" Laura said. "Hi, we're trying to solve a mystery but we were wondering if you had any headstones that has the numbers three or fifteen on them?"

Wayne nodded and a smirk formed on his face as if to say, okay that's a good point.

"Besides," Laura added, "do you honestly think it's a good idea that they know we're poking around?"

"No," Wayne replied, "but it might get us out of here a lot quicker. Come on."

They started walking toward the office building.

"I sure hope you know what you are doing," Laura said.

"Don't worry," Wayne said with assurance. "I have an idea."

"Care to fill me in?"

"Let's just say we are cousins researching our family tree," Wayne said.

Laura gave him a look of skepticism.

"It'll work," Wayne said. "Just follow my lead."

Laura snickered. "Whatever you say, cuz."

They walked through the entry door to the office and it appeared empty. There was a counter to their right yet nobody was behind it. They walked up to it. There was no bell to ring for service and no signs that they would return shortly.

"Maybe they are gone to lunch or something," Laura suggested.

"Without a sign on the door?" Wayne said in puzzled tone. "It makes no sense."

They turned away from the counter and looked down the only hall leading into the office hoping to spot someone when they heard a voice behind them.

"Pardon me," the voice said.

Laura jumped and let out a small yet quick scream, making Wayne spin around to see a man standing behind the counter.

"Oh dear, oh dear," the man said with his hands raised. "I am so sorry. I did not mean to startle you."

"Jesus!" Laura said.

The man was slim. He appeared to be in his early forties and wore a black and white tuxedo.

"Please do not take this the wrong way," Wayne said, "but how did you get behind that counter?"

"Oh, I was here. I was just looking for a cufflink that fell off my sleeve. See?" the man replied and showed the sleeve with the missing accessory.

"Ah," Wayne said. "Well maybe you can help us out."

"Yes?" the man said.

"My cousin and I are researching our family tree and are looking for a long-departed uncle. From the information we have, he is buried here."

"I see," the man said. "What is your uncle's name?"

Unaware of the name, Wayne had to think quickly.

"Um," was all he managed to say.

Wayne glanced at Laura for, casually dropping the hint that he needed her assistance.

"Oh my God," she said in a tone of annoyance. "Do you mean to tell me you forgot to write his name down?"

"Well...I must have but..."

Laura sighed heavily and glared at Wayne.

"How can this poor man help us now?" she said. "We came all this way and now we have to go back and get our uncle's name and come back."

"Please," the man said, unable to help but feel sorry for Wayne. "Let's all come down. Maybe I can still help you. Do you have any other information other than he is buried here?"

"Well," Wayne said. "We do have the numbers three and fifteen."

"Okay," the man said. "Perhaps I can find something under one of those numbers. Please wait here for a moment while I check into it."

Laura breathed a well-acted sigh of relief.

"Thank you so much," she said.

"Not at all," the man said and went down the hall.

They watched until he turned the corner.

"Hey, that was pretty good," Wayne whispered.

"I knew drama class in high school would come in handy one day," Laura whispered back in reply.

Shortly, the man reappeared holding a book in his hands and paced it on the counter.

"Now don't get your hopes up quite yet," he said, "but I think I found something."

"Yes?" Laura said inquisitively.

"Under number fifteen – which is a mausoleum – I have a Frederick Brown."

"That's him!" Wayne said without hesitation.

Laura gasped. "Are you sure?" she asked excitedly.

"Positive," Wayne replied. "That was the name I wrote down."

"There," the man said with a smile. "You see? Now you can go and visit with your uncle and not have to worry about coming back."

"Thank you so much," Laura said happily. "We really appreciate you help."

"You are entirely welcome," the man said. "I hope you enjoy your visit."

"We will," Wayne said. "Thanks again."

They turned and headed for the door when Wayne suddenly stopped and turned back to the man behind the counter.

"Oh, I'm sorry but which way?" Wayne asked.

"Not at all," the man said and pointed almost directly behind him. "Straight down and to the right."

"Thank you," Wayne said and walked out the door. Laura waited for him beside the office out of earshot. "See?" Wayne said. "I knew it would work."

"You got lucky," Laura laughed, "and it never would have worked without me."

"Over-actor," Wayne snickered.

"Hey," Laura said giving him a light smack on the shoulder.

Wayne laughed.

Following the man's directions, they walked all the way to the end of the narrow road and turned right. Wayne immediately spotted number fifteen. There were two others alongside it and suddenly he realized what the numbers in the riddle meant.

"So that's it," he said.

"What is it?" Laura asked, puzzled.

"Three-fifteen," Wayne said. "Three mausoleums but fifteen is the one we're looking for."

"Impressive," Laura said. "But frankly that only leads to another question. What are we looking for?"

They looked at the structure. The old-fashioned bricks appeared to be discolored and worn down by years of weather. The name Brown and the year A.D. 1939 were above the door. The door itself was bronze and had wide antique metal hinges. It also a keyhole with a separate metal handle. To Wayne's surprise it also had one small window. To his understanding most crypts had no windows. He stepped up to it and tried to look inside but was unable to see anything. The glass was tinted so that only mirror images of the outside were visible.

"Something that has to do with a verse," Wayne replied as he stepped away from the window. "I just hope it's on the outside. You look along that side and I'll look on this side."

"What if it is not on the outside?" Laura asked.

Before replying, Wayne looked around to make sure no one was within earshot. "Then we will have to go in."

"What?" Laura whispered with a look of shock on her face. She had no idea that Wayne was actually willing to break the law to find his answers. Yet, at the same time, she had a feeling that he would say that. She wanted to ask if the words jail-time meant anything to him, but instead she said, "I really hope you know what you are doing."

"So do I," Wayne replied with an understanding nod. "All right, let's get to work."

They each chose a side of the mausoleum and started searching the bricks for any form of writing. After only a few brief moments, however, they met behind the structure with empty results. Without saying a word, Wayne bowed his head in disappointment and headed back to the front of the structure. Laura followed him and when they got there, Wayne looked at the lock on the door. He never picked a lock before in his life and wondered what made him think he could start now.

"How do you propose to get in there?" Laura asked curiously.

Once again, Wayne casually looked around to see if anyone was nearby. They were still alone.

"I see no other choice but to try to pick the lock," he replied.

Laura closed her eyes and bowed her head. *I knew he was going to say that,* she thought.

Wayne walked up to the old door and knelt down to see if he was able to see through the keyhole. He saw nothing but darkness.

"There must be a way to pick this thing but I have no idea how," he said.

He then searched his front and back pockets and to his surprise, he found a handkerchief. He wondered how it ended up there but quickly snapped himself back to reality and unfolded it. Draping the handkerchief over his right hand he placed it over the doorknob but before he tried to open it, he took one final look around to make sure no one was around. Seeing no one, he carefully tried to open the door and was disappointed but not surprised to find it locked.

Unbeknownst to Wayne, Laura reached into her purse and pulled out a hairpin and a pair of tweezers. She placed her free hand on his shoulder.

Wayne was so concentrated on the door that he nearly jumped out of his skin. Even though he knew she was behind him he had no idea if it was someone else. He spun around to see Laura standing there and exhaled a heavy sigh of relief.

Her index finger rested on her lips but the look on her face said she was sorry for startling him.

"Good God, Laura!" Wayne said as he clutched his heart. "Don't take this the wrong way but…please, don't do that again."

"Sorry," she said, handing him the hairpin and tweezers. "Try these."

"Right," Wayne said, gently plucking the items out of her hand.

He turned back to the door and bent the tweezers until it was straight. He then placed one end inside the bottom portion of the lock and the hairpin at the top portion. Carefully and slowly, he moved them around hoping to feel anything inside the lock move but felt nothing. He paused, took a deep breath and tried again gently pressing in all directions. Precious seconds ticked by and still nothing happened. Losing patience, he pulled out and grunted in frustration.

Laura kept watch in case anyone approached. She was nervous and had a bad feeling in the pit of her stomach that someone would see them.

Wayne did his best to keep calm and patient and he tried again. Ever so slowly he toyed with the lock until finally he felt something give in the top portion of the lock. He was not sure what it was but to him it felt like a small spring.

Okay, I think we are getting somewhere, he thought. *Now let's see if we can be so lucky on the bottom end.*

Keeping the hairpin against the spring, he then fiddled with the bottom portion of the lock and once again he felt something give. Holding the two ends in place, he then wondered what to do next.

Do I turn it left or right? he wondered. *The latch is facing my left so it must be to the right.*

Something caught Laura's attention and she turned. She was not certain what it was at first. Her breath caught in her throat as she listened carefully and realized it was the faint sounds of voices.

Oh my God, she thought.

"Hurry, Wayne," Laura coaxed in a low voice. "I think someone is coming."

Keening his ears, Wayne slowly turned the lock to his right and was happy to see he was making progress.

Good, he thought. *Yes...good...good.*

Laura listened as the voices slowly drew closer. As far as she knew, they could have been less than fifty feet away.

"Wayne?"

"I hear them," Wayne said. "Almost there."

A few more seconds ticked by and the voices drew closer and closer. Now Laura was really nervous.

"Dammit Wayne," she whispered in a panicking tone. "We are going to get caught!"

Finally, Wayne heard the lock click and cautiously pushed the door open. The hinges were rusty so he had to carefully nudge it open with his shoulder. It creaked loudly in protest.

Laura was keeping her eyes on the direction of the voices and made sure she was unable to see anyone. As soon as the door was open enough, she helped Wayne to his feet.

"Come on," she said.

They stepped inside and closed the door as softly as possible behind them. It squeaked again but not as loud as before. One of the first things Wayne noticed were two small windows at the back of the crypt.

"Well at least we will have a little bit of light," he whispered.

He then turned and peeked out the small window on the door and there was no one around. A sigh of relief escaped his lips.

"They sounded real close," he said, "but I think we're clear."

"A little too close for my taste," Laura commented. "I was sure we were going to get—"

Just as Laura was about to finish her sentence, Wayne spotted two ladies no more than ten feet from their location. He quickly turned and silenced her by placing his index finger to his lips. To him, they appeared to be somewhere in their mid-forties.

Laura wanted to finish her sentence and say 'caught' but instead she covered her mouth and held her breath.

Wayne turned back to the window only to see the two ladies standing in front of their mausoleum. They were not looking at the window but he quickly moved his eyes away from it anyway. He motioned to Laura that they were standing right outside and her eyes widened in panic.

"Calm down," Wayne whispered in an attempt to lower her anxiety.

He was about to say something else when a voice spoke up from outside.

"So would you like to go inside?" One of the ladies said.

Wayne and Laura glanced at each other as if to say, what did she say? It took a moment for their eyes to get used to the darkness and without moving, they hastily looked for a place to hide but there was nowhere to go. All they found was an old coffin on a stone altar in the middle of the mausoleum.

"No, I think I will pass this time," the other lady said.

"Are you sure? I mean, we came all this way just to see our father."

"I know, but I can see him another time. You can go in if you would like."

"No, I am fine. We will visit him from outside today."

Wayne and Laura breathed a quit sigh of relief.

While they waited for the daughters of the deceased to finish their visit, Wayne could not help but feel bad for what he had done. Breaking into a tomb was not something he thought he would have to do or wanted to do, but he had no choice. He knew that if he and Laura were caught there would be severe consequences. Growing up, he was no angel and did many things he was not proud of but never did anything as bad as this. He never spent time in jail nor did anything to even warrant an arrest. Until now. Glancing over to the coffin, he somehow knew breaking into the tomb would not be his only misdeed for the day.

God forgive us, he thought.

Several more minutes had passed before Laura realized how quiet it was outside. She gently tapped Wayne on the shoulder and he looked over to her. She motioned to the door with her eyes and he nodded, understanding immediately what she wanted him to do. He stood up slowly and peeked out the small window and found that the two women had left.

That was a brief visit, he thought.

"All right," Wayne said softly, "I am pretty sure they are gone."

"What do you mean – pretty sure?" Laura asked curiously.

"Well I do not see them," Wayne answered, "but for all I know they could be close by. Let's just do what we have to do and get the hell out of here."

"Amen to that," Laura agreed.

Wayne and Laura stood on either side of the casket and looked down at it. It was just bright enough for Wayne to tell that it was made of wood.

"Okay, you look along that wall and I'll take this one," Wayne whispered, indicating the wall behind him.

They separated and searched along the walls and ceiling to see if there were any writings or carvings on them. There was none. They joined at the far wall and looked at each other. They held their gaze for a few seconds and then looked at the coffin and back at each other again.

"Don't tell me what we need is inside that thing," Laura whispered and pointed.

"I'm not looking forward to this either Laura," Wayne whispered in reply, "but we have no other choice."

He walked over to the coffin and Laura slowly joined him at his side. They both hated and dreaded the thought of what they had to do.

Well, here goes nothing, Wayne thought.

At first it seemed locked, but Wayne managed to open it with a little force.

"Do you have your cellphone?" Wayne whispered. "We need some light."

Laura took out her cellphone and turned it toward the dead body.

The sight of it was horribly gruesome but entirely skeletal. No foul odor came from it. A man in an old tuxedo stared up at them with its empty eye socket's and open mouth. Laura gasped and covered her mouth with her hand as she turned away. She had never seen a real skeleton before. Carefully, Wayne searched the casket in hopes of finding anything with writing on it. He wrinkled his nose in disgust but continued searching. He found nothing. Pausing, he looked at each of the dead man's pockets – except for the ones inside the jacket. A dry gulp sounded in his throat. The very thought of ruffling through a corpse's clothes frightened him. With shaky hands, Wayne slowly and gently patted the dead man's pockets. He hoped to hear the sound of crumpling paper but heard nothing. Finally, he knew whatever he was looking for was inside the jacket.

"Did you find it?" Laura asked quietly, still with her back to him.

"Not yet, but I think I'm about to," Wayne replied.

Laura turned just in time to see Wayne cautiously lift the left side of the jacket. He quickly glanced at her. The look on her face made it seem as though she were about to pass out but she did not. Unable to watch, she turned away again.

Very slowly, Wayne dipped his left hand into the inner left pocket of the jacket. Finally, he felt what seemed to be a folded piece of paper. He began removing it but suddenly felt something crawl onto his hand. He gasped and froze in place.

"What is it?" Laura asked at the look of shock and fear on his face. "What's wrong?"

Wayne whispered his reply in a cracked voice. "I…I uh…think a spider crawling on my hand."

"Oh my God," Laura whispered as she took two steps back. "Please, whatever you do…make no sudden movements."

Wayne did not answer her. Because of his fear of spiders, he was scared stiff. He closed his eyes for a moment because his vision had begun to blur. Impatiently, he waited for the spider to leave his hand. To Wayne, the seconds felt like minutes but the large insect finally moved off. Making sure he had the piece of paper, he yanked out his hand and shook it – just to be certain he was free of the spider. In doing so, a small scream escaped Laura's lips. Wayne released a huge sigh of relief and noted the look on Laura's face. It was a look that told him if he ever did that to her again, he would be very sorry. Wayne silently acknowledged the look and nodded in understanding. Without touching the jacket, they took one final look at where Wayne's hand was. For a few seconds nothing happened, but just as Wayne reached to close the lid the dark grey spider's legs felt at the air before creeping its way up and onto the front of the jacket. They both shivered at the sight of it. Wayne slowly closed the lid to the coffin.

"Wolf-Spider," he whispered. "How it got in there is beyond me."

"A what spider?" Laura asked curiously.

"A Wolf-Spider," Wayne replied. "They range from light to dark grey in color, and from what I know of them, they usually hang out in dark and damp places like wood wiles. They are not poisonous but they are venomous."

"Good to know. Are you all right?" Laura asked quietly.

"Yeah," Wayne replied. "Actually, I am surprised it didn't bite me."

"Why?" Laura asked.

"Don't get me wrong," Wayne said. "I am glad it didn't, but they are usually very aggressive and bite when provoked."

"Okay, let's get the hell out of here before we're caught," she added.

Removing a handkerchief from his back jeans pocket, Wayne rubbed down the coffin to rid it of fingerprints. They moved for the door and Wayne looked outside before opening it. Seeing no one, he opened it and stuck his head out again to see if he could spot anyone nearby. They were in the clear and he scooted Laura out first and then followed. He closed the door behind him and looked at it to see if it revealed any type of tampering.

"What do you think?" he said. "Does it look like it's been opened?"

Laura took a good look at it and shook her head.

"Luckily no," she replied.

"Good, let's get out of here," Wayne said.

"Are you sure that piece of paper is all that you need?" Laura asked as they walked back to the car.

"I bloody hope so," Wayne replied. "God, forgive us."

At the respectable speed of ten kilometers an hour, they drove out of the cemetery and headed back down Woodstock Road, toward Laura's home.

Without looking at it, Wayne put the still-neatly-folded piece of paper in his front pocket.

"Well," he began, "at least we didn't spend the whole day there."

"True, but it was still creepy," Laura said. "We were very lucky that we didn't get caught back there."

"So very true," Wayne agreed and then added thoughtfully. "Why don't we go over to the National Library on Springhill Road. Maybe we could find out some valuable information there."

Laura nodded. "Good idea."

Chapter Six
Bad News, Worse News

Once Wayne and Laura got through all of the afternoon traffic, they arrived at the library. The parking lot was big enough for a small shopping center. There were many vehicles but it was far from full. They parked near the entrance and stepped out of the car. When they got inside, they headed for the computers, which were on the main floor. Laura sat at one computer, while Wayne sat at another right beside her. The first thing they had seen on the computer screens was the Google Internet search browser.

"It is a good thing that both of us have a basic knowledge of the Internet, huh?"

"Yes, it is," Laura quietly agreed. "What are you searching for first?"

Wayne thought about that briefly before he replied. "Haunted Houses of Edmundston, New Brunswick. Just a shot-in-the-dark but it is all I can think of right now. I think it is a book. And you?"

"The Wilmot Rural Cemetery," she answered.

"We were just there," Wayne whispered to her. "You're trying to find that mausoleum, aren't you?"

Laura nodded as her fingers type away. As she conducted her search, Wayne went on with his. To his surprise, a whole list of not only haunted houses but haunted places like castles and museums popped up as well. There were sixty matches for haunted places in their city alone. He had no idea where to begin. Sitting back, he rubbed his eyes, not looking forward to having to go through them all. Then he began. He clicked on the links one at a time and scanned through them slowly. Laura had already found an article on the mausoleum they just visited.

"This is interesting," she said in a low voice.

"What is?" Wayne asked as he leaned in closer to listen.

"Our mausoleum," she said in a low voice. "It was constructed in 1944."

"Are you serious?" Wayne said. "You found it?"

"That's what it says here," Laura replied. "Frederick Brown must have been a dignitary."

"Really?" Wayne said.

"It looks that way," Laura answered. "There is quite a bit of information on him from political events to some of the places he travelled to."

"Hmm, I wonder if…it could be that there is a link in this website on my screen with the year 1944," Wayne said.

He leaned forward in his chair and searched for a link for haunted houses in Edmundston, New Brunswick in 1944. It did not take long for him to find one but it was not the one he was looking for. The one he found was for a haunted hotel on Spadina Street in Fredericton.

No, that's not it, he thought.

He continued looking until he spotted a familiar-looking house and clicked on it.

"This one looks interesting," he said. "I just hope it's the right one."

He began to read, but noticed Laura watching him. He turned to her and smiled.

"What?" he said.

"Oh, nothing," she replied she replied with a gentle smile. "It's just, ever since this whole nightmare started, I don't think I have ever seen you this excited. You almost look and sound like a Paranormal Investigator."

Wayne laughed quietly. "Thank you," he said and then turned back to the computer screen, serious again. "This is it, Laura. This is the house. Listen to this Article:

"At first, I thought it was just a harmless joke about the house at 15 Birchcroft Drive, where two high school boys, aged fifteen to sixteen, claimed to hear creepy noises like howls, screams, and feel ice cold invisible hands touching them. Last Tuesday morning, I was sitting at my dining room table reading the morning paper, dated September 7, 1952. I found an article that stated these same two boys decided to break into the house to play a game of hide and seek. Someone who lived across or near that address had seen them breaking in and called the authorities. About ten minutes later the police arrived. They drove up to the house, stepped out of their cruisers and began walking toward the house. Suddenly, the two kids charged out the front door, screaming as if they had seen a chopped-up body. The two boys were apprehended without harm. The police questioned them, and the aforementioned sounds and unseen hands were all they spoke of. According to this article, the boys were so insistent that the house was haunted, that two of the four police officers went inside to check it out. Moments later, one officer walked out the front door as if in a trance. A few seconds after that the other officer was cata-pulted through the living room window onto the front lawn and died almost instantly. It was later reported that he died from a broken neck. Luckily the officer lived. Later, he claimed an unseen and extremely powerful force launched him through the window and…"

By this time, Wayne and Laura had stopped reading aloud. They were astounded at this information. They gave each other a look as if to say, what in God's name have we gotten ourselves into? They silently carried on reading.

Nevertheless, as I indicated in the beginning of this web page, I did not believe the story at first. So, after I finished work that same day, and after I had my supper, I headed out to 15 Birchcroft Drive I wanted to see this place for myself and prove them all wrong. It was quite dark when I arrived there. The first thing I noticed was the boarded-up living room window. Surprisingly, the front door was unlocked and I walked in. I will tell you right now, what I heard inside that house literally freaked me out! I have been spooked before but never like this. I was not even five feet into the place when I heard this blood-curdling scream. It was a woman's scream. In fact, it was so loud that I froze in place right where I stood. I was unable to move for at what seemed like ten minutes. It sounded as if it was right in front of me but nobody was there. Immediately following that, I clearly heard what sounded a little girl's laugh. When that stopped, I heard running footsteps as if they were right beside me. The loud footsteps changed to low muffled hops as if they were heading down into a basement. Finally, the part that made me too scared to scream, and amazingly too scared to even – pardon the term – crap in my pants. In the living room, two tiny little red dots caught my eye. For a very brief moment, those little red dots went away, but then they came right back. Now I could not even breathe. I was horrified and it was too dark in that corner of the room to see any type of human form. I was certain, however, that those red eyes did not belong to any human. Then silence. It was such a dead silence – that in a soundproof room where you could hear nothing at all. Suddenly, I heard this voice…a voice from hell itself. It was a deep masculine voice. It said to me in a husky whisper, 'Get out of my forsaken realm.' When I did not move – though I truly wanted to – it growled loudly at me, 'Get out!' Well believe me I booted it right out the front door while it was still open. Mentally, I did not even feel the ground while I ran as fast as I could, and never looking back. The only one other thing I can say to all who read this website is please, heed my kind warn-ing and stay away from this house. I am positive that this house is a gateway to hell. I created this website in 1988, thirty-six years after my incident. Of course, this is an extremely late warning and I do apologize, but websites had just started coming out in the late '80s. That house is full of haunting mysteries. So, if you value your sanity, stay away from it, please.

By N.H. In Edmundston, New Brunswick.

Wayne and Laura sat there in shock by what they had just read. Wayne knew that it all had to be true because of what happened to him. Though he did not see any red-eyed demon, he thought perhaps the spirit itself was haunting him. Remembering the piece of folded paper that he withdrew from the dead man's pocket, he reached into his pocket and took it out. He unfolded it and to his surprise, there were two sheets of paper. The first page was a letter and the other had two verses on it. He read the two verses to himself. As he read, the look on his face became one of deep concern:

I call upon the dark lord. Satan, keep thy word and punish this – your failed servant. He deserves not to dwell in this house above your world. Chain him to your fiery gates and allow him no escape. I beg of thee!

I call upon the dark lord. Satan, keep thy word and let this – your servant – be free. Unbind his unbreakable chains and let him return to righteousness. I beg of thee!

Recite the right verse. N.H.

With a somber look, Wayne lowered the piece of paper to his knees.

How will I know which one to recite? Wayne wondered. *Only one of these sounds good but why do I have to do it in the first place? More importantly, what will happen if I recite the wrong one? How do I know if he was righteous or not?*

Laura placed her hand gently on Wayne's knee.

"Wayne?" she whispered. "What is it? What does it say? Is it bad?"

Wayne folded the note back to the way it was and put it back in his pocket.

He replied softly. "I will read it to you later. This is not the place, nor the time."

"But—"

"Remember the riddle?" Wayne interrupted in a whisper.

"Yes."

"Recite the right verse, it said."

"Yeah, but—" Laura said in an obvious puzzled tone.

"If I read from this now," Wayne interrupted, "the last thing we need is for something bad to happen: especially in the presence of this place and all these people." He placed the piece of paper back in his pocket.

"Well, you do have a point there," Laura said understandingly. "Where do we go now?"

"Well for starters," he said, "let's head out and grab a bite to eat. My treat. Then, I will tell you all you want to know about what's on that little note."

Laura grinned. "You never cease to amaze me, Wayne."

"Really?" Wayne said.

"Yes really. You are one man I know could be right in the middle of a world crisis, and still think about his stomach."

Wayne shrugged with half a smile. "Consider it my first theory of mystery solving. Never try to solve one on an empty stomach."

"What's your second theory?" Laura asked.

"Stay alive while solving it." Wayne stood. "Come on."

Well, I asked, said the look on Laura's face.

Even I should have seen that coming, she thought, rolling her eyes.

They walked out of the library and headed for Laura's car.

Wayne did not know how to tell Laura that he had to go back to that house. He knew that if he said anything about it, she would indeed become very worried. Laura unlocked the doors and they got in.

They drove to the nearest Wendy's, which was only a few short blocks away. Wayne ordered a large coffee with a barbequed steak sandwich, covered with sautéed onions and cheese. Laura ordered a double-bacon cheeseburger with fries and a small coke. As soon as they sat down and took their first bite, they closed their eyes and quietly sighed at how good they were.

"So," Laura said. "Now are you going to tell me what was on those pieces of paper?"

"Okay," Wayne reluctantly replied, "but you won't like what I have to say."

"I don't care. Can you please just tell me what is going on? The suspense is killing me!"

"Well," he began, "first of all, the guy who created the website is not the same guy who was in that mausoleum in the cemetery."

"What?" Laura said quietly, surprised. "Who was in that antique coffin then? How can you be sure?"

"Let's just say, this note says it isn't. Remember the guy's initials on the website?"

"Yes," Laura replied, "the letters, N.H."

"That's right. The same initials are on that little piece of paper. Also, I am certain the red-eyed demon in the living room is probably the evil that warned me to stay away from the last bedroom. Nonetheless, there is one problem."

"Problem? What problem?" Laura asked quietly, already sensing she would not like the answer.

Wayne answered in a whisper since the restaurant was a little more than half-full. "I have to figure out how this N.H. fellow died and somehow help him rest in peace. Also, I have to recite the right verse from this note, but I have no idea when or where to say it. Nor do I know what will happen if I read the wrong verse."

Wayne was obviously right. Laura did not like that answer at all. She rubbed her temples and leaned back in her chair. "How will you do that?" she asked. "And who was in the coffin of the tomb that we broke into? Does he have anything to do with all of this?"

"I have no clue, honey. Perhaps you should just read this," Wayne said as he handed her the two sheets of paper.

Laura read them quietly and slowly shook her head in disbelief.

"Oh my God," She said in a fearful whisper. "How are we going to figure this out?"

Wayne answered. "It seems, in order for this thing to stop haunting me is to free it from the house."

"Free it?" Laura repeated in an anxious tone. "What if you free this thing back to life?"

"There are two verses on that note but as long as I recite the right one, we should be fine. I hate to say this, but we have to go to 15 Birchcroft Drive All I ask is that you wait in the car and let me take care of this. Okay?"

"I really hope you know what you're playing with inside that house. Those spirits are not live people only looking to play hide and seek."

"I know, Laura," Wayne said, "but you know this is not something that I have control over."

Laura bowed her head. "I know," she sighed.

They ate the rest of their food in silence. Wayne wondered what else could happen to make their already bad day even worse than it actually was. He thought about the possible repercussions that could happen if he read the wrong verse.

Why is this happening to me? Wayne wondered. *Why could I not have just stayed out of that house in the first place?*

Chapter Seven
Mysteries of the Letter

After a leaving Wendy's they decided to make their way our way over to 15 Birchcroft Drive They rode in silence. For one reason or another, Wayne found it rather disquieting. They caught just about every read light that they approached. That only made their trip to the haunted house that much longer.

Finally, about a half hour later, they had arrived at 15 Birchcroft. At first, they remained seated in Laura's sporty Mazda and stared at the house. Wayne played Laura's earlier remark back in his mind when she said:

I really hope you know what you are doing.

Wayne realized he did not know what he was doing – scientifically or otherwise. He did know that he was about to mess with a paranormal time bomb. A time bomb that he also knew could easily go off if he made a serious mistake.

Even if I read from the right one, he thought, *what would happen then?*

Wayne looked over at his good friend.

"Well," he said. "Wish me luck."

Laura gave him a gentle smile. "Good luck, and come back safe, okay?"

"I will do my very best," he told her. As Wayne opened the passenger side door to step out, he stopped and leaned over to kiss Laura on the cheek. "Don't worry. I'll be back before you know it, honey."

Laura gave him a look that virtually pleaded with him not to go. Obviously, she was worried about him and the situation. She hugged him tightly. This surprised Wayne for a moment but he hugged her back. She let him go and he stepped out of the car, closing the door behind him.

Wayne made his way toward the front door of the creepy house. By this time, it was late in the afternoon. He looked up at the sky and noticed that the sun had begun its descent. He assumed it was between four and four-thirty in the early evening. Arriving at the door, he placed his hand on the doorknob and turned it. Oddly enough, the door was unlocked. As Wayne stepped into the house, he was surprised to find it completely quiet. He found that very interesting. The first time he entered the house, it was alive with the front door unlocking and opening on its own. He heard the sound of breathing as if some-one had run for miles. He witnessed a shadow of a human man and a riddle in blood. Not to mention, he had an eerie discussion with an unexplained phe-nomenon. Slowly, he made his way upstairs. Wayne was still somewhat leery about the upper level because of what happened. In fact, he was not too crazy about the whole place, period. Passing the first bedroom, he headed for the second. Once there, he found the door wide open and stepped inside. Scanning the room thoroughly up and down along the ceiling and walls, he found nothing. He also expected the bedroom door to slam shut as before, but nothing hap-pened.

That is odd, Wayne thought as he stared at the door. *Why is nothing hap-pening?*

"Hey! Are you here?" he shouted into the darkness.

He waited for a reply but no reply came. Suddenly, he remembered the letter from the tomb. Withdrawing the letter from his front pocket, he opened it.

"All right, I know you want me to read your letter. I also know I have to solve your murder before I can choose which verse to read. It says:

'If you have found my letter, then my riddle has succeeded in aiding you. However, the body in the casket which you have invaded is not my own. There is no name or initials on the tomb or coffin as to whom it belongs. Nathan Christopher lived at 15 Birchcroft Drive from 1934 to sometime in late 1951. In my many days of research, I discovered that Mr. Christopher was deep into Satan-worship. A newspaper article, of the Edmundston Exclusive, dated February 1, 1950 stated that they found a twenty-six-year-old woman dead in the attic of the house. Her throat was slashed twice and had three stab wounds in her heart. In an earlier article, dated February 13, 1940 they found a six-year-old girl dead in the cellar of the house hanged by her ankles. The girl had been horribly tortured to death with an old-fashioned razor blade. Thankfully, the press – as well as Authorities – did not go into overly graphic details. To find out more about these two unfortunate incidents, you should be able to find some information in the archives of the National Library in this city. Now, I imagine you are wondering how I died. This is why I had warned you about the third bedroom and to avoid it at all cost. I cannot tell you how I died. I can tell you that I right after I wrote this letter I broke into the tomb. I placed the letter in the jacket's left inner pocket of the person in the casket and then went back to the haunted house. I was murdered on that same day.

PS.

How do you know I am not lying? If I had survived, I would have gone back to the cemetery to reclaim this note. You never would have found it. You, as the chosen one, must figure out how I died before you can proceed with choosing from the verses below.'"

"This is my problem," Wayne said. "How am I supposed to figure out how you were murdered? I'm not an investigator, I told you that!"

Only silence responded as he stood there and waited.

To blazes with this, Wayne thought with an impatient wave of his hand.

Frustrated, he turned and headed for the bedroom door to leave. However, before he could get out, an unseen force slammed the door shut. The white blur flashed before Wayne's eyes as he felt it whoosh past his nose. It slammed with such force that it echoed throughout the room. Stunned, Wayne stopped dead in his tracks. Just a few seconds later, he managed to touch his nose lightly. He breathed a sigh of relief when he found it there.

"Look around you," a male voice said in a gentle whisper.

"What?" Wayne replied as he looked around the room. "I don't see anything."

"Look around you," the voice added, "and trust that which is inside you."

"All right," Wayne said in a frustrated tone. "Here is a question for you. If this, Nathan Christopher actually butchered those two people, including you, why am I still alive?"

"Because," the voice said in a slightly louder whisper, "you are the chosen one."

"Oh, don't give me that 'chosen one' crap!" Wayne said angrily. "Why must I be the one to help you? Why me?"

From out of nowhere, a strong wind continuously passed through him. Wayne gasped in terror and threw up his hands as if to shield himself from it. He hoped it was from outside but he glanced at the window and it was closed. He shut his eyes and prayed it would stop – but to no avail. The gusty wind was just powerful enough, that it made him step backward until he leaned against the wall near the door. He cringed in fear with his eyes still closed.

"Okay!" Wayne shouted into the forceful wind. "Stop! Whatever it is you are doing – make it stop! You win!"

As abruptly as it began, it stopped and silence filled the air. Wayne's breath caught in his throat. His heart pounded rapidly in his chest. He stood there for a moment, still holding his hands out in front of him. Slowly, he opened his eyes, expecting to see more writing in blood – but there was nothing. Wayne lowered his hands to his side. On instinct alone, he turned to look at the bedroom door. It remained closed. He was just about to look away when a faint click caught his attention. Wayne watched in awe as the door slowly open.

With his back still against the wall, he slowly yet nervously sidestepped toward the door and backed out of the room. As he entered the hallway, a deep sigh of relief escaped his lips. Unable to help himself, Wayne looked toward the third bedroom. He could not help but wonder what was behind it. Reluctantly, he walked toward it. Hesitantly, he reached for the doorknob but held his hand barely an inch from it. He shook his head and spun around. At a brisk pace, he headed down back downstairs to the main level and to the front door. Just as he reached for the door, a voice stopped him. It sounded like a little girl, and very close by. Wayne whirled around once again.

"Where are you going mister?" the voice said more clearly.

Slowly, Wayne scanned the area around him but again there was nothing to see.

"Hello? Who is there?" Wayne asked, hoping that a lost child had perhaps made it into the house and needed help getting out.

"Come, into the cellar. I have something to show you," the small voice requested, adding a slight giggle.

Cautiously, Wayne passed the living room and looked inside it. Seeing nothing but an empty room, he moved on. It was getting darker in the house and he knew it would not be long before darkness filled every room. Wayne approached a slightly open door. It was dark inside and all he was able to see was beginning of a stairway. It led down into the cellar. He paused and took a deep breath. Then slowly, he opened the door the rest of the way. Rusty hinges creaked in protest. Cautiously, he made his way down the old steps.

The cellar was not deep at all and he had no choice but to crouch down. The floor appeared to be made of sand. Wayne brushed his hand over it and it was. The dark cellar was dank and had an unpleasant musty odor. He wrinkled his nose at the smell. Suddenly, something caught his attention in the center of the room and he looked at it. From where he crouched, the object looked like a thick piece of rope. Carefully, he made his way over to it, looking all round so that he would not be surprised by the little girl.

Reaching the area where the hanging rope was, Wayne noticed the noose. At first, he thought it was a hallucination. He placed his left hand on it to prove to himself that it was a figment of his imagination. To his astonishment, it was very real.

The article on that website was right. The noose is still here but it makes no sense. Why is it still here after all these years? You would think the authorities would take it for evidence.

Just then, Wayne noticed a different type of smell in the dust-ridden air. The more he sniffed it, the more he was certain it was something other than mildew and old plywood.

No, that cannot be, he thought. *It smells like…like…blood.*

Still looking at the noose, he let go of the rope and placed his hand on the ground underneath it. As soon as his hand touched the floor, he felt something warm, mushy and sticky. A look of confusion appeared on his face. Reluctantly, he looked down. A puddle of dark liquid was forming before his very eyes. Wayne rubbed his fingers together and then smelled them.

"Holy Christ!" he said in a shocked whisper. "It is blood!"

Forgetting all about the low ceiling, Wayne stood quickly and whacked his head. Grabbing his skull, he dropped to his knees and gritted his teeth. He writhed on the floor and wanted to scream out in pain, but he remained silent.

Another giggle sounded through the air.

"Who are you?" Wayne asked, still holding the top of his head.

"You have heard of me," said the voice. "I would like to show you what happened to me."

Before the girl could say another word, Wayne quickly made his way to the stairs. As soon as he was able to stand, he leaped to his feet and charged up the stairs. He ran out the front door – nearly knocking poor Laura over.

"Whoa!" Laura said, surprised. "Wayne, are you okay?"

Still holding his head from foolishly whacking it into the low ceiling, he kept walking but replied. "No. Let's just…take a little walk. I really need some air."

"Hey!" Laura said as she caught up to him. "What happened in there?"

"You don't want to know," Wayne replied.

"You're damn right I want to know," Laura argued. "Look at you! One hand is holding the top of your head and the other is covered in blood!" Then she softened a little and gently held Wayne's arm. "Come on. We have to get away from here. Let's go back to my place and you could get cleaned up."

"We have to come back sooner or later," Wayne said.

"I know," Laura said gently. "But we will come back with clear heads, okay?"

Wayne stopped and stood motionless for a moment. He stared at his bloodied hand and shook his head. He could not help but laugh.

"What's so funny?" Laura asked, sounding concerned.

"I have never in my entire life seen anything like that at all," Wayne said. "I can't believe I even had the guts to go through with it."

"You're a lot braver than I am," she agreed. "Now, let's go home for a while and freshen up. Please?"

Wayne finally relented and followed her back to the car. They got in and he gave the house one final look before they drove away. He could not help but wonder what would happen next.

Chapter Eight
Home Away from Home

Laura unlocked the door to her apartment. They stepped inside and removed their footwear. She looked at his bloodied hand and wanted to ask more questions, but did not.

"You go ahead and wash up," she said. "I will get you a towel and a face cloth."

Without answering, Wayne headed down the hall to the bathroom.

Laura went into the kitchen and sat at her table. She wondered what happened in that house. She knew it had to be something bad because there was blood on his hand. The image of Wayne charging out of the house played back in her mind.

It was as if the house was on fire, she thought. *He got out of there in a real hurry.*

Suddenly, Laura remembered that she was supposed to get Wayne a cloth and towel. Standing from her seat, she went to the linen closet and picked out the two items. As she neared the bathroom door, she heard the water running. She knocked and opened the door slightly.

"Wayne?"

No reply came. Silence was not something she wanted to hear at that moment.

"Wayne, are you okay?" Laura asked a little louder.

"Yes…yes, I'm fine, thank you," Wayne replied.

Laura breathed a quiet sigh of relief.

"Here, I brought you a towel and cloth. I'll put it right here, on the sink, okay?"

"All right," Wayne replied. "Thank you, Laura."

"You're welcome," she said. "I'm going to wash your clothes."

"You don't have to do that," Wayne said.

"It's only two loads," Laura said, "and I have a few things to wash too. I don't mind at all."

"Okay then," Wayne said. "Thank you."

Laura took his clothes and then went into her bedroom to get more articles of clothing. She brought them into the kitchen. Her washer and dryer were behind two folding doors. She opened them, turned on the washer, and began separating the colors.

While the washing machine did its job, Laura made a pot of coffee and filled two cups for Wayne and herself.

Laura was sitting in the middle of the sofa when Wayne walked into the living room, wearing a man's dark grey robe. He sat down beside her.

"I took the liberty of making you a coffee," Laura said.

"Thank you dear," Wayne replied half-jokingly.

She giggled. "You're welcome. Feel better?"

Wayne nodded, sitting down beside her. "For the most part, yes, except for my head."

"What happened, anyway?" Laura asked.

"Are you sure you want to know?" Wayne asked. "It's way too creepy."

"Yes," she replied. "I want to know everything."

He took a sip of his coffee, and then told her all about his recent visit inside the haunted house.

"Until I got upstairs into the second bedroom and read the letter, the house was so quiet. It was like an empty shell. I heard no sounds and it did not feel like anyone was watching me. I felt no spiritual presence at all. When I finished reading the letter and nothing happened, I got fed up and turned to leave. That was when the house decided to come to life. Just as I approached the bedroom door, it slammed shut. It barely missed my nose. The voice told me to trust my instincts and look around myself. Again, I told it that I was no paranormal investigator and asked why he picked me."

"What did it say to that?" Laura asked.

"Because I was the chosen one," Wayne replied. "Anyway, I got a little mouthy with it."

"Pissed it off, did you?" Laura said knowingly.

"It certainly did not like my answer, no," Wayne said. "A strong gusty wind continuously passed though me. It even backed me up until I was against the wall."

"Oh my," Laura said as she leaned back her seat. "I am guessing it was not a breeze from outside?"

Wayne shook his head. "No, the window was closed. Needless-to-say, I begged it to stop and admitted – again – that it won. Then silence. I heard a very faint click and looked at the bedroom door. I watched in awe as it slowly creaked open. I backed out of the room and quickly made my way back down-stairs to the front door. When I got there, I reached for the doorknob but stopped when I heard another voice."

"Our ghost?" Laura asked.

"No," Wayne replied. "This time it was a little girl's voice. She coaxed me into the basement. There was barely enough light and I had to crouch down, but I found the rope that held her ankles."

Laura leaned forward in her seat again. "You mean the little girl that was found back in 1940?"

Wayne nodded. "But suddenly I smelled something different in the air; something sweet. Moreover, before I knew what was happening, I looked down and a puddle of dark liquid formed before my very eyes. I stuck my hand in it, and smelled it. It was blood, Laura. Of course, this caught me by surprise, so I stood up too quickly and whacked my head on the low ceiling."

"Ouch!" Laura said, touching the top of her head with her right hand. "That couldn't have tickled."

"You're right about that," Wayne replied as he felt the top of his head and winced. "This little bump is going to turn into a nasty big bump soon."

"Oh! That reminds me," Laura said as she stood up and made her way to-ward the kitchen, "I made an ice-pack for you. You really should be trying to keep the swelling down."

"I don't need an ice-pack," Wayne said stubbornly.

"Yes, you do!" she shouted from the kitchen.

Wayne was about to reply, but thought better of it.

"Here," Laura said as she walked back into the living room. "Put this di-rectly on the bump. Go on."

Wayne placed the ice pack on his head and winced again.

"That's a good boy," Laura added as she sat back down beside me. "This time, when we go back, I am going with you."

"Laura," Wayne began but she cut him off, somewhat upset.

"No way! You asked me to stay out of this once and I did that for you. Do not dare to ask me again! From now on, I am not letting you out of my sight!" She paused for a moment, calming down a little, placing her right hand on the back of my neck. "I'm sorry, honey. It is just that you mean so much to me. I do not want to see you get hurt or killed. Since this whole thing started, I have been worried about you. So, let's do this together like we talked about in the first place. Let's put our heads together and do whatever we have to do to solve this thing. Then, we could get on with our lives and forget this thing ever took place."

"All right," Wayne said. "You're right. I have been taking this thing way too lightly. From now on we'll do it all together."

"Good," Laura said as she hugged him. "So, what has to be done now? Do you have any ideas?"

"Well," Wayne said with a tired sigh, "before I got all gutsy with the unseen force from the second bedroom, it told me to trust my instincts and look around myself."

"What do you think it meant?" Laura asked curiously.

"I'm not sure," he replied. "Yet, I am pretty sure that it has something to do with the third bedroom, or around it."

"You mean this thing gave you a hint?" Laura said, surprised.

"All I know is it told me, 'this is why I warned you about the third bedroom.'"

"So what do you think?" Laura said.

"Well, if this Nathan Christopher character had died some time back in 1952 and the murder took place in 1986; wouldn't he have to possess a living body to commit a murder?"

"I thought you said possession was a thing of the distant past?" Laura said.

"Yes, I did," Wayne replied. "Though I have read and seen in some documentaries that anything is possible, even without Satan-worship."

"What exactly are you getting at?" Laura asked as she gently placed her nearly empty cup on the coffee table.

"Of course, this is just a shot-in-the-dark, but what if someone – anyone at all – went into that house on the same night N.H. was murdered? Is it possible that Nathan Christopher's spirit possessed the intruder? That might be something to go on."

"Any idea who N.H. Is yet?" Laura said.

"No, not yet," Wayne replied.

"How could he be so sure Nathan Christopher is the one? Could he be wrong?"

"Why else would he break into someone's tomb and place a note on the dead body? Why would he explain what that devil-worshipper had done in the past with those two other human sacrifices? Something tells me, he wouldn't do that just for the fun of it."

"If we went back to the library, we may be able to find out more about the house, Nathan Christopher and N.H." Laura suggested.

"What do you think we should do first, go to our nightmare house or to the library?" Wayne asked her.

"We should go to the library first," Laura replied.

"You think so?"

"We may need permission to look at the files or newspaper clippings in the archives, but nonetheless, if we had more history on the house and its ghostly occupants, we might be better equipped to piece this puzzle together. Right now, neither of us has anything real solid to go on," she concluded.

"You're right," Wayne said with a quick nod, still holding the ice pack on his head. "We should go now while the library is still open."

"When does it close?" Laura asked as we threw on light jackets and footwear.

"Ten o'clock. We should still have three or four hours left to do some homework," Wayne said as they walked out the front door.

Chapter Nine
Emily

At that particular hour, traffic was not much of a problem. In no time at all, Wayne and Laura arrived at the library. They stepped out of the car and went into the huge building. Barely ten feet inside, Wayne stopped and scanned his surroundings.

"Wayne?" Laura said.

"We have to find the special computers," Wayne said.

A puzzled look formed on Laura's face. She was unable to see any.

Wayne clarified his statement. "They do not look like normal computers. I do not know the technical name for them, but they look like bulky boxes with computer screens. They are meant to show newspaper clippings."

"Just in case, we should ask for permission first," Laura suggested.

"Indeed, we should," Wayne said. He looked toward a woman standing behind a counter. "Come on."

Laura followed him.

The woman behind the counter had long salt and pepper hair wrapped into a bun. She had her back to them as her fingers ruffled through a Rolodex.

Wayne quietly cleared his throat. "Excuse me, Miss?"

The woman turned to face them and smiled politely. "Oh. Hello," she said. "Do you need some assistance?"

Her name-tag read, Emily. She was wearing a plain ankle-length tan dress with tan high heels. The heels made her as tall as Wayne.

"Actually, yes we do," Wayne replied. "We were wondering if we needed authorization to look for information on a house. This would be somewhere between the 1930s and 1950s. We were hoping to look at some old newspaper clippings."

"That really depends on the situation," the librarian said. "Can you give me a general idea as to what you are looking for?"

Wayne looked at Laura and then back to the librarian. "It is somewhat difficult to explain, and it may seem a little far-fetched."

"Try me," the woman challenged as she leaned her elbows on the counter.

"Recently, I went into a house on Birchcroft Drive It gave me a few good reasons to believe in ghosts and I would like to do some research on it."

The librarian's face revealed a look that said 'are you kidding.' She leaned in closer to Wayne and lowered her voice.

"Are you referring to house number fifteen?" she asked curiously.

"You've heard of it?" Laura said.

"Unfortunately, I have," the librarian replied. "Please, accompany me. Jo-anne, could you please take over until I return from helping these nice people?"

"Of course," the woman answered.

She led Wayne and Laura to a closed door marked 'Authorized personnel only.' Withdrawing a small key ring from her pocket, she unlocked the door and allowed them to enter. Along the four walls were file cabinets and book-cases. Closing the door behind her, she motioned to the two chairs in front of a desk. The room was spacious. There were three desks, one along each wall with computers and telephones on them. Behind each desk on the wall was a beautiful landscape painting.

"Please, sit down," the librarian said.

She sat first, followed by Laura and Wayne.

"First, I will start by saying you both ought to steer-clear of that house," Emily began. "That whole place is nothing but a nightmare."

"Unfortunately, we can't do that," Laura said gently.

The librarian sighed heavily. "I should not be telling you this but I see no other choice. It was about a month after my thirteenth birthday. One night, my father sat me down and told me he needed to get something off his chest. He said when I was three years old; my mother went to a party and never returned home. For so many years, I thought she had abandoned us. I guess that after annoying him for so long he finally decided to tell me the truth. He also told me the police found her body one year later at that house. Her mutilated body was found in the attic strapped to some type of twisted sacrificial machine. Her throat was slashed twice and had three stab wounds in her heart. I was abso-lutely devastated." She paused briefly to compose herself. "I'm sorry. I have not been quite the same since then."

"Oh my God," Laura said quietly. "We are so very sorry."

"It's not your fault," the saddened woman said softly. "I also found out some other things about that house. Nathan Christopher was the last to own it. I also know it is very haunted by his evil spirit. That is why I warned you both to stay away."

Wayne sat back and listened intently. Yet he was uncertain if the librarian was being completely honest with them. He wondered if it was possible that she was simply trying to scare them off.

"How are they sure that it's his spirit, though?" Laura asked curiously.

"From newspapers and tabloids dating back to the year 1940 when a six-year-old girl was tortured to death in the basement of his home. All of the evidence pointed to him yet he was never charged."

"May I ask you a personal question, Miss…?" Wayne said.

"Please, call me Emily." she said, pointing to her name-tag.

"Emily," Wayne continued. "Your mother murdered in the year 1950. Correct?"

"Yes," Emily replied, somewhat stunned. "How did you know that?"

"Well, as I said, it's a pretty long story," Wayne answered. "I can also see this is very hard on you, so we won't take up much more of your time. Can you help us? Are there any type of documents here that can give us some history on Nathan Christopher?"

"You are still going through with this, aren't you?" Emily said with a grim look on her face. She shook her head. "Wait right here," she added. Standing, she walked toward the back of the room.

They waited patiently for Emily to return. Wayne wondered what Laura was thinking as his eyes drifted to her. He knew her well enough to know that she wished it was all over and they could get on with their lives. Not that he blamed her. He wanted it all to be over with too.

Emily returned to the desk and placed a thick leather-bound book titled 'Haunted Places of Edmundston, New Brunswick – Based on true accounts' in front of them.

"Everything you need," Emily said, "will be in this book."

"Emily," Wayne said, "we thank you for your time and patience. You have been a very big help."

"You are entirely welcome," Emily replied. "I caution you though; some of the accounts are exceptionally graphic. Please, be careful. You must not take this house lightly. And if you need more information, the news-scanner is open to you."

"Thank you," Laura added as they stood. "Your help is greatly appreciated."

Wayne and Laura left the office. They found an unoccupied two-person chair and sat down together. They sifted through the pages until they found what they were looking for. Wayne spoke.

"Ah, here we are," he said, pointing to the page.

"The House of the Soul Keeper?" Laura said.

They read each article together. Each one more graphic than the other just as Emily said they would be. The written occurrences spoke of labored breathing, voices, bleeding messages along with bleeding walls, shadowy human figures, screams and a child's laughter. It also spoke of the third and final bedroom. One person, who remained anonymous, called it *'The Devil's Room.'* The article read:

I remember when I first read that 15 Birchcroft was haunted. My reaction was 'oh wow! This I have to see for myself!' Two nights later, I paid a visit to the house and what I found literally scared the daylights out of me! As soon as I walked up to the front door, it opened on its own, though very slowly. There was nobody there. I hesitated at first, and then walked into the house. About five feet in, all I felt was the sudden forceful whoosh of the door slam shut behind me. Already I was spooked. As my eyes became used to the dark I continued through the main hallway into the kitchen. I heard this weird noise – like the sound of someone looking for a midnight snack in the refrigerator. At first, I did not see anything and assumed my mind was playing tricks on me. For a moment, I just stood there waiting and staring at the refrigerator, but nothing happened. Then I heard a faint giggle. A child's giggle and it sounded as if it were coming from inside the refrigerator. I could not believe my ears. Then, I could swear I heard the words 'don't be afraid. Let me out. It is so cold in here!' Right after those very words, something began thudding against the door like a-slightly-rapid heartbeat. I panicked. I lunged for the refrigerator door and swung it wide open. My jaw dropped as I stared in horror at what stared up into my eyes. It was a slit-up body of a young girl. She must have been between five and eight years old if I were to guess. Suddenly, I heard a much clearer giggle close behind me. I whirled around but no one was there. I looked back in the refrigerator and she was gone. I honestly thought I was beginning to lose my marbles. I slammed the door shut and quickly headed for the front door. Just as I passed the stairway that led upstairs, I heard my name. I heard it as clear as day. I asked who was calling me – but no answer came. I crept up the staircase until I reached the upper level. I heard my name again but muffled this time, as if it came from behind a closed door. The first two doors were wide open, but not the last one at the end of the hall. Reluctantly I walked up to the closed door. My hand barely touched the doorknob when it abruptly swung open. Then I saw it. Outside the bedroom window, a man hung from a noose. It rocked slowly back and forth. My breath caught in my throat. I slowly backed up, spun myself around and ran out of the house. I went to the side of the house where I saw the hanging body – but it was gone. I never went back to that house. Since that night, I swore to all-mighty God that I would become a priest and I have done just that.

Father Anonymous.

Wayne closed the book, thoughtful about what he had just read. He looked at Laura and she seemed just as perplexed. Laura spoke.

"That house is pure evil."

"I don't think any other word could describe it," Wayne added in a low voice.

"Excuse me," a female voice said from behind them, "but the library will be closing in about five minutes."

Wayne and Laura turned to face a young woman. To Wayne, she seemed barely older than twenty years of age. She wore black slacks and a white blouse with a name-tag that read Megan O'Leary. Her long dark brown hair cascaded over her shoulders.

"Thank you," Wayne replied. "Would there be any way my friend and I could sign out this book?"

The woman looked at the book and shook her head. "I'm sorry, sir. This book is a class C. Special authorization is required from our records department. May I ask how you came across it?"

"What does the C mean?" Laura asked.

"Classified," replied the young woman.

"Ah! In that case, a woman by the name of Emily retrieved it for us," Wayne said.

The young woman smiled. "Emily is the head of our record department, but she is gone home now. If you would still like to sign-out the book, you could come back tomorrow. I am sure someone will be able to help you then."

"Thank you so kindly." Wayne said as he handed her the book.

They left the library and made their way to Laura's car. It was just about the only vehicle left in the parking lot.

"Are you hungry?" Laura asked.

Wayne did not reply. Laura looked over at him. Clearly, he was in his own little world. She tried to get his attention again.

"Earth to Wayne."

"Huh?" was all he could say as he turned to her.

"Welcome back," Laura said. "I asked if you were hungry."

"Oh! Sorry Laura, I must have been deep in thought."

"Yes, you were," Laura agreed. "What is on your mind?"

"I am not I believe Emily's story," Wayne replied.

"Why would she lie about something like that?" Laura asked, obviously shocked by his comment.

"I do not know. I was thinking maybe she was just trying to scare us."

Laura thought about that and wondered if he was actually right.

"But, now that you mention it," Wayne said. "Yes, I am sort of hungry."

"Okay," Laura said. "Would you like to go back to Wendy's or somewhere else?"

"Wendy's will do just fine for me," Wayne replied. "But if you would like a different menu, it's up to you."

"Wendy's it is," Laura said.

She fired-up the engine and they drove out of the parking lot.

Chapter Ten
Facing the Darkness

As they approached Birchcroft Drive, Wayne wondered if the man described as hanged outside the third bedroom window could be the same man as their tormentor. To Wayne, it seemed too much of a coincidence to be two different people. So far, he knew of three people who died in that house – two of which were female.

They turned onto Birchcroft and parked across the street in front of the house. They stepped out of the car and looked around.

"You were right Wayne," Laura said. "Even now, this road is in complete darkness. But why though?"

"I'm not sure, but I am willing to bet it has something to do with this place," Wayne replied, indicating the ghost-filled home with a nod. "Come on, let's get this over with."

Laura walked by his side to the front door. Like clockwork, the door slowly creaked open. A shiver crept up her spine. She squeezed Wayne's hand firmly, silently telling him she was scared.

They stepped over the threshold and Laura turned on the flashlight. As they passed the living room, she flashed the light into it. There was nothing but an empty room. Not surprised, she flashed the light down the hall and they continued slowly until they reached the entrance of the kitchen. Laura flashed the light along the floor from one corner to the other. Numerous cockroaches scattered into dark corners to hide from the intrusion. They noticed the old refrigerator and stove. Silently, Wayne motioned Laura to stand by the old oven. She obeyed and shown the light on him. Wayne placed himself about five feet in front of the refrigerator and waited.

"What are you doing?" Laura asked in a whisper.

"I'm just curious to see if anything will happen," he answered back.

Laura knew exactly what he was referring to and leaned back against the stove. She held the light on the old icebox and hoped nothing was inside it.

They waited patiently for a moment or two, but nothing happened. The spirits remained quiet. That surprised Wayne even more considering all he had been through lately. Curious now, he slowly approached the lower door of the refrigeration-unit. He wanted to see for himself if the body of the little girl was in it.

Laura watched in anticipation as his right hand drew closer and closer to the handle.

Wayne clutched the handle and pulled the door open, only to find it empty. He released a small breath of relief.

Laura Suddenly felt several light tugs on the lower part of the back of her jacket. A very faint – yet irregular – clicking sound toyed with her hearing. Her breath caught in her throat. She did not know what was trying so eagerly to catch her attention, nor was she overly eager to find out. She briefly wondered if her mind was playing tricks on her but the tugs grew fiercer and the clicking sounds rapidly grew louder. She panicked. Unable to stand it anymore she screamed and leaped forward into Wayne's arms.

"Whoa!" Wayne said as he grabbed her. "What's wrong?"

Laura did not answer. Instead, she spun around and swung the light to the top of the stove. A substantial group of dark-furred mice squeaked in protest as the light blinded them. They crawled over each other in a frenzy as if looking for a dark corner to hide in. Every time they looked into the light, their tiny eyes glowed.

"They were trying to…catch my attention," Laura said, shivering. "At least now I know what it was. God, I hate mice! Do I have any on me?"

"Give me the light," Wayne said.

Laura quickly handed him the light and turned around.

Wayne noticed the small rips immediately and was surprised. He had no idea such small creatures could do so much damage. He then looked for any mice on her but found none.

"Well?" Laura said.

"No, you're clear," Wayne said as he gently patted her back. "You should be thankful though. I don't know how long those mice have been here, but they are obviously very hungry."

Laura breathed a sigh of relief. "Let's just do whatever we came to do and get out of here," Laura suggested.

"Amen to that," Wayne quickly agreed.

"You lead the way," Laura said.

They left the kitchen and headed for the stairs. The squeaks of the mice quickly faded away. The front door remained open. They stopped at the base of the stairs. Wayne turned to Laura.

"Are you sure you want to go through with this?" he asked.

"I thought we agreed that we are in this together," Laura said.

"I know," Wayne said, "but maybe you should wait outside. I do not want anything to happen to you."

"No," Laura argued. "I'm going with you."

Wayne was about to reply when he thought better of it. Slowly, he led the way as they climbed the stairs.

Halfway up, Laura felt an ice-cold gust of wind pass through her. She gasped loudly.

This startled Wayne and he spun to face her.

Embracing herself, Laura stared into his eyes with fear.

"That's it," Wayne said, "I want to you outside, right now – before something really bad happens to you."

"Didn't you feel it?" Laura asked in a whisper.

"Feel what, honey?" Wayne said almost nervously.

"The wind," Laura said.

"No, I didn't," he whispered. "Do you feel all right?"

"Yes…I think so."

"Nevertheless, I still want you to get to safety," Wayne added.

Again, she shook her head no. "Together," she said stubbornly.

Wayne bit his tongue and shook his head.

Why does she have to be so stubborn? he wondered.

They continued to climb the stairs until they reached the top. They turned toward the third bedroom, but instead Wayne led her into the second bedroom.

"Let's see if we can shed some light in here," Wayne whispered as he flashed the light along the walls for a light switch.

He found a switch and flicked it on. They were both surprised to find out the house still had electricity. Wayne turned the flashlight off. They looked around the room and took a few steps inside. The one thing that captured their attention was a message in dripping blood. Neither of them moved a muscle as they read the message:

You may have discovered my satanic past, but you will never free my children from eternal damnation!

Suddenly, Wayne felt a light tap on his right shoulder. Nearly scaring him out of his shoes, he quickly spun to face whatever it was. It was only Laura. He had forgotten she was right beside him.

"Honey, don't do that to me!" he said, though a little harsher than he meant to.

"I'm sorry! I'm sorry," Laura said as she raised her hands in the air, quickly realizing she made a faux pas. "I thought you might want to see this," she said as she turned and nodded to indicate the now closed bedroom door.

Wayne went to the door and tried his best to open it but it would not budge. Even the doorknob would not turn. It was as if he attempted to move a brick wall with a door-handle.

"What's wrong?" Laura asked with apparent concern.

"The door," Wayne replied, beginning to panic, "it's stuck. It's stuck good."

"Here, let me try," she offered.

Wayne stepped back two feet and let her fight with the stubborn door for a moment. She could not get it open either. Now they were both in a state of panic.

They turned away from the door and looked at each other briefly. Wayne then scanned the room for something – anything that would help get the door open. Laura, on the other hand, spotted the only window in the room and rushed to it. She did her best to open it – but to no avail.

"My God," she cried in a loud whisper. "We're trapped!"

Suddenly, the lights went out in the room. It was so dark that they could not see their own hands in front of their faces. Laura screamed. Wayne's heart pounded in his chest. He fumbled with the flashlight, but an unseen force ripped it from his hand. He heard it smash against a hard surface.

"Laura?" he said, but no reply came. "Can you hear me? Say something so I can find you."

Wayne felt around in the darkness, barely moving a foot at a time. He then heard a faint thud and stopped dead in his tracks. He listened closely to see if he could hear any other signs of her whereabouts. All he heard was silence.

God please, let her be all right, he thought.

"Laura? Honey, please, talk to me," Wayne pleaded.

A hunch made him turn around slowly. As he began to turn, a white light caught his peripheral vision. His eyes swung to it. What he witnessed shocked him and he took two steps back.

Laura was pinned upside down on the far wall by an unseen force. The light revealed nothing else in the room but her and her body was in the form of a crucifix.

Wayne was speechless. His mouth moved yet nothing came out. At the same time, he wondered why the demon was attacking her and not him. He ran to help her, but stopped just a foot or two away.

"Laura?" he said in a broken voice.

Wayne stared at her face and noticed a small amount of movement in her lips. He bravely lunged forward to try to help her but a split second before reaching her he was hurled back across the room. Swatted away like a pesky fly. He landed hard against the floor and rolled uncontrollably to the opposite wall. A stinging pain pinched his right shoulder. Wayne stayed down for a moment, grumbling under his breath as he clutched his shoulder. Slowly, he got to his feet and looked back at the wall. Laura was still there.

"You bastard, you let her go! I'm the one you want! You don't need her." Wayne shouted as he watched on helplessly.

The white light that covered his good friend went out. A deep demonic giggle resounded throughout the room. The light came back, but this time it was red and covered only Laura's face. Her eyes were closed but then they snapped open. Glowing red eyes stared back at Wayne. A chill ripped through his spine as he watched in fear. The evil that now lived inside her spoke in a low growl.

"Leave this place and never return, or you will suffer their fate."

"I told you to leave her alone Nathan! I'm warning you!"

The demon laughed and replied. "Pitiful fool! So easily, I could tear this soft little neck off its body and throw it at you. Leave, before I change my mind."

Almost as suddenly as the red light appeared, it vanished and a sickening thud resounded throughout the darkness. The lights turned back on and Laura lay motionless on the floor, where just a moment ago she was suspended in the air.

"Laura!"

Wayne ran to her side and checked for a pulse. He breathed a sigh of relief when he found one. He picked her up, draped her over his strong shoulders and left the room. Carefully, he made his way down the stairs and out the open front door.

Chapter Eleven
A Glutton for Punishment

Wayne gently laid Laura's limp body on the tall cool grass. He double checked her pulse and was thrilled – not to mention extremely grateful that she was still alive. Wayne shook her left shoulder and tried to wake her up.

"Laura? Can you hear me?"

Wayne smiled from ear to ear as she slowly began to stir.

"Thank God," he whispered with a sigh of relief.

Laura's eyes fluttered open. She looked up at him and smiled. Yet once she moved her eyes and tried to get her bearings, that smile quickly faded and she trembled.

Wayne could only imagine what was going through her mind. Gently, he made her look at him and he smiled down at her.

"Hi there, beautiful," he said to her softly. "It's all right. It is gone now. You are completely safe."

"What happened?" Laura asked groggily. "How did I get out here? Where is here?"

"You don't remember?" Wayne said. "You are on Birchcroft Drive in front of Nathan Christopher's old house. Are you okay? What's my name?"

Laura shook her head to clear the cobwebs and slowly sat up. Wayne helped her get to her feet and steadied her for a moment until her balance returned. He waited for her reply.

"Your name is Wayne. Yes, I am all right…I think."

"Good, because for a time there you were pinned against the wall in the second bedroom, and—"

"And what?" Laura asked curiously.

"Well, you were possessed with Nathan Christopher's spirit. I ran to save you, but something very powerful threw me back like a ten-pound sack of potatoes."

Laura placed her hands over her face and sighed heavily. A sudden, yet gentle breeze played in her hair.

Wayne tried to find the right way to tell her he had to go back into that house. He quickly ran potential answers around in his head, but found no easy solution. He spoke carefully.

"Laura, sweetie, I have to go back."

"Go back where?" Laura said, obviously clueless as to what he meant.

"Into the house," he answered calmly.

"Are you out of your mind?" Laura said in a low husky voice as she gripped Wayne's shoulders. Her eyes filled with fear. "Look at what just happened to us in there! You almost got yourself killed and I was possessed by a demon. We both could have easily lost our lives. I can't do this, Wayne and I won't let you go back," she paused for a moment to catch her breath before she continued. "This N.H. gave you a choice – either solve his mystery or be haunted for all eternity. Frankly, I would rather see you alive and tormented than see your obituary in the papers. I don't want you to die!"

"I am not going to die," Wayne said calmly. He knew Laura was fighting back tears and the last thing he wanted to do was make her cry. He tried to be comforting. "This is something I must do."

"No, you do not have to do this!" Laura shouted. She grabbed him by the wrist and led him away from the house. "Come on, I'm taking you away from this place. This house is making a stunt man out of you, and eventually you are going to pull one stupid stunt too many. Now, get your ass in the car! We are going home."

Seeing how upset Laura was, Wayne wasted no time. They sped away and headed back to Laura's place. He could not blame her for being spooked by what happened. On the other hand, he realized he was not very scared anymore. On the contrary, he was much more eager to face Nathan Christopher, and anything else got in his way.

Once they turned back onto Woodstock Road, Laura finally began to slow down. She glanced at Wayne.

"Look," she said in a much calmer tone. "I'm sorry I flipped out on you like that. Now I know how you felt when you first went into that house. It scared the hell out of me. Then, I find out that I was temporarily possessed. I really don't want to go back to that god-forsaken place – and above all – I don't want you to go back."

Wayne listened with understanding to everything she said.

Why didn't I just keep my big mouth shut? he wondered. *I should never have gotten her involved in this.*

Laura added, "Don't get me wrong, though. There must be some way we could help N.H. from outside the house. The only question is, how?"

"I'm not really sure if that's possible," Wayne replied as he watched the road through the windshield. "Unless of course, you know a ghost-shop around here with experts on the paranormal."

Laura grew quiet for a moment as she thought about that.

"Actually," she said, "there is one place I can think of, the only problem is that it's all the way across the city."

"How long do you imagine it would take to get there?" Wayne asked.

"At least an hour," Laura replied. "Give or take a few minutes,"

"Is it really that far?" Wayne said.

"Uh-huh," Laura said, keeping her eyes on the road. "With any luck they have something that can help us solve this thing."

"I hope so," Wayne said.

At that moment, Laura made sure both sides of the road were clear of traffic and did a U-turn, heading back toward Birchcroft Drive.

Surprised, Wayne looked at her. He never thought she would have wanted to take a long trip at that late hour.

What would the point be of heading up there right now? he wondered. *Certainly, the stores are closed by now.*

The only possible answer he could think of was she hoped this place was open twenty-four hours a day.

As if she read his mind, Laura answered. "I just thought it would be nice to beat the morning traffic and get an early start."

"Oh, I see," Wayne said.

"That's okay, isn't it?"

Wayne shrugged and smiled at her. "Of course, it is. Besides, you are the driver. You do realize, of course, that at this hour the place is probably closed?"

"No, it's not," Laura claimed. "It is open twenty-four hours a day."

"Are you sure?"

"Yes."

They drove past Birchcroft and continued down Woodstock Road, through the suburbs and into the countryside. Wayne opened his window halfway. A moment later, Laura did the same. There were mainly farms out that way. The moon was just bright enough to reveal the crops of corn. He could not help but smile as the sweet country air filled his lungs.

Laura sighed quietly. "Ah, smell that fresh air," she said.

"I know," Wayne agreed, "I love the country, only I can't afford to live here."

"No?" Laura said.

"Not really," Wayne replied. "I'm sure some of the property can be a decent price but you need a vehicle just to get from one place to another."

"Well," Laura said, "I can see what you mean to needing a vehicle around here. The farms seem to be fairly long walks in between."

Once again, Wayne looked out my window. For a moment, he forgot the reason they were even driving out here in the middle of nowhere.

Laura gasped and slammed on the brakes.

On instinct alone, Wayne threw his hands forward against the dashboard.

"Whoa!" he shouted.

"Sweet Jesus!" Laura said, shocked by what she saw over the steering wheel.

In their path, a young female stood motionless and stared at them. She was roughly five feet away. She was wearing a white knee-length dress but it was covered in blood. They did not recognize her at first, but after a few more seconds, Wayne knew exactly who it was. He spoke in an awed whisper.

"Oh my God, it's her!"

"What?" Laura said. "What do you mean? Who is she?"

"The six-year-old girl from 15 Birchcroft," he answered. "The one who was slowly tortured to death in Nathan Christopher's cellar."

"Are you serious? How can you be sure?"

"Dead serious," Wayne replied. "Look at her face."

Doing as instructed, Laura took a good look at her face and finally noticed the many scars. Her eyes widened. Almost each one of the scars overlapped with another. She wondered how any human being – no matter how disturbed and twisted – could do such a vile thing to a child and possibly enjoy it. Her stomach turned in disgust at the disturbing images that filled her mind. She looked away and closed her eyes.

Never taking his eyes off the little girl, Wayne opened his door and slowly stepped out of the car. He felt that if he made any sudden moves, it would scare her off.

Laura turned off the engine and cautiously followed his lead. To her surprise, the young girl had no interest at all in her and concentrated only on Wayne.

Silently, Wayne gestured to Laura to stay right where she was, by the driver's-side of the car. With caution, he hesitantly approached the spirit. The little girl did not move an inch but watched his every move with a cold lifeless stare.

"All right," Wayne said in a gentle, yet somewhat shaky voice, "you have my attention. What is it that you want from me?"

I want you to find my body, the spirit said without moving her lips.

This took Wayne by surprise. For a brief moment, he wondered if he actually heard anything. He snapped a confused look at Laura and then back to the girl.

Yes, you are the only one that hears me, the little girl added.

"I did not know that ghosts can be telepathic," Wayne said.

There is much you do not know about the spirit world, Mister Wayne Saunders.

"How can we help you if we do not know who you are?" Wayne asked. "Can you tell us your name?"

My name is Wendy Saint-Pierre, said the haunting voice.

"Is your body here somewhere, Wendy?" Wayne asked. "Do you know where your killer left it?"

A look of confusion formed on Laura's face as she listened intently.

Wendy slowly turned her head to the right. She lifted her right arm and pointed into the darkness. They looked in that direction. Laura spoke.

"I'm not sure, but that looks like an old barn. Luckily the moon is so bright, or we would probably have never seen it."

"Very true," Wayne agreed. Without turning to face the little ghost he asked. "Is that where your body is, Wendy?"

Wendy Saint-Pierre gave no reply. She only stood there, expressionless and silent.

Wayne and Laura turned back to her but she had already vanished. Now only an empty road lay before them. They got back in the car and sat there, staring in the direction of the barn.

"So, what do you think?" Laura asked.

"We should check it out. Who knows, we may actually find her."

Laura restarted the car and turned into the driveway that lead to the barn. She turned on the high-beams to get a better view of the barn and their surroundings. Running along both sides of the gravel-entryway was a wooden pole-wire type fence. Some of the poles were slanted and some of the wires were broken. To her, it appeared built in the mid to late thirties. They parked in front of the barn and stepped out of the car. They decided to keep the headlights on so they could see. They stood there for a moment and scanned the area. They saw nothing that seemed out of the ordinary. Several crickets hummed their nightly tunes. Laura broke the silence.

Wayne grabbed the flashlight from the back seat and turned it on. "All set?"

"As ready as I will ever be," she answered.

They walked toward the barn door. The gravel crunched under their feet. The door was unlocked and Wayne swung it open. He moved the flashlight across the interior.

Wayne went inside first and Laura followed behind him. The flashlight revealed a few old rusty farming tools and accessories. A shovel, hoe, and a rake hung on the left wall. A ladder rested horizontally on the rear wall, and the right wall held an old fertilizer dispenser and a gardening hose.

"Maybe she is on the ceiling," Laura said.

Wayne pointed the light upward, in hopes that finding Wendy Saint Pierre would be that easy. He guided the light along the entire ceiling and found nothing but old beams. They moved a little deeper into the barn, flashing the light along the floor now. It was mainly dirt and hay.

Wayne sighed. "There must be something we're missing," he said softly.

"Yeah," Laura agreed. "The only question is what?"

"Could you hold this?" Wayne said, holding the flashlight out to her. "I'm going to need both hands for this."

"Sure," Laura said.

Wayne knelt down and sifted through some of the hay, with hopes he would uncover some sort of clue or a body.

Laura shed the light in front of him. She wondered if the little spirit was playing with their minds.

Even if she was, why would she? Laura wondered. *She would have nothing to gain by misleading us.*

"How are we supposed to find anything in this mess?" Laura asked.

"To put it mildly," Wayne said, "with luck."

They searched every inch of the old barn but found nothing to indicate where Wendy Saint-Pierre had been buried. Laura broke the silence.

"Maybe, there is a chance we…might be…looking…" she stammered.

"Laura?" Wayne said as he turned to look up at her. "Are you okay?"

"The door to the past has been closed," she said in a slow trance-like-tone, "but I cannot tell you where it is."

Something in her voice did not sound right to Wayne. Puzzled, he got to his feet and placed a hand on her shoulder. He tried to look into her eyes, but was unable to see them clearly in the darkness of the barn. Nevertheless, he knew something was not right and hoped she was just tired.

"Honey," Wayne said, "why don't you go sit in the car and rest for a while? I could do this myself."

Without saying a word, Laura turned and headed for the open door. Wayne pointed the light along the floor so that she would not trip and fall. Once she was outside, he turned back to the matter at hand and continued his search for Wendy. As he searched along the floor he wondered if what Laura said had any meaning. He flashed the light along the walls of the barn once again. There were no doors to speak of.

She must be tired, he thought. *Hell, I must be tired because that voice did not sound like hers.*

Unbeknownst to Wayne, Laura made her way back into the barn and slowly walked to the far-right corner along the same wall as door. There she waited silently in the darkness.

There must be something here...some type of clue, Wayne thought as the hay noisily crunched under his feet.

The minutes passed and Wayne was getting nowhere. He thought about taking a break and wondered how Laura was doing. He stood with his back to the door about fifteen feet away from Laura's position. Suddenly, he heard a something that sounded like a loud thud. It startled him and he whirled toward the door. There was nothing there. He slowly backed up toward Laura's corner pointing the flashlight at the door.

Laura remained quiet and perfectly still. She wanted to say something but had no control over the voice or movements.

Just as Wayne neared the corner, he turned to face it and the flashlight shown on Laura's face. He cried out and fell to the floor, crawling away in a complete panic.

What the fuck was that? he wondered, quickly trying to get to his feet but then suddenly it hit him. *Wait...was that Laura?*

Still on the ground, he stopped panicking and flashed the light back to the corner. He was more than relieved to see that it was Laura standing there. He breathed a heavy sigh and got to his feet.

"Laura, honey I really wish you wouldn't sneak around like that. It scared the hell out of me."

Laura still remained silent.

Curious, Wayne made his way over to her.

"Laura?"

Just as he placed his right hand on her shoulder, the toes of his left foot bumped into something solid. He looked down and wondered what it was. Kneeling. he brushed the hay away to reveal a handle of sorts.

Is this what I think it is? he wondered.

Finally, Laura moved away from the corner and gently took the flashlight out of Wayne's hand. She walked about five feet and turned to hold the light for him.

He shoveled the hay away with his hands and to his surprise, he uncovered a rectangular-shaped-trapdoor. Wayne could not believe it, yet there it was. He tried to open it from the position he was in but it would not budge. He stood up, adjusted himself properly, and tried again. Using his strong legs, he finally managed to open the heavy trap door. The rusty hinges creaked in protest. He carefully rested it against the wall.

Laura shined the light inside the now open floor, revealing the skeletal remains of a young child.

Wayne squatted down to get a better look, but quickly realized without science, they could not identify the body as Wendy Saint-Pierre.

"We should get the authorities out here," he said. Laura remained silent. He turned, thinking that perhaps she had not heard him. "Wouldn't you agree?" he added.

"Is that her?" Laura asked breathlessly.

"I think so," Wayne replied, "but right now there is no way to be sure. I was just saying we should get the police out here."

"Really?" Laura said in a confused tone. "Oh. I…I agree of course. There is a police station not far from here."

"Are you sure you are all right?" Wayne asked.

"I am fine. Just tired I guess." Laura said. "The last thing I remember is walking back in here."

Wayne quirked his left eyebrow. "That's it?"

Laura had no idea what happened, nor could she explain it.

"Yes, but never mind that now. So, what do we do now?" she asked.

"Well," Wayne said as he turned back to the eerie sight of the corpse, "we can't just leave her here. Would you be willing to go and get them while I wait here?"

"Yes, I can do that," Laura said.

"Are you sure you're okay to drive?" Wayne said.

"Yes, I am fine. What are you going to do?"

"I'm going to guard the body."

"Guard the body?" Laura said somewhat sarcastically. "Who would take it?"

"With everything that happened lately," Wayne said, "it wouldn't surprise me if someone is just waiting for us to leave."

"Yeah, I guess you have a point there," Laura said. "Okay, I will be back as fast as I can."

Wayne walked her to the car and opened the door for her. She got in and fired-up the engine. After making sure her legs were out of harm's way, he gently swung the door closed.

"Back before you know it," Laura said.

"I'll be here," Wayne said. "Be careful."

"I will," she said.

Wayne watched as she drove down the lane way and turned onto the road. He could not help but wonder why Laura acted so strangely.

I wonder if our little friend, Wendy Saint-Pierre had something to do with it, he wondered, looking back toward Wendy's body.

Chapter Twelve
A Day at the Office

Lieutenant Paul Jennings approached his desk at a slow walk. He passed many of his fellow officers. Some were too busy to notice him while others nodded their greeting. In one hand, he held a cup of coffee. In the other, a black folder labelled Police Reports. Paul's supervisor – detective James Wilson – gave him the job of reviewing the reports. It was not one of his preferred tasks, but he had no choice in the matter. His partner – Sergeant David Mansfield – somehow magically appeared by his side.

The sergeant was six feet tall with a stalky build and in his mid-thirties. He was in the force for eleven years and became Jennings' partner two years ago.

"Report review night, huh?" the sergeant said.

"Yeah," Jennings replied. "I hate these things."

"Oh, come on Paul. They can't be that bad."

"Maybe you should try these," Jennings said, holding the folder out to his partner.

"Nah, that's okay," Mansfield said. "I already have a report to read."

Paul gave his partner a side-look and grinned. "You do?"

"Yeah my own," Mansfield quipped.

Jennings laughed. "You are such a smart ass."

Jennings placed the folder and his coffee on his desk and sat down. His partner sat across from him. Just as he reached for his coffee, his telephone rang. The look on his face stated he was not surprised. He picked up the receiver.

"Jennings," he said.

"Hello Lieutenant, this is Officer Jim Paisley at the front desk. I have a woman here by the name of Laura Barns. She informed me that she and her friend just found a dead body."

Sympathetic to the news, the lieutenant closed his eyes and shook his head slowly. Even after twenty years on the force, it was something he never enjoyed hearing. Nor could he imagine any normal person in or outside of the force who liked those words; except of course for homicidal maniacs and the criminally insane. He had a feeling it was going to be one of those nights. And for him, that was never a good thing.

"I'll be right out," he said and hung up. He looked over to his partner. "Come on Dave. A lady in the lobby said she found a dead body."

The officers stood from their seats and headed for the front desk.

Laura waited patiently at the front desk. She wondered how she would explain the child's body, and how its ghost led them to it. No real answer presented itself. Every possible way she thought of explaining it – nothing would come out the right way.

"Someone will be here shortly," said the officer behind the desk.

Laura simply nodded her acknowledgement.

Lieutenant Jennings and Sergeant Mansfield approached the front desk. They spotted Laura and walked up to her.

"Miss Barns? I am Lieutenant Paul Jennings and this is my partner, Sergeant David Mansfield. I understand you found a dead body?"

"Yes sir," Laura replied. "My friend and I found it in an old barn not far from here."

The two officers looked past her but did not see anyone. They glanced at each other and then back at Laura.

"My friend is waiting at the barn where we found the body," Laura commented.

"May we ask how you came across it?" Mansfield asked.

Laura hesitated, but replied. "It's not so much a question of how – as it is more a question of whom."

The two officers exchanged looks again.

"I'm sorry Miss," Jennings said. "What do you mean?"

Again, Laura hesitated but tried to quickly think of a believable story instead of just blurting out that a ghost just popped out in the middle of the road and stopped them. "Well, we were driving along and my friend decided he needed to pee so we stopped at a barn…" she paused as the officers stared at her with blank looks. "Oh God, okay, you probably will not believe me but a ghost kind of told us where to find it."

"Ma'am have you been drinking tonight?" Lieutenant Jennings asked.

"Absolutely not," Laura replied somewhat insulted. "And, we are not certain, but we think the body belongs to a Wendy Saint-Pierre."

"That's impossible," Mansfield said.

"How so?" Laura asked.

"I recall reading about her funeral many years ago," Mansfield replied. "Her body was buried underground in a cemetery and laid to rest."

"Nevertheless," Jennings said, "there is a dead body out there that requires our attention. Would you mind showing us where you found it?"

"Not at all," Laura replied. "Whenever you are ready."

"Lead the way," Jennings said. "Is this barn far?"

"No, actually, it is not far at all," Laura replied.

They walked out of the station. Laura went to her car and the officers headed for the lieutenant's cruiser. She pulled out of the station and the officers followed.

Chapter Thirteen
Unexpected Reward

Wayne leaned against the weather-worn barn and stared out at the cornfields. In the distance, he heard the faint sound of sirens. Deep down he knew they were doing the right thing by getting the authorities involved. As they drew closer, he wondered what type of questions they would have. He knew some of the answers would not be easy to explain. To kill time, he went back into the barn to take one more look to make sure the body was still there. With the flashlight in hand, Wayne walked up to the trapdoor – which he left open – and looked inside.

"That's a good girl," he said. "Now don't you go disappearing on us. I promise, somehow I will free you from your prison of hell."

Wayne knew they were headed in his direction. The sirens were getting louder by the second. He went back outside to await their arrival, and watched the cruisers flashing lights as they approached. They turned into the driveway. Their headlights shined on him as they parked in front of the barn. Simultaneously, they stepped out of their vehicles.

"Wayne," Laura said as Wayne walked toward her and the officers, "they don't think that body belongs to the little girl, Wendy Saint-Pierre. This is Lieutenant Phil Jennings and his partner, Sergeant David Mansfield."

Wayne looked at the officers. "What do you mean? Are you sure?"

"Sir," Lieutenant Jennings said, "according to our files, Wendy Saint-Pierre's body was buried in the Wilmot Rural Cemetery in the summer of 1940."

Wayne thought about that for a moment. He motioned the officers to step inside the barn with him. He showed them the dead body as they beamed their flashlights inside the trapdoor.

"May we ask how you came to the conclusion that this body belonged to her?" Sergeant Mansfield asked.

"You honestly would never believe us if we told you," Wayne said.

"Try us," the lieutenant said. "We might surprise you."

Wayne looked over to Laura and she spreads her arms as if to say 'I tried to tell them'? "All right," Wayne said. "Does either of you gentlemen believe in ghosts?"

"Excuse me?" the sergeant said.

"Actually," Lieutenant Jennings said, "I do."

"Since when do you believe in the spirit world Paul?"

"When I was a kid, there was a ghost that used to haunt my home. Even years after I left it continued to haunt me," the lieutenant claimed.

"Really?" Laura said.

"Oh yes. Some nights that thing still scared the crap out of me."

"I thought you didn't believe me," Laura added.

"Well, truth be told, it is not something we hear every day around these parts," Sargent Mansfield replied.

"Well," Wayne said, "what if I told you there is a ghost of a little girl who claims to be the spirit of Wendy Saint-Pierre? She stopped us about hundred-feet away from this very barn and claimed her body was here."

"Oh, come on," Sergeant Mansfield said with skepticism.

Wayne added. "Good sir, if you think I am joking, you are sadly mistaken. In case you are wondering, I am thirty-two years old – not seven. If I told you about everything we have seen, heard and read within the last few days – I am sure you would believe us."

"I believe you," Lieutenant Jennings said reassuringly.

"Thank you," Wayne said. "I apologize if I seem rude. The last few days have been very difficult for us."

"It's all right," said the lieutenant. "You both appear to be a little worn. Why don't you go on home and get some rest? All we need is your contact information and you may go."

"Yes officer, we were just on our way to do that when this happened," Laura lied.

Wayne and Laura gave the appropriate information. They were walking for the door of the barn when Wayne turned.

"Lieutenant Jennings?" he said.

"Yes, Mr. Sanders?"

"Do you think there is a chance you could let us know who that is, when you find out?"

"Don't see why not," Lieutenant Jennings replied, taking out his notepad and pen. "What is the number you could be reached at?"

"Actually, we're just going to stop at a motel for the night," Laura said. "But we will call you with the number as soon as we get there."

"May we ask why you are so interested in this individual's identity?" Sergeant Mansfield asked with scrutiny.

Wayne thought quickly. "Well, if we really did meet up with Wendy Saint-Pierre out on the road," he said, nodding toward the end of the driveway, "then we feel that she needs our help."

"My extension," Lieutenant Jennings said, writing it down on his notepad, "is eight, seven, zero, two."

"Thank you," Wayne said, taking the slip of paper.

"You're welcome. Good night, Mr. Sanders."

"Good night," Laura replied as she and walked out of the barn.

At Laura's car, they stood by their separate doors.

"Wayne?" Laura said. "Maybe Lieutenant Jennings is right. Maybe we should stop somewhere and get some rest. It has been a very long day and we are both tired."

"I suppose," Wayne agreed.

They got into the car and without saying another word, they drove off into the night.

It was not long before they drove up to a Motel named, *The B and B*. They stepped out of the car and walked up to a sign on the wooden-porch. It read:

The B and B, you will always come back to.

"That remains to be seen," Wayne grumbled under his breath.

Laura sighed. "Come on Mr. Grump. Let's go see if they have a room. I'm tired too."

Wayne rang the doorbell. While they waited, he turned and looked out into the night. All he wanted was to nestle into a nice warm bed and sleep. He was certain Laura wanted nothing more than to do the same. To his surprise, no one answered the door.

"Maybe they're fully booked," he said.

"The No Vacancy sign is not lit up," Laura said.

"Maybe they just didn't hear the buzzer," Wayne commented.

At that moment, the door opened. They turned to face a man appearing to be in his late fifties to early sixties wearing a grey bathrobe. He was slim and stood roughly five foot six.

Laura cleared her throat. "We are so sorry for disturbing you at this late hour," she said.

"No apology necessary," the man said. "I take it you and your friend need a room?"

"Yes," Laura agreed. "Would you have one available? We've had an extremely long day and could use a good night's sleep."

"Actually, yes we do," the kind old fellow said. "It's a double bed though."

"That will do just fine," Laura said. "Thank you."

"Okay," the man said. "Come on in and I'll get you the key."

After they signed in and paid for the room. They obtained the key to room number ninety-four and turned to leave. Just as they were about to walk out the door, they heard a female voice speak.

"Who is that, Reggie?"

To which Reggie answered, "Go back to sleep dear. It is only a nice young couple visiting for the night."

Wayne and Laura glanced at each other and smiled. They continued on their way and drove along the row of rooms until they reached theirs. To them, it appeared to be a very quiet area. There were only five other vehicles parked in front of their rooms – or near them. Wayne unlocked the door and they stepped inside. Laura easily found the light switch and flicked it on. The room was not as tiny as they had anticipated. It was actually a fair size. It had wall-to-wall dark green carpeting with sheer white curtains. There were matching lamps on the end-tables. There was a long rectangular dresser in front of the bed and a tall narrow one beside it. On one side of the long dresser was a twenty-one-inch television set. The other side had a white touch-tone telephone. They removed their footwear and walked across the room. The carpet was plush and thick. Laura sat on the edge of the bed and Wayne located the bathroom. The bathtub had double-glass doors.

"This is a pretty nice room," Wayne claimed as he found Laura staring at a beautiful painting on the wall above the headboard. "Now, there is a gorgeous piece of work. Where's the frame?"

"It's a Mural," Laura said. "I've never seen one in real life before."

"What is a Mural?" Wayne asked curiously.

"A painting where only a wall is the canvas," Laura said.

"Oh, I see," Wayne said as he took a better look at it. "Wow, it looks so life-like."

Wayne turned and picked up the telephone. He dialed the Police Station and listened to the options. He then keyed in Lieutenant Paul Jennings' extension. On the third ring, a man's voice answered.

"Jennings," the voice said.

"Paul Jennings?" Wayne asked curiously.

"Yes, that's right," the lieutenant replied. "Is there something I can do for you?"

"Actually, yes, there is. My name is Wayne Sanders. We met earlier. I was wondering if you found anything out about that body in the barn."

"Oh yes. Mr. Sanders, I was hoping you would call. The body did indeed belong to, Wendy Saint-Pierre. We had the body picked up, taken to the coroner's laboratory and the dental records matched perfectly! Also, I have more good news. I spoke with my commanding officer and he said that the Wendy Saint-Pierre case was never solved. It went cold. However, since you and your lady-friend found the body, there is a five-thousand-dollar reward."

"Are you serious?" Wayne asked, astonished.

"Yes, indeed I am," the lieutenant replied. "You could come down to the station in the morning to claim it. You will need to provide some identification though."

"We'll do that, thank you," Wayne said.

"You are welcome. Good night sir," Lieutenant Jennings said.

"Good night."

Wayne hung up the receiver and stared at it in shock.

Wow! Five thousand dollars? That will help with lots of things, he thought.

"Well," Laura said. "What did he say?"

Wayne cleared his throat. "Through dental records, they found out it was indeed Wendy Saint-Pierre's body in the barn."

"Wonderful!" Laura said happily. "So why do you seem so surprised?"

"In the morning, we are going down to the Police Station to claim a five-thousand-dollar reward."

Laura's eyes widened. "A five-thousand-dollar reward?"

"That's right," Wayne said as he went around and sat on the other side of the bed, "five big ones."

They lay back on the bed, too lazy and tired to bother getting undressed.

Wayne reached over and turned off the light. He could not help but wonder what would happen tomorrow.

Laura spoke through the dark.

"Wayne?"

"Yes, my dear?"

"Is it possible, that it could all be this way?" she asked.

"What do you mean? Finding bodies and getting rewards for them?"

"Yeah," she said.

"No honey," Wayne answered. "I think there is so much more to it than that."

"Think so?"

"Think about it. That little girl and – as far as we know – two others were brutally murdered in that house. How did their bodies get to wherever they are now? Wendy's body was hidden in a barn. Lord knows where the others are.

Did Nathan Christopher do it all himself or did he have help? And, why did the spirits choose me to help them?"

"Those are good questions. Hopefully, time will tell the answers," Laura commented.

Silence filled the room after that as they slowly drifted off into sleep with thoughts and images of the unforgettable events that took place that night.

Chapter Fourteen
Horror Before Day Break

It was still dark when Wayne's eyes snapped open. He turned to look at the digital clock on the night table on his side of the bed. It was ten minutes after five in the morning. He turned onto his side toward Laura. She had her back to him. He wanted so much to wrap his arm around her. For a brief moment, he wondered if he should or not. He did not want to disturb her or possibly even scare her. On a whim, he gained the courage and carefully placed his arm around her waist. Laura stirred a little, snuggled into him and placed her hand in his. Wayne's heart pounded in his chest at the mere sensation of her body against his.

"I've been wondering when you would come around," Laura said softly.

"You mean you wanted me to get closer?" Wayne asked curiously.

"Wayne, ever since this whole paranormal mystery started, I've felt a little closer to you each day." She paused, gliding her fingertips back and forth along the back of his hand. "Now I know I'm not alone in my feelings."

"You're right," Wayne said. "My feelings grow deeper for you with each passing day too."

Laura turned to face him. Slowly, she brought her beautiful face closer to his.

Wayne tried to focus on it. He was barely able to see her looking into his eyes. He wondered what they searched for: perhaps images of them. Maybe she wanted to tell him something but was too afraid to.

"I will be right back, okay?" she said. "I have to pee. Can you turn on the light?"

"Sure," Wayne replied.

He rolled over and turned on the light. The brightness of it made his eyes squint immediately in protest.

Oh! Damn, I hate that, he thought.

Laura made her way into the bathroom and closed the door.

Wayne laid back and closed his eyes for a moment. He wondered what was on Laura's mind. Suddenly, he heard what clearly sounded like glass shattering. A split second later a blood curdling scream. He bolted from the bed and lunged at the still closed bathroom door. He placed his hand on the brass knob but paused.

"Laura?" Wayne waited briefly for a response, yet none came. "Honey? Can you hear me?" Still no answer. "I'm coming in!"

Without further delay, he slowly opened the door. The bathroom was shadowed in darkness, but the light from the end table slowly cast a faint glow. The first thing he noticed was Laura's hand. It pointed toward what he assumed was the bathroom mirror.

"Laura?" Wayne said softly.

Gently, he took her wrist in his hand. The only sound Wayne heard was a quiet yelp of pain. Immediately he let go of her wrist and flicked on the light. He looked on in horror as the light revealed Laura's bloody hand and face. Her right hand reached up to hide her eyes.

"Sweet mother of Jesus," Wayne said as he looked around the bathroom and down at the glass-covered floor. There was blood all over the sink and floor around her bare feet. "Come on. Let's get you out of here. Take my hand and watch your feet."

He sat Laura down on the edge of the bed and motioned her to stay there. Then he threw on his shoes went back into the bathroom. He fumbled around for anything that would help with her wounds. He did not see a first-aid kit or any bandages so he grabbed two hair-towels and two face cloths and ran the cloths under warm water. He went back to Laura's side.

"Okay, let's have a look," he said.

He checked for any glass that may have entered her skin. Not seeing any, he wiped her hand as best he could and wrapped it up in the towel. He then used the other face cloth to clean her face. There were two small nicks on her left cheek and one about an inch long on her right, one on her forehead and a narrow gash just above her left eye.

"Well, you have some nasty little cuts but I don't see any glass. Here, rest this against your face, sweetheart," he said as he handed Laura a hair-towel. "I'll be right back."

Wayne went back into the bathroom and used the other hair-towel to brush the glass away from the bathroom's entryway. He shook out the towel in the bathtub and then placed it flat by the door. He then went around to the other side of the bed and got on the telephone to the innkeeper. It rang on the receiving end a few times before a man picked up.

"Hello? This is The B and B Motel."

"Yes, is this, Reggie?" Wayne asked.

"Yes. May I help you?"

"This is Wayne Sanders in room ninety-four."

"Oh! Hello Mr. Sanders, is everything all right?"

"Actually no," Wayne said. "There has been a bit of a mishap here and I need a first aid kit and I need it as soon as possible," Wayne said in one breath.

"I have one right here in the office. What hap-?"

"No time to explain," Wayne said. "I'll be right over."

Without saying goodbye, Wayne hung up and knelt down in front of Laura. He dabbed away more blood from her face as the cuts still bled.

A slight whimper escaped her lips.

"I know honey," Wayne said sympathetically. "I am sorry, but they have to be cleaned. I am going to run to the rental office and get a First-Aid kit. Okay? You just rest here and I will be right back."

Wayne tried to be quiet as possible as he marched out the door. He then ran as fast as he could to the registration office. Reggie was waiting for him outside with a First-Aid kit. He seemed genuinely concerned.

"What happened?" he asked.

"Sorry, Reggie. No time to explain right now, but as soon as I get her patched up, I'll tell you everything."

With those words said and before Reggie could object, Wayne whirled around and dashed back the room.

Laura was still sitting on the edge of the bed, right where he left her. As Wayne approached her, he noticed she was still staring straight ahead in fear and silent as ever.

"You poor thing," Wayne said as he knelt in front of her and began cleaning up her face and hand with sterile wipes. To his surprise, she did not make a single peep, nor did she try to pull away. He always knew women were tough but it was as though she felt nothing. "You know, I think we are both going to need some therapy after all of this is said and done." He paused for a brief moment and slowly waved a hand in front of her eyes. Not once did she blink. "Laura? Please, talk to me. Say something."

Her mouth moved slowly as she still stared as if in a hypnotic trance. "That face…"

"You've seen a face?" Wayne replied softly as a sudden look of concern formed on his face.

Finally, she blinked. "I will never forget that face as long as I live."

Wayne brushed Laura's long hair away from her face so he could finish tending to her wounds. He suddenly noticed a small chunk of glass just below her left cheekbone.

How the hell did I not see that? he wondered.

Wayne studied it closely for a moment and wondered if he should try to remove it. It had barely protruded the skin but he had no way of knowing exactly how deep it was. He decided it was best to let a doctor remove it.

Oh yeah, that is so going to leave a mark, he thought with certainty.

Looking down at the first-aid kit, he picked up a triangular bandage and a gauze pad. He thought back to his first-aid training. It was two years ago, but he quickly remembered what to do. Placing the narrow ends of the triangular bandage in his right hand, he rolled it around his fingers with the other hand until it looked something like a large thick ring. He then removed it from his hand and wrapped the opposite – loose end – inward so that it would stay securely around the wound. Then he took the gauze pad and pushed it gently between the now circular bandage to form a tent. Carefully, he then placed it over the open wound on her cheekbone and taped it.

"You are lucky though," Wayne said. "This could have been a whole lot worse. Do you want to talk about it?"

"No," she said, as if disappointed in herself.

"Okay," Wayne said.

Finished now, Wayne picked up the bloody towel and face cloth and stepped into the bathroom. Leaving the door open, he tossed them into the tub. He turned to the sink to wash his hands but stopped himself as a thought occurred to him.

Should I really leave those there? Wayne wondered. Reggie will definitely ask questions if he finds them lying around. He might think I beat her.

Calmly, he looked around the bathroom and found a garbage pail with a black garbage bag in it. He removed the garbage bag, placed the bloody linen inside it and tied it closed. Feeling a little more at ease now, he then turned back to the sink and washed his hands thoroughly. Unable to help himself, he looked at the medicine-cabinet that once held a mirror in it. It made him wonder what happened. Her words 'that face' played back in his mind repeatedly.

Could she be talking about the face of Nathan Christopher, he wondered. *Could she be talking about our ghost N.H?*

A moment later, Wayne finished up and went back to Laura. She was still sitting in the same place on the bed with a shocked look on her face. To him, the poor woman looked as though she had been hit by a car. Nevertheless, he admired her strength. Concerned, he knelt down beside her. Never before had he seen her that way.

"Are you going to be all right?" he asked her softly.

For a moment, she remained quiet and stared off into her own little world.

"I don't know," she finally replied, never taking her eyes away from that unseen world. "I've never faced anything like that before in my life."

"It's okay Laura. It's gone now," Wayne whispered comfortingly. "Wow! It must have been really ugly to make you think you could never sleep again. Did it say anything to you?"

She looked away from him to stare at the wall again. "Yes, it did, but I can't talk about it right now."

Wayne nodded understandingly. "All right. We should get you to a doctor. You definitely need medical attention. I will drop the keys off at the rental office. When I come back, we will leave. Okay?"

"Okay," Laura said.

Wayne closed up the first-aid kit and walked out the door. He left the door unlocked and walked briskly to the rental office. He had to think of a quick story to tell Reggie. If he told Reggie what really happened, he would probably never believe him and call the police. Wayne hated lying, but was able to see no alternative.

As if Reggie heard him coming, he opened the door of the rental office and stepped outside.

"Now will you tell me what happened?" he asked.

Wayne handed the first-aid kit back to Reggie and he accepted it.

"She is going to be fine," Wayne said. "She just needs a few stitches."

"A few what?" Reggie repeated.

Keeping his composure, Wayne quickly thought of a lie.

"Well, this is rather embarrassing, but my girlfriend uses a small mirror when she showers."

A puzzled look formed on Reggie's face.

"The way she explained it to me," Wayne continued, "was that she somehow neglected to rinse off all the soap and she slipped."

Still puzzled, Reggie cocked his head to the right.

Somehow, I get the feeling I am not going to like this, he thought.

"You see, she went down face first with the mirror in her hand. The mirror shattered and splashed up into her face."

Reggie opened his mouth to say something, but instead he shook his head slowly and pointed westward.

"There is an all-night clinic straight down this road. You will see it just after the third intersection."

"Thank you," Wayne said.

Reggie nodded.

As Wayne turned and walked away, Reggie shook his head again.

I guess it is true what they say, he thought. *You can never be too old to hear something new.*

Wayne found Laura waiting for him in the car. He opened the driver's door, got in, started the engine and headed for the clinic.

Chapter Fifteen
From the Hot Seat to the Mirror

On the way to the clinic, Wayne drove through the first intersection. He was a little concerned with what the doctor would think and say.

"There is an all-night clinic not far from here," Laura said.

"Don't worry. I know where it is," Wayne said.

"How do you know?" Laura asked curiously. "I had no idea you knew this area."

Wayne laughed with a single small grunt.

"I don't," he replied. "Reggie told me."

They drove through two more intersections and arrived at the clinic. Wayne pulled into the six-car parking lot and stepped out of the car. He went around to help Laura out. They then made their way to the entrance of the clinic. Even at that early hour before the break of dawn, they could tell it was a quaint country-style facility. The light by the front door revealed a wooden porch with three steps. Two potted plants hung from the eave. The only sounds they heard were their footsteps on the gravel and the steps as they creaked objectively. Wayne opened the door and they went inside. Almost immediately, they heard a woman's voice.

"Oh, my goodness, what happened?" A woman wearing a nurse's uniform approached them. She appeared to be in her mid to late thirties. She stood roughly five foot two with auburn hair and had a very caring way about her. Gently, she took Laura by the hand and shoulder. "Come," the nurse added, "let's get you looked at right away."

Wayne watched as she guided Laura down the hall. Turning, he found the waiting room and took a seat. Across from where he sat was a bookcase filled with books and magazines. Standing, he went to see if there was anything of interest. A National Geographic magazine with a picture of an Egyptian mummy mask on it caught his attention. He took it and went back to his chair. He leafed through the pages until he found the article on the mummy mask.

"Now, this seems interesting," he said. "An article on King Tut."

After reading only a few sentences, Wayne suddenly felt a very warm sensation in the seat of his chair. At first, he thought nothing of it and continued reading, but after a few more seconds, it felt even warmer.

"Whew," he said, fanning himself with the magazine. "Man, is it just me or is it getting really warm in here?"

Then, almost as quickly as it started – it stopped. Wayne sat there with a confused look on his face. He stood and felt the seat of his chair. To him, it seemed a normal temperature. He sat back down again.

"Weird," he commented as he continued to read.

Suddenly, the seat of his chair became too hot to handle. His eyes widened in surprise as he gasped and leaped out of the chair. He grabbed his behind and spun around to face the chair. He stared at it in disbelief.

Either I am losing my marbles or I am in dire need of sleep, he thought.

Almost reluctantly, Wayne placed a hand on the seat of the chair. To his surprise, it was cool again. He shook his head in confusion.

Now it's as cool as a cucumber, he thought. *How is that possible?*

"Are you all right?" a feminine voice asked.

Startled, Wayne spun around.

"Oh! I am so sorry," the nurse said. "I didn't mean to startle you."

"That's…that's okay," Wayne said as took a breath. "How is my friend doing?"

"She is still with the doctor. May I get you anything? A glass of water, perhaps? You seem as though you could use one."

He wanted to say, 'I could use much more than that' but instead he replied. "No, I'm fine, thank you."

"Are you sure?" the nurse asked.

"Oh, yes," Wayne replied. "Actually, is there a washroom I could use?"

"Of course," the nurse replied. "It's the very last door on the right at the end of the hallway."

"Thank you," Wayne said and excused himself.

He had no trouble finding it. The light was already on and the door was open. He went inside and locked the door behind him. Turning slowly, Wayne faced himself in the mirror and leaned his hands on the sink. He stared at himself and leaned his head slightly to the right. He could not help but notice just how tired he had become. Sighing heavily, he bowed his head and closed his eyes.

Dear God, please help me get through this, he prayed. Give me strength and help me fight this evil, he prayed. Laura especially needs your help and guidance now more than ever. Ever since this whole thing began, she has been in a very bad way. I know the last time we spoke was long ago; but I ask – no, I am not asking – I am begging for your help.

His prayer completed, Wayne opened his eyes and lifted his head. To his surprise, darkness surrounded him. Deep down he knew something was not right and prepared himself for another paranormal scare. He stared in awe as the mirror revealed horrific images of fire and brimstone, human-like figures with distorted faces being torn to pieces by an unseen force. Every one of their blood-curdling screams rang through his ears. Wayne tried to turn away but could not move. He tried to cover his ears, but an unknown force somehow stopped them only inches away. He tried to close his eyes but something held them open. What he witnessed next would be something he would never forget for the rest of his life. Insects – hundreds of them – began crawling up the mirror. To Wayne, they looked like small beetles. The eerie yet entrancing sound they made was like a swarm of various insects together. In a very brief time, Wayne felt jittery. He felt as though the insects were crawling all over him. He wanted to turn and storm out of the washroom – but could not. Finally, the mirror turned to darkness and quiet returned to the washroom. He thought it was over and released a heavy sigh of relief. He was wrong. A face so ugly and so disturbing appeared and glared back at him through the mirror. Wayne cringed in fear and backed away slowly until his back touched the door. Its eyes were a brilliant fiery red. Two long curved horns protruded from its forehead. It had yellow jagged teeth, no ears, no hair, dark gray wrinkled skin covered mainly in scars and looked very angry. It spoke to Wayne in a deep raspy voice.

"Pathetic little human pig! You live because I allow it. Soon I will tire of toying with you. Then you will join us. and I will bring you before the Lord of Darkness. He will be pleased to make you suffer."

Suddenly, Wayne's fear was replaced with anger. He glared at the demonic face defiantly.

"Leave us alone!" he shouted angrily. "Let those trapped souls go!"

The only reply was an eerie slow laugh as it smiled back at him. The devilish face vanished and the lights flickered back on. Wayne shielded his eyes until they became used to the light. His reflection stared back at him. He whirled around to face the door and fumbled with the handle until it unlocked and opened. He lurched into the hallway and found he was not alone. Laura, the nurse and the doctor were waiting for him.

"Wayne," Laura said. "Are you okay? We heard you shouting."

"You look as though you've seen a ghost," the doctor said, obviously concerned. "Why you're as white as a sheet!"

"No, I'm fine," Wayne replied. He brought his fingers up to massage his temples. "It's just one of those nasty little migraines that won't go away. That's all."

"Perhaps, you should accompany me to my office. Let me examine you, yes?" the doctor suggested kindly.

Taking one small step back, Wayne replied. "Really, that won't be necessary. I'll be fine."

"Come now," the doctor said calmly. "Don't be bashful. It will only take a moment or two."

"Maybe you should, Wayne," Laura said, concerned yet chastising. "Maybe you should let the good doctor have a look at you."

Wayne looked at the three of them for a moment, unable to help but feel their concern. Finally, he relented.

"All right," Wayne said, letting the doctor lead him away.

After making a few turns, they arrived at his office. The doctor opened the door and let Wayne enter first. Much to Wayne's surprise, it was a large room. He expected one of those closets with a table-bed and a cheap looking stool. He also expected a small counter with a sink, but there were none. The office appeared as though it was meant for a psychiatrist. Brown carpet covered the floor and a comfortable brown settee rested in the middle of the room. A few feet away, a black leather chair faced the settee in a diagonal position. A beautiful cherry wood desk faced a massive bookcase, which covered one whole wall. Not one single shelf was bare.

The doctor wondered what was going through his mind. He wondered what Wayne had seen in the washroom. Not to mention what made him yell.

"Please," the doctor said, pointing his left hand at the settee. "Lie down and relax."

Wayne did as instructed.

"Mr. Saunders, you look exhausted. Is there anything in particular you would like to tell me?"

"What do you mean?" Wayne asked.

"Well, for starters," the doctor said as he picked up his medical bag and withdrew a small pen-light, "I heard you say the words 'leave us alone' and 'let those trapped souls go.' Focus on this tiny light please."

Wayne obeyed and followed it from right to left, then down to the tip of his nose.

The doctor proceeded to feel Wayne's forehead and found it to be cool.

"Hmm," the doctor grunted. "No fever and you seem quite lucid."

"Doctor?"

"Please call me Ben."

"Are you a medical doctor or a shrink?"

Ben chuckled. "I am a little of both actually, but I am much more an M.D."

"I see," Wayne said.

"Obviously, something scared the crap out of you, but I also think you are just overtired. I want you to go home and try to sleep. Yes?"

Wayne nodded. He heard those words before. "Well, it has been a very hectic week."

"Are you having trouble sleeping?"

"Sometimes I have nightmares," Wayne said.

"Do you recall these nightmares?" the doctor asked.

"No," Wayne replied as he sat up. "Everyone has bad dreams."

"Nevertheless, if you continue to have sleepless nights, I want you to come back and see me, okay?"

"All right," Wayne agreed.

"Good," Ben said. "Now, let's go see your friend and tell her what's going on."

They found Laura and the nurse waiting in the waiting room. They looked up as Wayne and the doctor approached.

"Well," Ben began. "Besides being fairly exhausted, Wayne should be just fine. He told me he has been having some nightmares. Do you know someone who could keep an eye on him? If they continue, I want to see him again."

"I will. Thank you so much Ben," Laura said as she stood up.

"You are most welcome," Ben said.

Wayne shook the doctor's hand and they made their way to the door where they entered the clinic. Wayne opened the door for Laura and let her pass first. The doctor and the nurse stood behind them.

"Remember," Ben said, "if those nightmares return—"

"You'll be the first to know," Wayne replied, then joined Laura on the walk-way.

"Did you tell him?" Laura asked as they neared the car.

"About the haunting? No. Did you?"

"No, I couldn't bring myself to."

They got into the car with Wayne at the wheel. He started the engine and drove off into the night.

Chapter Sixteen
The Surprise Sister

They continued on their way to the police station. On the horizon, the sky was beginning to show signs of dawn. Wayne took his eyes off the road to glance at the clock. It was seven O'clock in the morning. He wondered how long they were at the clinic.

"It didn't seem that long," he whispered.

"Huh?" Laura said.

"I was just wondering how long we were at the clinic," Wayne said. "I mean, it's seven in the morning and it feels – at least to me – like we've been there for only an hour."

"You know, you're right," Laura agreed.

"By the way," Wayne said, "How many stitches did you need? I forgot to ask you."

"Only a few," Laura replied. "Ten on my face and six on my hand."

"That's a lot more than just a few. I thought you said only a few. A few equals three," Wayne said in a teasing tone.

Laura shrugged. "Slight miscalculation I guess."

"I'm just teasing," Wayne said. "You are actually very lucky."

"I am? How am I so lucky?"

"It could have been worse. It could have been much worse."

Laura grew quiet.

To Wayne, it seemed as though he insulted her. Of course, he had no intention to. He slowed down as they neared the police station.

"Ah, here we are," Wayne said as he pulled into the parking lot.

"Wayne?"

"Yes, my dear?"

"What did you see back at the clinic in the washroom?"

"Possibly the same thing you did," he answered.

"Possibly?" Laura said curiously.

Parking the car, Wayne opened the door and stuck one leg out before he replied.

"That face you saw, did it have red eyes, roughly seven-inch horns, no hair and no ears?"

"Yes, that was what I saw."

"Then, that brings one question," Wayne said.

"What's that?"

"Why did the mirror explode in your face and not mine?" Wayne asked curiously.

Laura raised her hands as if to say 'I don't know' and grinned. "Maybe he likes you."

"Ha ha ha," Wayne replied with his head tilted. "Well, at least your sense of humor is back."

Laura giggled as they stepped out of the car. Once they were side by side, she reached for Wayne's hand and he placed his in hers. They smiled at each other. To Wayne, it seemed even through all their hardships – their love was growing stronger with each passing day. They entered the police station. The gray tiled floor appeared polished to perfection. Straight ahead was a desk with two officers sitting behind it. A sign marked 'Information' hung above it. Wayne and Laura walked up to the desk. The officer to their left seemed much younger than his partner. His short black hair had not one strand out of place, and his shirt appeared neatly pressed. The name Geoffreys was on his name-tag. His partner, on the other hand, appeared as though he just woke up. His greying brown hair was disheveled and his shirt had some wrinkles here and there. The name Frankfurt was on his name-tag.

"Good morning," Officer Geoffreys said. "May we help you fine folks?"

"Good morning," Wayne replied. "My name is Wayne Saunders and this lovely lady is Laura Barns. We are here for the reward for finding the body of Wendy Saint-Pierre."

"Oh yes," the young officer said. "Lieutenant Jennings informed us you would arrive sometime today. We will require two valid pieces of photo iden- tification before we can give you the reward."

"Yes, of course," Wayne said, reaching for his wallet.

Laura did the same.

They pulled out their drivers' licenses and health cards and handed them to the young officer.

"Thank you," he said.

Officer Geoffreys reviewed the cards very closely and then returned them. He opened a drawer and withdrew an orange letter-size envelope and handed it to Wayne.

"Here you go, and congratulations."

"Congratulations?" Laura asked, slightly surprised.

"Yes ma'am," Officer Frankfurt said. "You both found a little girl that – most unfortunately – has been deceased for sixty-eight years. A crying shame."

"May I ask a question?" Laura said.

"Absolutely," Officer Frankfurt said.

"Was her killer ever caught?"

"Sadly, no he was not," Officer Frankfurt replied. "Whoever the killer was, he or she was very smart. According to the case file, no clues were ever found."

"The main thing is that you found her," a female voice said.

Wayne and Laura turned to face a woman who appeared to be in her late fifties. Her gray hair flowed down just past her shoulders. She wore a pink day-dress with white running shoes, and a white purse draped over her right shoulder.

"I was ten when I began my search," the woman continued as she slowly walking toward them. "Of course, I never found anything. I finally gave up three years ago. Now, two people – to whom I am exceptionally grateful to – found her at long last."

Wayne and Laura glanced at each other, and then back at the two officers behind the desk. Officer Frankfurt spoke.

"We beg your pardon folks. Somehow, we forgot to mention Ms. Saint-Pierre would be by to give her thanks."

"Ms. Saint-Pierre?" Laura said.

"I am – was – her sister," Ms. Saint-Pierre said. "My name is Cathy."

"Ms. Saint-Pierre," Wayne said, "please accept our most sincere condolences."

"Thank you," she said. "At least now I can move on with my life," she paused with a slight chuckle. "What is left of it anyway. Well, I believe I have said all I came to say and I really should be going. Thank you once again."

"You are very welcome, Ms. Saint-Pierre," Laura replied.

Wayne merely raised his right hand and nodded a farewell before she turned and walked out the door. For what appeared to be a long moment, they were all quiet. Wayne broke the silence.

"Will you gentlemen need anything else from us?"

"No, Mr. Saunders. You are free to go."

"Thank you," Wayne said. "Come on honey, it's a long way home."

They headed for the door and stepped out into the bright morning sunlight.

Chapter Seventeen
The Clue from Another

"I don't know about you," Wayne said as they got in the car, "but I'm starving."

"Yeah, me too," Laura agreed. "Usually, I never feel this hungry."

"Well, I'm sure that's because you take really good care of yourself. I mean, you eat three square meals a day. You have a little snack in between and sometimes a little junk food too."

"Hey!" Laura said with a giggle. "How do you know so much about my habits, huh?"

"Because I'm smart," Wayne replied.

"Oh, I see. Smart ass," she added.

Wayne could not help but laugh.

Laura stared at him for a moment before she laughed with him and slapped his left shoulder playfully.

"Cut that out," she said as her laugh mellowed. "Let's get serious here. We have to figure out what we are going to do next."

Wayne's laughing slowed to a halt and he patted her left knee.

Laura looked down at his hand and then up into his eyes. She smiled briefly but grew serious.

"I'm sorry, Laura you're right. Look, we know Wendy Saint-Pierre was saved. We also know it is possible that N.H. was saved. Lord knows, I have not seen or heard from him since I read that letter. So now—"

"Wait a minute," Laura interjected. "I'm pretty sure I know the answer to this, but I'll ask anyway. You never found his body, did you?"

"No," Wayne replied. "I would have told you if I did. Why?"

"Because, if you are right and Wendy is free – wouldn't we have to find all the bodies? You see what I am getting at? Wendy led us to her body, but the only thing N.H. led us to was a cemetery, and a corpse that was not his own."

Wayne grew quiet for a moment.

If Laura is right and we do have to find all the bodies, then we have no time to lose. On the other hand, there is only way to find out if N.H. was actually saved. We will have to go back to that house, he thought.

Wayne felt a slight pressure in his sinuses and bowed his head. He applied pressure to the top of his nose with his fingers.

"Are you okay?" Laura asked me.

"Yes, I'll be fine," he replied, then inhaled and exhaled a deep breath. "I hate to say it, but we have to go back to the house on Birchcroft."

"I knew you were going to say that. Then again, I knew we would have to go back eventually. It's to find out about N.H., isn't it?"

"Yes."

Laura sighed heavily. "Okay, but can we go back after breakfast? I really am hungry."

Wayne smiled at her tiredly. "Of course, honey. I could use some hot coffee myself."

"And a huge breakfast," she added.

"You bet your ass," Wayne said.

They went on their way. The scenery passed them by. They were very impressed by the beauty of many properties. Neatly mowed lawns, flowerbeds, almost perfectly trimmed hedges, various types of rock and vegetable gardens and trees from pines to maples and birches. Some had white picket fences and others did not. Not one house seemed as old as a weather-worn barn. Wayne almost felt as though they were driving through the French-Quarter in New Orleans. He never went there, but heard it was very nice.

"Beautiful, isn't it?" Laura said.

"Uh huh," Wayne agreed. "There is only one thing wrong with it."

"What's that?" Laura asked.

"Not all that much civilization around," Wayne replied. "I mean, you need to drive for at least, what – fifteen to twenty minutes just to reach the first mall or theatre? Not to mention, there are no grocery stores around."

"True. But on the plus side, you get away from all that city noise and most of the pollution."

Finally, they pulled into the first restaurant that they found and went in to eat. Everything on the menu looked delicious and reasonably priced. Laura ordered a stack of French toast and Wayne ordered what they called a 'Hill-O-Pancakes Platter.' The pancake dish consisted of six full sized pancakes. They were stacked one on top of the other. Between them was a blend of fruit, bacon, sausages and hash browns. A seemingly happy yet mature waitress jotted down their orders.

"Excellent choices," she claimed and smiled. "I hope you have a very good appetite, sir. That is a lot of food for just one person."

Wayne chuckled. "Don't worry about me. You bring it and I'll eat it."

Both Laura and the waitress laughed.

"Okay. I'll be back shortly with your meals," she said, turning to walk away but then stopped. "Oh!" she added. "Would either of you like some coffee?"

Both Wayne and Laura agreed.

The waitress went on her way and returned quickly with their coffees.

"Thank you," Wayne and Laura said simultaneously.

"You are very welcome," the waitress said and walked away again.

They sipped their coffees and chatted quietly while the cooks prepared their meals.

Before long, their food arrived. The steam emanated scrumptious aromas of freshness.

"That was quick," Wayne commented.

"Good service, means happy customers," the waitress cheerfully replied. "And good healthy food means happy bellies. So please, go ahead and dig in while it is still hot. Enjoy! If you need anything just raise your hand."

Laura took a second look at Wayne's plate and raised her eyebrows. She was shocked at the amount of food on it.

Wayne noticed the look.

"What?" he asked.

"Are you really sure you could finish all that?"

"There is not a doubt in my mind," Wayne replied with a grin and a wave of his hand.

They virtually ate in silence as they enjoyed their meals. Occasionally, they glanced at one another and smiled.

"You know," Wayne said after swallowing a bite of food. "Thank god this place isn't one of those fast-food joints, where they sometimes let the food sit and go cold."

"Mm hmm," Laura moaned in agreement with a mouthful of food.

They continued eating until they were finished.

Wayne was about to raise his hand for the check when a woman in the parking lot caught his eye. He was not sure who it was, but she looked vaguely familiar to him. She walked toward the restaurant. As she drew a little closer, he found that she looked a lot like Cathy Saint-Pierre. He looked at Laura and then back to the woman.

"What is it?" Laura asked.

"See that lady?" Wayne said as he pointed to her.

"Yes," Laura answered. She did not recognize her either. "So?"

"Does that look like Cathy Saint-Pierre to you?" he asked.

She looked again, but this time she looked harder.

"Well?"

"Wayne, I think you are imagining…no, wait…you're right, it is her!"

Cathy Saint-Pierre walked into the restaurant. She scanned the place until she noticed Wayne and Laura. She made her way over to them.

"Hello once again," she said. "Please, forgive my intrusion but—"

"No intrusion at all," Laura said. "Please, sit down and join us."

Turning, Cathy grabbed a chair and sat between them.

To Wayne, she seemed nervous, but was unsure as to why.

"Ms. Saint-Pierre," Wayne said.

"Please, call me Cathy."

"All right, Cathy it is then," Wayne replied. "Please don't take this personally, but how did you know where to find us?"

"It is a very long story. You may not believe me – but I will gladly tell you."

"Well, you obviously made it here and found us," Laura claimed. "So, of course we will believe you."

"Yesterday afternoon, I was taking a nap and had some kind of weird dream. Maybe it was a vision – I am still not sure which. I saw this place, and the two of you sitting right here in these very seats."

Wayne and Laura glanced at each other.

"A male voice spoke to me, but did not speak in full sentences."

"What do you mean," Wayne asked.

"He spoke as though reciting a riddle. When I awoke and got my bearings, I wrote it down quickly. I tried making sense of it but I could not. Nevertheless, I knew it involved the two of you. So I knew I had to find you and give you this," Cathy said and handed Wayne the riddle.

Wayne read it aloud:

"All these years, hidden so well, still filled with anger and tears for no one ever found me to tell. Four fields of a work affair, yet one stands alone. A silo seen by air – and a tree limply weeps for the unknown. I venture along a path – certain birds point the way. If not found by second sunset – face my wrath. If you succeed – live free to fight another day."

"Well, that doesn't sound nice," Laura commented.

"No, it certainly does not," Cathy added. "But what does it all mean?"

Wayne knew it was another piece of the puzzle to their mystical journey, but he did not want to alarm poor Cathy. Thinking quickly, he folded the little note neatly and placed it by the trash accumulated from their meals.

"In all honesty Cathy I think it means absolutely nothing," Wayne said as sincerely as he could.

"What do you mean, it means nothing?" Cathy politely challenged as she looked from Wayne to Laura. "It all seemed and felt so real."

Laura opened her mouth to speak and Wayne immediately noticed it. Without being noticed, he gave Laura a motion of silence. Laura caught on and simply smiled.

"Cathy," Wayne began, "you really shouldn't concern yourself with such gibberish. As far as I'm concerned, it was just a freaky dream."

"Perhaps you're right," Cathy said. "But how did I know where to find you?"

"Coincidence I'm sure," Laura replied.

"Please, don't get us wrong. We greatly appreciate you finding your way here to caution us about this," Wayne said as he pointed down at the riddle.

Cathy sat quietly as she thought about Wayne's words. She wondered if he was right and it really was just a dream.

"Well, okay. If you are sure it means nothing, then I guess it means nothing."

"Good. Now, since you are here, why don't you join us for some coffee or tea," Wayne suggested openly.

"Oh, no thank you," Cathy laughed, politely waving away the kind gesture. "I had my fill this morning."

"Perhaps a little something to eat then," Laura said. "Don't be bashful. Nothing says we shouldn't at least be friends."

"No, thank you. I am fine really, but if it is any consolation – for finding my sister and bringing her peace – you also brought peace to me. For that, I shall always consider you my friends."

"We are indeed honored," Laura said.

"So are Wendy and I," Cathy responded with a smile and stood. "Hopefully, the next time we meet it will be under better circumstances."

Being the man he was, Wayne stood and forwarded his hand in friendship. Cathy shook his hand.

"I'm sure we will," Wayne said with certainty.

Laura stood and followed Wayne's lead. "Yes, I am sure we will indeed."

With that said, Cathy Saint-Pierre turned and made her way toward the door.

Wayne and Laura watched as she got into her car and drove away.

"Why didn't you want her to know?" Laura asked.

"I did not want her to get caught up in all of this," Wayne said. "Lord only knows what would happen to her. I mean, you know as well as I do, Nathan

Christopher would trap her spirit somewhere in that God-forsaken house. I'm sure he would torment her to no end."

"Well, if you put it that way, I guess you have a point," Laura said.

"Of course, I do. If she knew everything that we know, she probably would have gotten involved a long time ago. Like me, you have seen and read about that place. God knows, she would probably be dead by now like Wendy and the others. Would you really want her to get involved? Would you really want her to take the chance and wind up joining Nathan Christopher's collection of souls?"

Laura was quiet for a moment.

"Of course, you wouldn't," Wayne said knowingly.

The waitress approached their table and refilled their coffee cups.

Laura picked up the riddle and opened it. She read it again.

"From what I gather," she began, "fields of a work affair, mean farms. There are three farms between here and home: that I know of anyway. It also says one stands alone. It refers to a path with certain birds that point the way, and a tree that weeps. What type of a tree weeps?"

She handed the piece of paper to Wayne. He thought about it briefly before speaking again.

"If I were to guess – I would say a weeping willow."

Suddenly, Laura gasped and placed her face in her hands.

"What's wrong?" Wayne asked.

"We had better get moving," she said.

"Right now?" he asked, not particularly thinking of her reasoning.

"Yes, right now. Are you forgetting about the last sentence of the riddle?"

"Not at all," Wayne replied as he patted her hand gently. "It said 'if not found by second sunset'…I know."

"Okay, good, so you do remember. Do you also remember that Cathy had the vision yesterday afternoon?"

Wayne was still clueless. He knew he should have understood what Laura was getting at, but he could not help it.

Laura continued in a concerned whisper.

"We now have less than ten hours before the second sunset."

"All right," Wayne said gently, "let's try to remain calm. I'll pay the check, and then we'll go, okay?"

Laura nodded her agreement, trying her best to relax.

Wayne raised his hand and he looked for the waitress. She emerged from the kitchen and headed to their table.

"All done?" she asked.

"Yes," Wayne answered. "Everything was delicious."

"Absolutely," Laura added. "Our compliments to the chefs."

"Oh, I'm so glad you enjoyed it. I'm sure the chef will appreciate the vote of confidence," the waitress commented as she handed Wayne the check.

"Ah! Here. I'll pay that right now," Wayne aid. Wayne reached into his front pocket and pulled out his wallet. He handed her a twenty. The check was for eleven dollars and fifty cents. "Please, keep the change."

"Thank you so much. You two have a great day."

"We'll do our best," Laura said.

As the waitress walked away, Wayne could not help but think about their current task. He put his hands together and placed his elbows on the table. He joined his index fingers into a pointing position and brought them to the tip of his nose. That was what he did when he was deep in thought.

Laura knew what that meant and watched him curiously.

"What's on your mind?" she asked.

"I think it would be a good idea if we picked up a few supplies along the way," he replied.

"Good idea," she said. "What did you have in mind?"

"Water and a shovel," Wayne replied.

"Water I get, but why a shovel?" Laura asked.

Wayne lowered his voice. "You never know where a body could be found. I doubt we will need it, but you never know."

"All right. Let's get going," she said.

They stood from their table and headed for the door.

They walked toward Laura's car and Wayne glanced to his left.

"There should be a home hardware not far from here," Laura said.

"Yes, I think I noticed one about a mile back that way," Wayne replied pointing to his left.

They got into the car, started it and drove off in that direction.

Chapter Eighteen
A Bird's Point of View

It was not long before they found a hardware store. Wayne went inside and bought a shovel and two large bottles of water. They continued driving until they found the first farm. It was a wheat farm. The first two things they looked for were the silo and willow tree. Almost immediately, Wayne spotted the silo.

"Well, there is the silo," he said, pointing. "Now where is the willow tree?"

"I don't see it anywhere," Laura said.

They were just about to give up when Wayne suddenly pointed at something behind Laura.

"What is that?" he asked curiously.

Laura checked her mirror quickly but could not see anything. She had to open her door and get halfway out to look.

"Do you mean those four trees way over there?" she asked.

"Yeah," Wayne said. "Do any of them look like a willow to you?"

"I can't tell from here," Laura answered.

Getting out, she headed to the rear of the vehicle. She opened the trunk and began rummaging through it.

Wayne's curiosity was peaked. He stepped out of the car and went to see what she was doing. Before he could ask, she somehow anticipated his question.

"I am looking for my binoculars, but I cannot seem to find – ah! Here we are."

"Good thinking," Wayne said with a nod. He wondered why he did not think of that himself. "You're so resourceful."

"Now, let's have a look," Laura said as she held the binoculars up to her eyes. "No willow tree. All I see are two pines, a maple, and what seems to be a fir of some sort."

"Can you see anything that could possibly indicate we are at the right place?"

Very slowly, she turned in the direction of the farm.

"Some sparse trees and shrubs but nothing else," Laura said.

"Then we should head to the next farm," Wayne said.

"I guess you're right," she agreed, lowering the binoculars. "Let's get going."

On the way to the second farm, they drove through more of the same types of towns. This time, they found houses and properties not nearly as nice as the others before. In fact, some of the properties were very unkempt. There were lawns with nasty burn patches, some were so long that young children could have easily hid in them were long and littered with toys, others were littered with children toys. A number of homes looked like old shacks with very noticeable patches on the rooftops. A few were a completely different color than the actual house. Some had ivy growing up the walls and appeared as though they had no windows. Some had picket fences that were either worn down by years of weather or they were never properly cared for with an occasional wood-finish or paint.

"How could people let everything go like that?" Wayne said.

"Let what go sweetie?"

"Their properties and homes," he clarified.

"Oh," Laura said. "Some people just don't care, I guess."

Wayne glanced at the clock on the car radio. There was roughly seven hours of daylight left. To him, time seemed to tick away quickly on that particular day.

"Here we are," Laura said as she pulled over.

They stepped out of the car and looked around. On Wayne's side of the vehicle, there was nothing but thick brush. On Laura's side was a wide field of short grass. It had a number of large burn patches on it. Laura reached into the back seat and brought out the binoculars. She scanned the field very slowly from left to right.

"What type of farm is this?" Wayne asked.

"I'm not sure. This time I don't even see a silo," she said, sounding somewhat discouraged. "And you know something else? The only possible way we would see any type of bird would be if it were flying. I mean, did you see any type of bird at the other farm?"

"Actually, now that you mention it," Wayne said, "no."

The Laura added. "I am starting to wonder if this one is just a wild goose chase."

"We still have two farms left," Wayne stated, trying his best to be optimistic. "Something has to turn up."

"And what if nothing turns up? What happens then? You die?"

"Laura," Wayne replied calmly, "I am not going to die. If nothing turns up at the last farm – if it actually is a farm – we retrace our steps. We go back in exactly the same direction we came. Except this time, we turn over the stones that we left untouched."

"Meaning, we should look over the same fields twice?"

Wayne shook his head. "No, I mean we should look in places other than the farms."

"Oh," Laura said. "Well, like where?"

"I don't know," Wayne replied, "but there has to be something we are missing here."

Once again, they went on their way.

Wayne wondered if Laura was right and it really was a wild goose chase. He had no reason to believe it was. When Cathy found them in the restaurant – he knew there had to be good reason. He looked out his window. Deep down, he felt Laura was just being paranoid.

Why else would Cathy go through all the trouble of finding us, he wondered.

He thought about the riddle and the possibility that they were going about it all wrong.

The scenery passed by, now with exceptionally few houses. There were several homes with barns. Some had horses, others had cows and sheep but there was not much else to look at other than some thick brush and sparse patches of tall grass.

Wayne turned his attention back to the road. In the near distance, a small green sign caught his eye. He was not able to see clearly it from where they were. As they drew closer, he realized it was an airplane. He had a hunch it would not lead them to an actual airport, but he was certain it would lead to a smaller one. Suddenly, the answer hit him like a ton of bricks.

"That's it!" Wayne said in a surprised whisper. "That's the sign we need."

"Huh? What are you talking about?" Laura asked in a puzzled tone.

"Turn the car around. I think I found what we are looking for,"

Laura pulled over, did a U-turn and drove slowly until he told her to stop.

Wayne stared at the back of the back of the sign until they were close enough.

"Okay, pull over here," he said.

Laura pulled over and stopped. She wondered what caught his attention so abruptly.

Wayne got out of the vehicle, looked both ways to make sure there were no vehicles approaching, and seeing none, walked over to the sign. He stared at it and couldn't help but smile. It was then that he knew they were not looking for an average field.

Laura joined his side and looked up at the sign too.

"You see that?" Wayne said.

"Yes, it's the sign of an airplane. So?"

Wayne's smile widened. He wagged his index finger at it.

"I would love to meet the son-of-a-gun who put that there."

"Are you okay?" Laura asked as she took a step back. "You're starting to scare me."

"Don't be scared," Wayne said. "Do you know why I want to meet him?"

"No," Laura replied.

"Because he is freaking brilliant!" Wayne said excitedly. "I want to kiss him right on the lips!"

"Well, that's…nice," Laura said with notable curiosity. "Wouldn't you rather kiss me?"

"Don't you get it?" Wayne said as he pointed to his left temple. "Remember those birds you were asking about earlier?"

"Yes. What about them?"

"Planes are metaphorically known as birds. N.H. does not want us to look for his body in a farm. He wants us to look in an airfield," he concluded.

Laura thought about that for a moment before she replied.

"Are you sure? I mean, that could take days."

"As sure as the devil has horns," Wayne replied. "Come on. We may not have that much time left."

"How do we even know that is the right place to look?"

"We don't," Wayne answered. "But we have to hope that it is."

They followed the signs to a secluded airfield on Park Road. They parked on the opposite side of the entryway and got out. Wayne opened the back door and grabbed the shovel. They walked up the entryway. To their surprise, there was nobody around. Laura spoke.

"Correct me if I'm wrong, but isn't there normally someone around to watch over the place?"

"You mean like a security guard?" Wayne asked.

"Yeah, or some sort of caretaker," Laura said.

"Maybe in there," Wayne said as he pointed to a large house-like structure roughly fifty feet away.

"Should we find out?"

"Let's not and say we did," Wayne answered as he continued to walk. "Right now, we have bigger problems."

"There are the planes," Laura said pointing to them. "Are those Cessna's?"

"Yes. Every last one of them," Wayne said. "They seem to be pointing at that building."

Eight planes stood side by side in a diagonal line. Each one was a different color. Two were white with blue stripes. Two were yellow with black stripes. Two were red with white stripes and two were orange with red stripes. They walked toward them. Wayne spoke.

"I always thought the Cessna were really cool!"

"Me too," Laura agreed. "Some have only one long seat, making it a two-man plane; others have two long seats, making it a four-man plane."

"Some have two separate seats with one long seat," Wayne added. "Way cool!"

Laura placed herself between two of the planes and focused on where they pointed. She emerged and walked in that direction.

"Come on," she said. "They are pointing to the left side of the building – not at it."

Wayne followed her until she stopped just passed the side of the building. To their disappointment, there was only brush.

"I don't get it," Laura commented. "There is nothing but foliage. There is no path here."

"Wait," Wayne said when he spotted another Cessna about thirty feet away. He pointed to it. "Over there."

Parked at an angle, the propeller faced the bushes. For no apparent reason, Wayne ran to reach it quickly. Sure enough, a narrow path lay before him.

"It's here!" he shouted back to Laura.

He waited patiently as Laura ran to his side. When she arrived, Wayne was crouched down and staring into the path. He was unable to see much because the trail veered off to the right about ten feet into it.

"Okay Sherlock, let's go find us a dead body," Laura said.

Wayne stood from his crouched position and held his hand out to her. Laura accepted it with a smile and they ventured into the path. At first, Wayne thought the trail would be easy to navigate. It turned out he was seriously mistaken. The foliage quickly became so dense that they felt as though they were in a jungle. Some smaller trees had numerous branches that cross-crossed in front of them. The lowest branches reached just below their knees. They tried to push through them but it proved too much of a task.

"This is going to take us forever," Laura commented. "There must be another way."

"I agree," Wayne said. "We could go around but we may lose the trail, and if we lose the trail, who knows how much time we will have left? I see only one way through this."

"You mean, crawl under it?" Laura said.

"Exactly," Wayne said.

Laura gave him a look suggesting that he was joking.

Wayne noticed the look and shrugged his shoulders as if to say he was sorry. He got down on his knees and stared at the low gap between the branches and the ground. Getting his clothes dirty was something he was used to in his line of work.

Laura watched as Wayne made his way under the branches. As soon as his shoes disappeared, a heavy sigh escaped her lips. She did not feel like crawling in dirt but deep down she knew he needed her. Carefully, she got down on her hands and knees and worked her way under the branches.

Once they were able to stand, they found more branches to push through. They were relieved though. Many of the branches were old and brittle. Only a select few were young and full of leaves. Wayne was doing his best to be careful not to let any branches escape his grip too soon. If he did, they would snap back and whip pour Laura in the face. They cleared the second obstacle and the trail widened up.

"There. That wasn't so bad, was it?" Wayne said.

"Speak for yourself," Laura replied in a grumble.

"Oh, come on," Wayne said as he turned to face her. He was about to say more but stopped when he noticed the look on her face. It was a glare that could have killed him if it were possible. He looked her over from head to toe and she was covered in dirt. Quickly, he turned back to face the path ahead he slapped his hands together. "Well. We should keep going."

Every two minutes or so, Wayne searched for clues along both sides of the path. He hoped something would turn up soon. They carefully passed through more branches. This time they were fuller than before. In fact, Wayne continuously tried to peek through to the other side, but was unable to see anything. Suddenly, he bumped into something solid.

"What the… What's this?" Wayne said.

He carefully lowered his hands to feel what it was.

"Did you say something?" Laura asked. "Why did we stop?"

"Yes," Wayne replied. "I just bumped into something and it seems to be blocking our way. I can't see what it is, but it feels like a fallen tree."

"Great. What's next?"

"Maybe we can get under it," Wayne added.

I knew he was going to say that, Laura thought with a disapproving bow of her head.

Carefully, Wayne lowered himself – and the shovel – as close to the ground as possible.

The shovel gave him a few minor problems, but he made it. He moved forward with his hands until his whole body touched the ground. He slithered along the ground army-style until he cleared the tree and the remainder of the branches. The ground was no longer flat and the trail led upward. The hill itself was covered in long grass and weeds. It was not very high, but it was steep.

"All right, Laura come on through," he said as he stood up and moved out of the way.

Wayne sat at the base of the hill and waited for her to emerge. He looked up at the sky and hoped the sun was still high enough to indicate they still had enough time. However, he could not see it from where he was. Standing, he climbed the hill a little more than halfway and turned to look for the sun again. He found it about halfway between the sky and the distant horizon.

That should leave us roughly a few hours to find N.H.'s body, he thought.

Laura was beginning to emerge from the bushes. Wayne hurried to help her.

"No wonder we couldn't see anything," she commented as she noticed the hill.

"Would you like to rest a little before we continue?" Wayne asked.

"No, I'm okay," she replied.

"Good. Let's move on then. I think we have a few hours of daylight left."

"How can you be sure? Neither one of us has a watch," Laura said.

"I'll explain at the top," Wayne replied. "Are you ready to climb?"

"I was born ready."

It took a few minutes, but they reached the top without incident. They turned to face the sun and Wayne pointed to it.

"In my first year of high school, my science teacher – as a special weekend project – made us study the sun by clocks and watches. On the following Monday he took us outside for a surprise quiz. For fifty minutes he tested us on time depending on the sun's whereabouts."

"Interesting," Laura said. "Did you pass the quiz?"

"I sure did. He gave me ninety-five percent."

"Excellent! But what happened to the other five percent?"

"It was around this time that I messed up," Wayne replied.

"Oh, well that's not—" Laura began but then stopped in mid-sentence. Her smile quickly faded as she suddenly realized Wayne just admitted that he could be wrong about the time remaining to find the body. The look on her face changed to something that said, are you freaking serious?

"Well," Wayne said as he clapped his hands together again. "Let's go see about finding that willow tree."

Her gaze followed him as he led the way forward.

They searched from where they stood and quickly spotted the big willow tree. It was slightly to their right, roughly forty feet away.

"Ah! There it is," Wayne claimed and pointed to it.

They went down the opposite side of the hill and made their way toward it. They were surprised to find no obstacles. It was just one straight line to the tree. They arrived at the foot of it in no time.

"So now what happens?" Laura said.

"Now we go to work," Wayne answered. "We figured out how to get here. Now we have to find out where to go next. N.H. led us to this tree, so there must be something of significance to it. Let me have a look-see."

Wayne went through the arching branches and walked up to the trunk. He circled it slowly and studied the thick bark for any signs. Halfway around the trunk, some odd markings caught his attention. His eyes widened and winced as he studied them.

"I think I found our next clue!" he shouted.

Laura quickly made her way to his side and eyed the markings with curiosity.

"It looks like a name," she commented.

"Not only is it a name," Wayne said, "but I think it belongs to N.H. And there is an arrow pointing that way," he added, pointing to his left.

"The name has to be abbreviated," Laura said. "I mean, what parents in their right mind would spell their child's name 'o.r.m.n.e.n.d.r.s.n.'?"

Wayne thought about that for a moment. He played the letters around in his head until the only possible solution appealed to him.

"Henderson," he said. "His name is Norman Henderson."

"Think so?" Laura said with uncertainty.

"What else could it possibly be?" Wayne replied.

"Okay smarty pants," Laura added "What do you think these three letters and three small lines beneath them mean?"

Wayne studied the letters r.w.s closely.

"Sewer," he said with confidence.

Laura looked at him, still somewhat confused.

"It means Norman Henderson is in sewer number three. Come on." he replied and charged away from the tree.

"Wait! How can you be so sure?" Laura asked as she followed closely behind.

They followed a dirt path that quickly led to a long narrow ditch. It was only hip-deep and bone dry. They looked left, then right and located the opening to the sewer. They went down into it and made their way to the sewer's opening at a trot. Once there, Wayne crouched down to see if he could spot Norman Henderson's body. To his disappointment, there was nothing to see but darkness. He hooded his eyes and looked deeper into the sewer. There was a very faint light roughly thirty into it.

"See anything?" Laura asked.

"Hardly," Wayne said, "just a faint light. There is really only one way to go about this."

"You're not seriously thinking about going in there, are you?"

"What other choice do I have?" Wayne replied as he turned to face her. "If you have any other ideas, now would be a good time to share them."

Laura shook her head, unable to give an answer. She turned away from him and folded her arms under her chest. Throughout her childhood, she had all sorts of nightmares about sewers. A number of times, Laura dreamt about being trapped in the pitch-black darkness of a sewer. She was crawling aimlessly in the dark with sensations of spiders crawling all over her and the squeaking sounds of rats. When she was old enough, horror movies added to those nightmares. She knew they were only movies but they still made her wonder.

Wayne wondered why she reacted that way. He wanted to tell her not to worry and that he would be fine, but did not want to risk her anger further. He ventured into the sewer.

Though the sewer was wide enough, it was a little less than three feet high. Wayne had no choice but to remain on all fours. He was barely half way to the faint light when the sewer began to smell. At first, he thought the odd odor consisted of some form of mildew with a hint of raw sewage. He thought nothing of it, deemed it normal and continued. Just a few feet from the light the odor was a little worse. Wayne wrinkled his nose in disgust but kept going until he reached the light. It was a small area – but he was able to stand. Just enough light shined through the manhole for him to make out an iron ladder that led to the surface. Slowly, he studied the four walls and floor that surrounded him. There was no dead body and nothing significant that would lead him to it, but he was not discouraged. Getting back on all fours, Wayne continued into the adjoining drainpipe. The pipe was the same size – but was also much darker than the first. In fact, it was so dark that he could not see anything at all. This made him crawl a little slower than before. Just a few seconds later, a thin spider-web draped over his face. Immediately, he stopped moving and cringed in fear.

"Damn!" he grumbled and frantically wiped it away with the backs of his hands.

I had to be stupid enough to come in here without a flashlight, he thought. *There is only one thing I hate more than spiders – and that is feeling their webs on my skin.*

Regaining his courage, he continued through the darkness. The stench of the sewer slowly increased with each passing moment. The uneasy feeling of nausea was beginning to set in. He tried to concentrate on other things.

So long as no more webs touch me, *I'll be fine,* he thought. *I just need to find Norman Henderson's body.*

Suddenly, a light breeze passed through him. It carried a stench so foul that it made him gag instantly.

"Oh my god!" Wayne said in a muffled voice as he grabbed his shirt and covered his mouth and nose. "What the…hell is that?"

Wayne held his breath for as long as he could and tried to think of a way to mask the foul odor. He searched his pockets for a handkerchief but found none. Obviously, he was unable to use his hands. They were coated with dust and dirt and who knew what else. As the seconds ticked by, he was beginning to feel somewhat light-headed. Suddenly, an idea popped into his mind. He removed his shirt and covered his nose and mouth with it. He inhaled deeply but it was too late. The nausea had become too much for his system to handle. He removed the shirt from his face and began vomiting in several vicious cycles. The gut-wrenching stench certainly did not help matters. Every time he stopped hurling and managed to take a breath, it would make him throw up again. Somehow, between hurls, he heard Laura's voice.

"Wayne? Are you okay?"

Wayne could not answer her. At least, not without throwing up again. He knew it would make her worry, but felt he had very little choice. He continued on, now breathing only through his mouth.

Chapter Nineteen
Eavesdropping Is a Virtue

On her first patrol that late afternoon, Sergeant Janet Polsen drove down Hillcrest Road. It was one of the roads that led to Aaron Airfield. Even before getting out of bed that morning she was certain it would be a boring day. Little did she know, that feeling was about to change. Nearing the intersection, she slowed to a stop. Almost immediately, she noticed a navy-blue Mazda. She turned onto Park Road and pulled up behind it. The young sergeant checked her rear-view mirror and the road ahead. There were no other vehicles around. She scanned the surrounding area and no one else was around. Her mentor – inspector Jack Percy – gave her several tips on how to find a stolen vehicle. One, they were normally found in the middle of nowhere. Two, damaged windows – only real professionals do not break windows. Three, in most cases, the keys are always be found in the ignition. With every stolen vehicle she ever found, those tips rang very true. She recalled one time where the owners were off having a picnic. Looking toward the airfield, she wondered if that was the case this time. To be safer than sorry, she picked up the C.B. radio.

"5442 to base," she said.

"Hey boss lady," a seemingly happy male voice said. "I hope we're still on for dinner tomorrow night."

The voice was that of her boyfriend and police dispatcher, Gregory Hanson. It was their first one-year anniversary that day. Unfortunately, since they were both working, they had no choice but to postpone the celebration.

The young sergeant smiled and shook her head. Ever since she became a sergeant six months ago, Gregory always teased her. Though not so much lately, to which she was very thankful. In the beginning, he teased her a lot because he was jealous. Being only twenty-five years of age, Janet became the youngest sergeant on the force. She was also three years his junior. He had been trying for two years to pain promotion to sergeant. Every time he thought he passed, he failed and remained a corporal. For the first few weeks, it put a real strain on their relationship. Then one day, Gregory apologized for his sour behavior and explained why he teased her so. He also admitted that deep down, he was always happy about her promotion. That same night, he took her out for a nice romantic meal and they were a happy couple again.

"Yes, we're still on," Janet said.

"Good. I hope you will enjoy what I have planned," Gregory said.

"I'm sure I will," Janet replied with a grin. Then she grew serious. "Can you run a plate check for me?"

"Can do. Fire away."

"Tammy – Norman – Victor – Sam – Seven – Niner – Six."

"Got it," Gregory said. "The vehicle is registered to a miss. Laura Barns. She lives at sixty 60 Nethervue Street in Edmundston, New Brunswick. Need the postal code and telephone number?"

"No thanks. I am at Aaron Airfield. Either Miss Barns is around here somewhere, or something is wrong. Has the car been reported stolen?"

"Negative."

Unbeknownst to the dispatcher, Detective Wilson was standing right behind him. He was not there for long, but heard enough to be suspicious. Immediately, the detective sensed Wayne and Laura were up to something. What exactly – he had no idea – but he was certain it had something to do with ghosts.

"I have to check out the airfield anyway," Janet said. "I'll see if I could find her."

Gregory was about to reply when a hand gently grabbed his wrist. He looked up and noticed the detective.

A puzzled look formed on the young corporals' face. "Sir?" he said.

"At ease," Wilson said as he gripped the radio. "Base to 5442."

"5442 go ahead," Polsen replied.

"This is Detective Wilson. Remain where you are. I am on my way to meet you."

"Sir?" Janet said, confused.

"As I said, don't move. I am on my way."

"Yes sir," Polsen said.

Wilson released the radio. He turned to leave and realized he forgot something. He snapped his fingers and pressed the radio again.

"Sergeant Polsen?"

"Yes sir?"

"If you see Laura Barns – more than likely – you will see a man with her. His name is Wayne Saunders. Let neither one of them leave. I have a few questions for them. Understood?"

"Crystal clear, sir," Polsen said.

"Good. I will not be long."

The sergeant kept her eyes on the navy-blue Mazda and placed the C.B back in its holder. She leaned back in her seat and wondered what was going on. Then she turned her attention to the entryway of the airfield and waited.

As time passed by, she wondered what her Gregory had planned for her for their anniversary. For their one-month anniversary, he took her dancing. On their sixth month, he bought her a ten-karat gold necklace and took her to see Cinderella. It was her favorite movie. On both occasions, she had no idea what to expect, but always enjoyed every passing moment with him.

Polsen was still watching the airfield entryway when she heard the sound of a car. The distraction turned her attention away from the airfield. She watched as Detective Wilson get out of his cruiser and approached her. He opened the passenger door and sat down beside her.

"Any sign of them?" he asked.

"Not yet," Polsen said. "Any possible way you can tell me what's going on?"

"Just playing a hunch," Wilson said. "I think they are looking for something and I want to be there if they find it. I am going to take a little walk. If they show up – I am on channel three."

The sergeant wanted to ask what it was he thought they were looking for, but left it at that.

"Yes sir," she said.

Polsen watched him walk through the entryway to the airfield and disappear behind the bushes. She wondered what possible hunch was going through his mind. She leaned back in her seat, knowing there was nothing left for her to do but wait.

Chapter Twenty
Something to Be Nervous About

"Wayne! Wayne can you hear me?" Laura yelled into the sewer.

On her knees, Laura peered into the darkness and looked for any sign of movement. There was none. Her patience was wearing thin as she waited for Wayne to reply. When he did not, she became even more concerned. She got to her feet and placed her hands on her head.

Where is he? she wondered. *I hope he is okay.*

"Laura Barns?" a masculine voice called out from somewhere nearby.

Startled and surprised to hear her name, Laura turned in the direction she thought it came from. At first, she was not sure who it was. From where the figure stood – she was only able to make out a man in a police uniform. Filled with a sudden wave of nervousness, she took a step back. Quickly, she glanced at the sewer and then looked back at the approaching authority figure. Laura was stricken with panic. As the figure drew closer, she was relieved to recognize the familiar face of Detective Wilson. She exhaled a deep sigh of relief. The last thing she wanted to see at that moment was an unfamiliar face.

"Ms. Barns," he said. "Please, don't take this personally but what are you doing here?"

"Detective," Laura said in a puzzled yet almost happy tone. At least, she was no longer alone but was curious as to how he found her. "How did you—"

"One of my fellow officers was patrolling this area and found your vehicle. She thought it was stolen and called in a plate-check. I was standing behind the officer who took the call. When I heard your name and where you were, I wanted to know what you and Mr. Saunders were up to. Speaking of which, where is he now."

Bowing her head slightly, Laura motioned with her hand to the open drain-pipe.

The detective looked toward the sewer. Puzzled, he looked back at Laura.

"Am I to understand he is in the sewer?" he asked inquisitively.

"Yes," Laura replied.

The detective was quiet for a moment. He thought back to the time he first met Wayne and Laura. It was in an old barn where they found the dead body of a young girl. Wayne and Laura were certain it was the body of Wendy Saint-Pierre. Later that night, the coroner – along with dental records – proved it true. Something told him it would soon be a similar situation.

"Did you two find another dead body?" he asked.

"No," Laura replied with obvious uncertainty. "At least, I don't think so. He has not answered me in a while."

The senior officer removed his two-way radio from its holster and spoke into it.

"Wilson to 5442," he said.

"Go ahead," Sergeant Polsen said.

"Do you have anything to open manholes?"

For a brief moment, the radio was quiet.

"Yes sir, I believe I do," Polsen replied with a hint of curiosity in her voice.

"Good. We are going to need it. Go to the back of the building and follow the dirt path in front of the two-seater airplane. Be careful. You will find some tricky spots, but stick to the path and you will be fine. Let me know when you make it to the top of the small hill."

"Ten four," the sergeant said. "I am on my way."

Polsen stepped out and went around the cruiser to the rear. She opened the trunk, pulled out a crowbar and made her way into the airfield. A relaxing nature walk was something she enjoyed. There was never a time that she did not enjoy one. During her years on the force, she knew Wilson to be a bit of an exaggerator and assumed he was doing it again. In all of her nature-walking experiences, she never found a dirt path so cluttered.

Walking past the two-seater plane, she found the narrow path and walked in. To her surprise, the detective was right about the tricky spots. Following Wilson's directions, she made her way through the path's frequent obstacles. In a matter of seconds, the front of her uniform was full of dirt. To her, it felt as though she was crawling through a dense jungle. Sargent Polsen hated getting her uniform dirty, but when duty called for it – she did what she had to do.

It did not take her long to arrive at the top of the hill. She brushed herself off and pulled out her walkie-talkie.

"5442 to Wilson…I am here," Polsen said.

"Good," Wilson replied. "Now look straight and to the right; you will see a willow tree. Go to it and then follow the narrow path to the right of the tree. It will lead you to a dip. Look to the right and you will find us."

"Copy that," Polsen said.

Obeying the order, Polsen walked up to the tree and found the path that led to her superior. She followed it. Once she arrived at the trench, she looked to her right and spotted them. She hurried over to meet them.

I wonder if that is Laura Barns with him, Polson thought.

"Ah good," Detective Wilson said. Immediately, he noticed her dirt-covered uniform but said nothing. He was well aware that she was going to get dirty. "We are going to follow these pipes and open each manhole until we find him."

"Someone is trapped in there?" Polsen asked.

"No. Someone is looking for a dead body," the detective replied nonchalantly as he turned back to the drainpipe's opening.

At first, Sargent Polsen thought he was joking and frowned. Ever since she had met him, she found his jokes to be somewhat twisted and warped. She hardly disliked him. In fact, she respected him a great deal as an officer. She just did not like his jokes too much. As Wilson and Laura climbed out of the trench and started following the sewer, Polsen realized he was not kidding.

"Are you Laura Barns?" Polsen asked as they walked.

"Yes Officer."

Does everyone know who I am? Laura wondered.

Chapter Twenty-One
From Darkness to Daylight

Although Wayne was still shaky, his breathing had returned to normal. Once again, he covered his mouth and nose with the shirt and continued through the darkness.

Man, I hope I never have to do this again, he thought.

To him, the seconds felt like minutes as he crawled. He wondered how much further the next manhole was. There was no sign of light at all and it was beginning to worry him.

After a few brief moments, Wayne was beginning to think he was lost. For all he knew, he may have accidentally turned into an adjoining pipe – away from the one he was looking for. But without a flashlight, there was no way for him to tell. Finally, he spotted a faint light in the near distance.

"Ah!"

He crawled faster toward it with high hopes of finding Norman's body. Another cobweb grazed his face, but he quickly shrugged off his fear and pressed on. Finally arriving at the light, Wayne slowly got to his feet and looked around again. To his right was another iron ladder that led to the surface. To his immediate left was a plain wall with nothing but a few cracks in it. His frustration began to mount. He stomped a foot down, but at the same time something told him to look down. He did so. Sure enough, something big lay lengthwise to the wall. It startled him at first, but he quickly regained his composure. The dim light showered the dead body and revealed nothing but its utter skeletal gruesomeness. Its empty eye sockets stared up at him.

"Ugh!" Wayne grunted in disgust and turned away briefly. He looked back down at it.

Norman Henderson I presume, he thought. *But you can't be the one with that foul smell. There must be a dead animal somewhere nearby.*

Suddenly, Wayne noticed the awkward way the arms and feet were placed. He knelt down to take a better look. However, as he drew closer the revolting stench was even more overpowering. That, along with the still fresh scent of vomit on his breath almost made him hurl again. Quickly, he stood up again and turned away. Carefully, he took a slow deep breath before he knelt back down.

Let's try this one more time, he thought. *Who would have thought the stench would be worse close to the ground?*

Wayne looked closely at Norman's wrists and ankles. He immediately noticed the metal clamps that bolted them to the lower wall and floor of the sewer. It shocked him as to how someone could be so disturbed and cruel to do such a horrible thing.

Well, Nathan certainly made sure you were not getting out, he thought.

From out of nowhere, another wave of nausea hit him. Unable to stand it any longer, Wayne held his breath, stood up and lunged for the ladder. He climbed up and forced the manhole open. Quickly, he climbed out and tossed his dirty shirt to the ground. Even though he was out of the sewer, he still held his breath. He walked about ten feet and dropped to his knees. Finally, the nausea was too much for him to handle. He threw up once again and let the fresh country air fill his lungs. Looking up at the sky, he noticed the sun was just moments away from completing its descent.

Dear God, I pray I never have to go into another sewer again, he thought.

Suddenly, he remembered Laura was still at the entrance to the sewer. He almost forgot and knew she must have been worried. Upset at himself, he closed his eyes and shook his head. He knew she would not be pleased with him. Nevertheless, he decided to rest for a few more minutes before going back to find her.

Chapter Twenty-Two
Lost and Found

Frequently calling out Wayne's name, Detective Wilson, Sargent Polsen and Laura followed the pipes of the sewer. They opened every manhole they discovered only to find it empty. To Laura, their search seemed to go on forever and she knew that daylight was running out.

Until finally, Laura spotted Wayne kneeling down beside a small bush. A smile of relief burst onto her face and she charged toward him.

"Over here!" she shouted to the officers.

The three of them ran over to Wayne's side.

"Honey, are you all right?" Laura asked as she placed a hand on Wayne's shoulder.

"Yes, I'm okay," he replied, but did not turn to see who else was with her. "Who were you talking to?"

"Detective Wilson and one of his officers," Laura replied.

"Oh," Wayne said. He got to his feet and turned to face them. "Sir, there is a dead body in the sewer. The killer used metal clamps to keep him from escaping – or washing out into the open. I'm willing to bet a lifetime of pay checks his name is, Norman Henderson."

"Where in the sewer?" Wilson asked.

"At the bottom of that manhole," Wayne answered and pointed.

Wilson walked over to the open manhole and looked down into it. He brought his left hand up to cover his mouth as he stared at the dead body. Sergeant Polsen wanted to see the body, but the superior officer politely discouraged her.

"What is that horrible stench?" Polsen said, covering her nose.

"Must be a dead animal somewhere nearby," Wilson replied. "It can't be our friend down there…looks much too old to smell like that."

Laura brought her face to Wayne's ear.

"What if it's not him?" she whispered.

"Then we just took a step back," he whispered in response.

Detective Wilson turned and walked back slowly toward them. The look on his face was of someone deep in thought.

"Whoever did this was very smart," he claimed.

"How so?" Laura asked.

"Mr. Saunders was right about the metal clamps," the detective said. "Dead or alive when he was put in there, he was never getting out."

"That way, the killer thought no one would ever find it." Laura said thoughtfully.

"That's right," Wilson said.

"Until we came along," Wayne added.

The detective grew quiet for a moment before he spoke again.

"Just out of curiosity," he said. "How did you two find this body?"

"Well," Laura began, but stopped and looked at Wayne as if for permission to continue. "It's a very long story."

"If you have some time, we will be happy to explain," Wayne added.

"All right," Wilson said. "Be at my office tomorrow morning. I will hear your explanation then. For now, why don't you two go home, or do whatever it is you kids do at this hour."

"You do not need us to stay?" Laura asked him.

"No," he replied with a slow shake of his head. "You two have done your good deed. Now please, let us do our job."

Without another word, Wayne and Laura left hand in hand and began making their way back to the airfield.

They remained quiet until they reached the top of the hill that led to the big willow tree. The beauty of the sunset immediately caught their attention. The top half of the sun had a bright halo of yellow. The sky surrounding it was a mix of orange and dark pink.

"Well, look at that," Wayne said. "Isn't that sky something?"

"It sure is," Laura commented. "And I can't think of anyone better to watch it with."

Once again, they crawled under the fallen tree and slowly fought their way back through the bushes. By the time they got back to the airfield, it was dark.

Wayne and Laura drove until they found motel. They drove up to the rental office. Wayne was just about to get out of the car when Laura placed her hand on his arm. She shook her head slowly and got out of the car. Wayne wondered why, but then realized he was shirtless, filthy and obviously a little smelly.

He waited patiently while Laura registered them. All he wanted to do was take a nice hot bath and wash up. A moment later, Laura emerged from the rental office.

She got back in the car and they drove up to room number thirty-nine. They got out of the car and went inside.

"I am going to take a nice hot bath," Wayne said.

"Not to sound harsh," Laura said, "but I think that would be a good idea. I, on the other hand, am going to the laundry-mat and wash our clothes."

"There's a laundry-mat near here?"

"I asked the guy at the registry office and he told me where to go," Laura replied. "It is not far. You go ahead and get out of those filthy clothes. Just leave them by the bathroom door and I'll pick them up."

"Okay," Wayne said, "Wait a minute. How are you going to wash your clothes? I imagine that would be quite tricky because you have no change of clothes."

"You let me worry about that." Laura said.

"I must admit, that would be interesting to see," Wayne added, folding his arms across his chest.

Laura laughed. "I bet it would," she said.

Wayne then made his way to the bathroom and closed the door softly behind him. He got undressed and then opened the door just enough to place his dirty clothes at the entrance. He closed the door once again and ran his bath. Sitting on the edge of the tub, he waited for it to fill. He looked at the mirror. Images of the disturbing horned face and hellish backgrounds flooded his mind. He remembered its words and their screams of agony. Unable to take anymore, he slammed his eyes shut and placed his head in his hands. He hoped that God would give them at least one night of peace.

Laura scooped up Wayne's clothes and put them into a large plastic bag. She knocked on the bathroom door.

"I will be back as soon as I can," she called out.

"Okay," Wayne replied.

Nodding, Laura turned and headed out the door.

Chapter Twenty-Three
The Next Morning

Wayne stirred as the fresh aroma of coffee and an assortment of hot foods tickled his nostrils. He turned onto his side and squinted at the bright morning sun.

"Well, look who's finally up," Laura said. "You should come and eat your breakfast before it gets cold."

"Breakfast?" Wayne said, curious as he turned to look at her. "Okay, you have my attention. That smells delicious."

"Yes, it does," Laura agreed. "Your clothes are at the end of the bed by your feet. I have to go pee."

With those words said, Laura scurried off to the bathroom and gently closed the door. Wayne got out of bed and dressed himself. Afterwards, he sat at the small two-person table. His intention was to wait for her, but somehow she anticipated his good gesture.

"Don't wait for me," she said through the closed door. "I'll be there momentarily."

Wayne looked down at the healthy portions of food in the Styrofoam container. The delicious aroma was driving him crazy. Unable to control himself anymore, he picked up his knife and fork and began to eat. There were three eggs, four sausages, four slices of bacon, hash brown and two orders of white toast. He was impressed.

"How much did all of this cost you?" Wayne asked with a mouthful.

"Three dollars and ninety-nine cents," she replied.

"Hmm," Wayne grunted with a surprised nod.

"I asked if they could give me a little extra for you," Laura said.

Wayne happily sampled each one of the different foods before him. He found them to be nothing short of scrumptious.

Laura emerged from the bathroom and sat across from him. She appeared to be in a good mood.

"Well?" she said simply.

"Everything is just wonderful," Wayne answered. "Thank you so much for this."

"Oh, there is no need to thank me," Laura commented with a smile and a wave of her hand. "Besides, I knew by this morning you would be starving since you went all night without eating."

"Did you sleep at all?" Wayne asked.

"A little," she replied. "When I got back, you were already asleep. I took a bath and watched a little television."

Wayne was curious. He wondered how she washed her clothes. If there was one thing he knew about her, she was no exhibitionist.

"Well, it's better than no sleep at all," he said. "So, now all we have to do is go to the police station."

"Oh! I almost forgot," Laura said. "Last night, I was fortunate enough to find a small pharmacy. I bought a few necessities."

"Mm-hm?" Wayne grunted with another nod.

They ate the remainder of their breakfast in silence and enjoying every tasty morsel.

Afterwards, they tidied up like good little renters and made the room spotless. Laura then took a few minutes to show Wayne everything she bought at the pharmacy. Toothbrushes, toothpaste, a small bottle of Listerine mouthwash, his and her deodorants, nail clippers, hairspray, styling gel and some anti-bacterial wipes. They finished getting ready and took their respective turns in the bathroom.

Wayne felt much better after brushing his teeth and used a few capfuls of the mouthwash. Then finally, they were on their way.

"Feel better?" Laura asked as they walked out the door of their room.

"Oh yes," Wayne said, "much better."

They drove over to the rental office and checked out. As they stepped out of the office, they took a moment to enjoy the morning's glory. It was a beautiful morning: not too hot and not too cool. The leaves showed off their autumn colors as a gentle breeze played through them. Several birds were singing their soothing tunes. It almost made them feel like staying a while longer to enjoy it all. Wayne spoke.

"You know, I think it would be nice if we came back here one day soon."

"You think so?" Laura said.

"Yeah," Wayne said. "It's so peaceful here."

"No argument there," Laura agreed as she took Wayne's hand in hers and smiled. "Come on. We should get going. I do not think the detective would appreciate us making him wait too long."

"Quite true," Wayne agreed. "Let's go then."

The ride back to the police station was quiet, yet relaxing. Their windows were down about half way. A soothing breeze of fresh air flowed through the car. Traffic was at a bare minimum. Laura turned on the radio and for a moment, there was nothing but idle talk about an upcoming political debate. Then the weather came on. It announced sunny skies with a high with nineteen degrees.

Before long, they arrived at the police station. They found a nice parking spot close to the station entrance and got out of the car. Taking each other's hands, they walked up the walkway. Wayne held the door open for Laura and they went inside. Detective Wilson was walking toward the information desk when he noticed them.

"Good morning," he said.

"And a good morning to you too detective," Wayne said.

"How are you this fine morning?" Laura asked him.

"Well, you two seem to be in a good mood. I am fine, thank you," Wilson replied. "Please, follow me."

Wayne and Laura followed the detective to his office. Once there, he opened the door and gave his guests the courtesy of entering first. Closing the door behind him, he then walked behind his desk and pointed with his right hand to the two chairs in front of it. Wayne and Laura sat obediently, followed by the detective. The lawman opened a drawer and pulled out two file folders with numerous papers inside them. He placed them on the desk softly.

"Now," Wilson said, "is there anything I can get you before we begin, some coffee perhaps?"

"No, thank you," Laura answered.

"I'm good, thanks," Wayne added.

"Very well," Wilson said. "Let's begin then."

The detective opened the folder and leafed through some of the papers, scanning them briefly before he continued.

"Firstly, we have Wendy Saint-Pierre. As I indicated to you before, we know neither of you had anything to do with her death. What we would like to know, is exactly how you came to find her body."

"Detective," Wayne began calmly. "We tried explaining this to you before."

"Ah yes, the ghost story. Mister Saunders, with all due respect – do you really wish us to believe that spirits led you to these two bodies," Wilson asked calmly, indicating the folder before him.

"Look," Laura added. "We know how crazy the story sounds but it's the truth."

"Maybe you just think it's the truth."

"What do you mean?" Wayne asked. "Sir, we are not a couple of young brats merely looking for attention. We are not schizophrenic, nor delusional.

What we have been through these past few days is enough to turn anybody in to a believer."

Detective Wilson eyed Wayne and Laura with skepticism. He was certain that there was a more logical explanation other than ghosts. He once believed in them as a child in his early teens. As often as he could he read factual articles, watched documentaries and even movies. In a short time, he hoped to see one in real life. The days turned into months and the months into years, he never witnessed a ghost of any kind. It turned out that most of the articles he read on so-called true accounts were hoaxes. He found out by reading books like *Haunting Hoaxes*. Eventually, he lost all interest in ghosts and stopped believing in them. Yet, now he was curious. He wondered if there was any truth to the youngsters' statements.

"I want to believe you," Wilson said. "I really do. I just don't believe in ghosts or the spirit realm."

"Then go to where the spirits are," Wayne respectfully argued. "We will take you there personally. Perhaps then you will believe us."

The detective eyed Wayne and Laura thoughtfully for a moment.

"All right," he said. "I will go to this place with you to this place and check it out. However, if I find out you are telling me fish-tales—"

"We're not," Laura interjected. "We swear."

"Very well," the detective said. "Where is this place?"

"Fifteen Birchcroft Drive," Wayne answered.

A gentle knock came to the door.

"Yes?" Wilson said.

An officer opened the door part way and peeked his head inside.

"I beg your pardon sir, but may I have a brief word with you?"

"Would you excuse me for a moment?" the detective asked his guests.

"Yes, of course," Laura replied.

Wilson stood and stepped out of his office. He closed the door softly behind him.

Wayne and Laura were quiet for a moment before Laura spoke.

"Think they're talking about us?" Laura asked.

"Don't know," Wayne said. "We will have to wait and see."

A moment later, the detective re-entered his office but kept the door open.

"It seems we will have to continue this later," he said. "Is there any way you two could come back in say…two hours?"

"Sure," Wayne answered. He and Laura stoop up. "Two hours it is then."

"Good. See you then," the detective said as we walked out of his office.

Wayne and Laura stepped out into the fresh air and debated on what they would do to pass the time.

"Want to take a drive?" Laura asked.

"For two hours? Not really," Wayne said. "Besides, where would we go?"

Laura laughed. "I don't know…around I guess. Are you hungry?"

"Nah, I am still full from breakfast. Want to take a walk?"

"For two hours?" Laura said. "Where would we go?"

This time Wayne laughed. "Around I guess."

"Oh!" Laura said in a laugh and smacked Wayne's shoulder. "Cut that out."

"Ouch!" Wayne said, though the smack did not really hurt. "Why? It's fun."

"Come on," she said, still laughing and pulling him by the wrist. "Let's go take a walk."

After just a few steps, Wayne stopped and arched his arm. Laura graciously accepted it and they walked on.

"Well, aren't you a gentleman?"

"I try my best," Wayne commented as they continued walking. "Learned it in school you know."

Laura laughed. "At what, the prom?"

"No, a class."

"A class?"

"Yeah."

"Dare I ask what this class was called?" Laura said.

"Sure, it was called stick out your arm or else."

Chapter Twenty-Four
History Repeats Itself

After their long walk, Wayne and Laura returned to the police station. They waited for Detective Wilson in the lobby. Beside the two officers sitting behind the information desk, they were the only ones there. However, after a few more seconds ticked by, an officer walked in with a woman on his arm. Her hands were in cuffs, yet she did not seem to put up any resistance.

Probably because of the size difference, Wayne thought.

The officer appeared to be at least six feet tall, and roughly two hundred and forty pounds. The woman, on the other hand, seemed only five feet tall and roughly one hundred twenty pounds. They walked straight past the information desk and disappeared behind a closed door marked *Bookings.*

"Humph! I wonder what she did," Laura said.

"You've got me," Wayne replied, "but I bet she's not in there for good behavior."

"Are you two ready?" a sudden voice asked.

Wayne and Laura looked to their immediate left to see Detective Wilson standing there. There were two other officers with him.

"Yes sir," Wayne said.

"Ready whenever you are," Laura added.

"Great," the detective said. "This is Officer Malloy, and this is Officer Jackson. Let's get going. We will follow you."

Walking out of the station, Wayne and Laura headed for their vehicle. They got in, started it and began their journey back to where their nightmares began. The detective and his men trailed closely behind. Wayne could not help notice Laura occasionally checking the rear-view mirror.

"Is something wrong?" he asked her.

"Nothing," she said. "I just hope nothing happens to them, that's all."

Wayne wondered why she said that. Then it suddenly occurred to him; memories of what they read at the archives. Everything that happened at that house and to those people flashed before his eyes.

"I just have this weird feeling," she said.

"Like history will somehow repeat itself?" Wayne asked.

"Yeah."

"Well, I hate to say this – I really do – but they wanted to know."

"I know," Laura said in agreement.

"I don't like this any more than you do," Wayne added, "but we have no choice."

Once again, they grew quiet. Laura concentrated on the road and Wayne turned his attention to the scenery. Some folks tended to their lawns and gardens. Others sat on their porches and enjoyed the shade. Some looked up as they drove by; others did not and continued as they were. The calming tranquility of the countryside still impressed Wayne. Deep down he knew it always would.

It did not take them long to get back to the busy streets of Edmundston. People were bustling about. Some were walking their dogs, some were jogging, and some ran errands. Traffic was certainly at a much higher volume than it normally was that time of day. In some areas it was bumper to bumper.

Eventually, they turned left onto Lepine Street. This meant they were much closer to reaching Birchcroft Drive The whole of Lepine Street was a thirty kilometer an hour school zone. They pulled up to a stop sign by a park. Wayne and Laura looked over to it and witnessed dozens of children playing. They appeared to be having a great time. They ran back and forth on the play structures, swung to and fro on the monkey bars and played tag. Their little yet loud screams placed emphasis on the excitement. There were even a few toddlers playing in a sandbox with their guardians or babysitters. Many adults were on hand to keep a close watch over the festivities.

"Looks like the whole neighborhood is there," Wayne said as he took one final look before they drove on.

"Yes, I noticed," Laura said. "Better outdoors on a beautiful day like today, instead of cooped up in the house watching mindless television."

They drove through two more short streets and finally made it to Birchcroft Drive They turned right and continued until they stopped in front of the haunted house. The lawmen pulled up behind them. Wayne and Laura got out of the car and waited for the police to join them. It seemed as though they were speaking amongst themselves. Wayne looked to Laura for answers, but she shrugged her shoulders in response.

"Maybe they are just letting their headquarters know where they are," she said.

Detective Wilson and one of the officers stepped out of the cruiser and joined them. The other officer stayed in the cruiser.

"Sorry about that," Wilson said.

"No problem," Wayne replied as he looked past him.

Wilson noticed the look and turned to glance at the cruiser, then back to Wayne.

"Just a little precaution," he said. "Always better to stay one step ahead in case something goes wrong."

"I understand. Are you ready?" Wayne asked.

"We certainly are," the detective answered. Nodding his head upward, he added. "The house appears abandoned: any idea who the last owner was?"

"I think we do, but there is no way to be certain," Laura replied.

"How so?" Officer Malloy asked as they began walking up the driveway toward the front door.

"We think the last owner was one, Nathan Christopher," Wayne said. "According to records at the library and archives, he owned the house a long time ago. If there were any other owners after him – we do not know of any."

"How long ago?" Wilson asked.

"You mean, when did he buy it?" Laura said. "To be honest we are not sure. We are sure that he died some time back in 1952."

At the front door, Wayne reached for the doorknob but paused, thinking it would open on its own again. This time, it did not. Delaying no further, he opened the door. The light from the outside lit up the empty hallway. It hardly surprised him to see billions upon billions of dust particles floating about. One by one, they stepped inside. It reeked of mildew and wet carpet. The house was obviously unhygienic.

Because of Wayne's previous experiences with the house, he could not help but feel leery. He cautiously led the small group to the living room. Once there, they stepped in and looked around. Wayne noticed the old paint had begun to peel off the walls in some areas. The ceiling appeared to hold a few minor water stains, normally caused by old leaky pipes. A part of him expected to see the red-eyed demon, yet there was nothing but an empty room with boarded up windows. Another part of him wanted to hear it breathe – but all they heard were the sounds of silence. Wayne felt somewhat disappointed.

"It seems your ghosts are shy, Mr. Saunders," the detective said.

"Let's check out the rest of the house," Wayne suggested.

"Maybe they only come out at night," Officer Malloy said. "Perhaps we should come back then, sir."

"No," Detective Wilson said thoughtfully. "These two brought us here for a reason. Let's stick around for a while and see if anything happens."

"Yes sir," Malloy agreed.

"You stay here," the detective added. "I am going to go with them. If you see or hear anything, you let me know immediately."

"Will do," Malloy said.

They went on to the kitchen and stayed there for a brief moment. Again, there was nothing to see but dust, moldy walls and filth. It appeared as though someone still lived there. There were several dishes left in the sink and on the counter. On the kitchen table – though bare for the most part – rested one single dirtied plate almost covered with live ants. What little was left on the plate was caked on and barely enough to feed a newborn baby, but the ants did not care.

Laura wrinkled her nose in disgust. The detective spoke.

"You would think someone from the last owner's family could have at least come in to clean up."

"Maybe he had no family," Laura said.

"Even at that," Wayne added, "a real-estate agent could have ordered it cleaned and repainted. At least, now we know the house never resold."

Wayne turned to face a closed door. He walked up to it and carefully opened it. The hinges creaked loudly in protest.

Laura covered her ears.

Wayne noted her reaction and stopped moving the door.

"Sorry," she said. "I just don't like that sound."

Turning his attention back to the now open door, Wayne noted stairs leading down to the basement. Even though the sun was still shining, the basement was so dark that they were barely able to see the steps. Detective Wilson appeared at his side and turned on his flashlight.

"Ah! That's better," Wayne said.

"A flashlight comes in very handy," Wilson said. "I'd better lead the way."

Slowly they made their way downstairs. When they reached the base of the stairs, they ducked at the low ceiling and waited. They detective swept his flashlight across the floor slowly. There appeared to be nothing but sand and dust.

"Nothing down here but dirt," he commented.

"Wait," Wayne said. "Shine your light at the center of the room near the ceiling?"

Doing so, the detective was surprised to see a short thick rope with a small noose at the end.

"What the hell?" he said curiously. "How did you know that was there?"

At first, Wayne did not reply. He only stared at the thick noose as disturbing memories of a tortured and bloodied young Wendy Saint-Pierre flashed through his mind. Frowning, he closed his eyes and shook his head slowly.

"Mr. Saunders!" Detective Wilson said, snapping him back to reality.

"This is what he used," Wayne grumbled as he stared at the rope.

"Who used it?" the detective said, slightly impatient now. "Used it for what?"

Wayne slammed his eyes shut. He could not believe he was about to blurt it all out, but was left with little choice.

"That rope is what—" he began but was cut off abruptly by the detective's two-way radio.

"This is HQ," a man's voice said. "Detective Wilson, please respond."

Wilson grumbled something under his breath before replying.

"This is Wilson. What is it?"

"Thank God," the voice said. "Sir, this is Lieutenant Phil Jennings. Listen to me very carefully. Everyone has to get out of that house, right now."

"What are you talking about, Jennings?"

"You wanted Corporal Bently and I to find out what we could on the address you gave us."

"Yes, and?" Wilson said somewhat impatiently.

"Sir, what we found out is nothing short of disturbing and apparently very real," Jennings claimed. "There is no time to argue. You all have to get out of there!"

"How do you know it's true?" Wilson asked.

"I will tell you when you are all safe outside," Jennings argued.

"You will tell me now, dammit!" the detective argued back.

"Long story short, we went to the Library and Archives."

"Library and Archives?" the detective said.

"Yes – and sir – things happened in that house. Things that you—"

The radio suddenly went quiet.

"Jennings?"

There was no reply.

"Jennings? Wilson to base, come in?"

Again, no reply came. This frustrated the detective even more.

"Damn! Okay, everybody out," Wilson ordered, pointing at the stairs behind them. "You two first, I'll be right behind you."

Wayne and Laura obeyed and headed for the stairs.

From out of nowhere, a loud crash reverberated through the basement and everyone stopped in their tracks. Once again, the detective pulled out his walkie-talkie.

"Malloy, what's going on?"

No answer came.

"Malloy, report!" Wilson prodded.

The radio remained silent.

"That's it," Wilson said, unable to take no more. "You two get behind me and you stay behind me. If I move, you move. If I stop, you stop, and wait for my signal. Understand?"

Wayne and Laura nodded their agreement to him.

"Good," he said as he pulled out his gun. "Let's move!"

Quickly yet carefully, the detective led the way up the stairs. Wayne and Laura followed close behind. They stopped behind him at the top step and waited for his signal. Sticking his head out, Detective Wilson looked both ways to make sure no one waited to surprise them. Seeing all was clear, he gave Wayne and Laura the signal to move forward. They followed him into the living room. Officer Malloy was no longer there and the room seemed much brighter than before. Detective Wilson turned to face the kitchen.

"Malloy?" he shouted. "Where are you?"

Wayne looked at the living room window and noticed the boards that once covered it were smashed through.

"Detective?" he said as his breath almost caught in his throat.

"Yes?" the lawman said as he turned to face him. "What is it?"

"I think we have a problem."

Following Wayne's eyes, he noticed the broken boards and gasped. A sudden feeling of disaster overtook him.

"Malloy!" he bellowed and charged for the window.

"Detective?" a male voice called from somewhere outside. "Come quickly."

At the window, he stared outside in shock and his face became sudden pale.

Wayne and Laura watched helplessly. They knew something horrible just took place. It was just a question of what.

The detective turned and walked toward them at a brisk rate.

"Everybody out," he ordered. When Wayne and Laura hesitated, he yelled. "Now!"

Immediately, Wayne and Laura spun and charged for the door. Laura reached for the doorknob and turned it, but it would not open. She then pulled at it frantically.

"It's stuck," she called.

"Here, let me try," Wayne said as he went to her side.

He turned the doorknob again and pulled harder, but still it would not budge. Losing patience quickly, Wayne shook the door as hard as he could.

Wilson joined his seemingly feeble attempt in trying to shake the door open – but to no avail.

A sudden low growl sounded through the house and we stopped.

Everyone stopped in their tracks and fell silent.

At that moment, Wayne knew why the door would not open. The yellow-eyed demon was finally making its appearance. Though they could not see him, Wayne knew he was there.

"We have to jump out the living room window," Wayne said.

"You don't want to go that way," the detective claimed. "Trust me."

"What other choice do we have?" Laura asked.

The detective thought quickly. "Get behind me and get down."

Wayne and Laura quickly obeyed. They moved back about five feet and crouched down beside the wall. Wayne held Laura in his arms to help comfort her. The first shot rang through the air and a small scream escaped her lips.

Nathan Christopher's low growl turned into an eerie giggle.

The second shot made Laura cringe. Wayne held her a little bit tighter and this time she held him back. A third shot rang out. Then silence. For a moment, Wayne and Laura stayed crouched down where they were and just held each other. The detective spoke.

"Come on you two!" he said. "The door is open. Let's get the hell out of here before whatever it is changes its mind!"

Wayne and Laura glanced at each other in confusion. Neither one of them heard the door open. Wasting no more time, they jumped to their feet and hurried out the door. Detective Wilson quickly followed. They ran for the street and did not turn back until they arrived there. The detective went right to the fallen officer's side and knelt beside him. Officer Jackson was with him as well. The long weedy grass of the lawn had been unattended for so long, that it was difficult to see the downed man. Laura spoke in a low frantic voice.

"I knew this would happen. I just knew it! Is that what you wanted?"

"Of course, that's not what I wanted," Wayne replied in the same tone. "All I wanted was a simple scare, if anything. Not for someone to be catapulted through a boarded-up window."

With each second that passed by, the ambulance drew closer. The two officers were beside themselves with concern.

Wayne felt horrible for Officer Malloy but he knew why Nathan did it. He did it to scare him away and make him forget about that God-forsaken place. Wayne shook his head slowly as he glared at the house.

"It's not going to work, Nathan," Wayne whispered. "This little war between us is far from over."

"There is the ambulance!" Laura cried out and pointed.

The ambulance stopped in front of the house. Two paramedics got out with a handbag and charged through the long grass to the officers.

Wayne and Laura watched on as one paramedic looked up at the officers and shook his head. At first, he did not understand what that meant, but then it hit him like a ton of bricks.

"Oh my God," Wayne said in a hushed voice.

Laura placed her left hand on his shoulder.

"It's not your fault," she said.

The paramedics went back to the ambulance and pulled out a stretcher. They placed the limp body of Officer Malloy on to it and carried it back to the ambulance. Detective Wilson got in with them and drove off without activating the sirens.

Officer Jackson walked over to Wayne and Laura.

"I was told to inform you; Detective Wilson wants to see you both in his office tomorrow at your earliest convenience."

Wayne remained silent and nodded.

Without another word, Officer Jackson turned and headed for his cruiser.

Wayne and Laura watched him drive away until he turned the corner. They looked at each other and then at the house. Laura got in the car but Wayne hesitated: but this time, it was it as the street that caught his attention. Wayne took a step back and looked both ways down the street.

With a puzzled look, Laura watched him. She rolled down the passenger-side window.

"Wayne? What's the matter?"

Wayne gave his head a little shake.

"Nothing," he said. "Just, every time I step onto this street, I never see anyone or anything."

"What do you mean?" Laura asked.

"Nobody," Wayne said. "No people…no dogs, no cats…no squirrels – nothing. It's as if this part of the block was abandoned long ago."

"Oh, I'm sure they're around here somewhere," she said. "Come on. Let's get out of here."

"It's just weird," Wayne added, "that's all."

Laura started the car and Wayne got in. He gave the house one final look as they drove off.

Chapter Twenty-Five
A Little Side Trip to Remember

Except for the vague hum of the tires, Wayne heard nothing else. He stared out his window, oblivious to the scenery. His thoughts were elsewhere. Though he was not technically responsible for the death of Officer Malloy, he felt responsible nonetheless. He only hoped the officer did not suffer. Pulling his eyes away from the window, Wayne looked at the clock. Fifteen minutes passed since they left the house on Birchcroft. This surprised him a little. To him, it felt as though it was only a few moments ago. He took a deep breath and released it slowly. For a moment, he closed his eyes and tried to relax.

"You know," Laura said. "What happened back there was not your fault."

"Yes, it was," Wayne said.

"Why would you say such a foolish thing?" Laura asked, shocked.

"Because, that is how I feel," he replied, turning to face her. "It was my idea to take them to that place out."

"And that makes it your fault?" she asked sarcastically. "Come on. Look, there is no way you could have predicted or prevented that."

Wayne lowered his head slightly and turned back to his window. Deep down he knew she was right.

"I'm sorry I snapped at you back there," Laura added. "The last thing I wanted to do was make you feel guilty. Besides, if anything, I feel just as guilty."

"Why?" Wayne asked.

"I was the driver and they followed."

"And that makes you guilty?" Wayne asked with the same sarcasm.

Laura grew quiet for a moment.

Wayne looked at her and noticed a small smile form on her lips.

"Touché," she said. "So, we're good then?"

Wayne laughed. "Yes, we're good," he agreed and turned back to his window.

"Would you like to go back to the motel?" Laura asked nonchalantly.

Wayne turned back to her. At that particular moment, her eyes were on the road. He held his gaze and waited patiently. He wanted her to see his reaction. Deep down he knew what she meant, but used it as a cheap pick up line.

Laura sensed his stare and turned to him.

Wayne moved his eyebrows up and down and grinned sheepishly.

Laura gasped and turned her attention back to the road. She laughed and shook her head.

"You are horrible," she commented.

"Yeah baby!" Wayne replied in his best Michael Myers impersonation.

Laura laughed again. "To the motel then," she said.

From their current position, the motel they stayed at the night before was not very far away. They looked forward to going back. Nothing paranormal happened there and they both hoped it stayed that way.

Wayne smiled and went back to staring out his window. He felt much better since he and Laura were communicating again. Suddenly, something in the sky on the distant horizon caught his attention. It was very dark compared to the partly cloudy sky above their heads. At first, he thought his eyes were playing tricks on him. He turned away, blinked a few times and then took a second look. The darkness was still there. He turned his attention to the road ahead. Curious, Wayne wondered if the news mentioned anything about a possible storm. No such announcement revealed itself. Again, he looked out his window. The darkened sky was a little closer now. A look of concern formed on his face.

"Maybe once we get back to the motel," Laura said, "we'll get something to eat."

"Sounds like a plan," Wayne answered in almost a trance-like tone.

"See something interesting out there?" Laura asked.

"Actually, yes," Wayne replied. "I'm not entirely sure, but those look like storm clouds over there."

"Storm clouds?" Laura said, puzzled. "What are you talking about? I don't see anything," Laura said.

Wayne leaned back in his seat and pointed with his right thumb.

"How about now?" he asked.

Laura's eyes widened. She pulled over to the shoulder of the road, but continued driving slowly.

"You are right," she said. "Where do you suppose they came from?"

"I don't know, but they are heading this way. And fast from the looks of it."

They stopped in front of an open yet somewhat woodsy area. Three adult pine trees stood proud. Each one separated by a length of at least six feet. Not far behind the trees, Wayne noticed several neatly stacked piles of wood and brick. He wondered what they were going to build. The area was big enough for a nice house, or another store of some kind.

But what type of store? he wondered. *There are already two jewelers, a television repair, a pawnbroker, a Tim Horton's and a gas station on this road.*

Wayne looked back up at the sky. The stormy darkness was much closer now. He knew it was only a matter of minutes before the storm would begin. It both shocked and amazed him to see a threatening storm brew so quickly. A second bolt of lightning struck down: this time, much closer than the first. Wayne rolled down his window to see if they could hear anything. To his surprise, all was quiet. In fact, it was a little too quiet for his taste. There was no ka boom from the lightning, no growling thunder and no wind. It reminded him of that first night on Birchcroft Drive The night he stood in front of Nathan Christopher's house. He still faced my window as he spoke.

"Do you hear that?"

"No," Laura replied. "Hear what?"

Instead of answering, Wayne allowed the memories of that night to play back in his mind. It was the only road in complete darkness. One minute, the leaves rustled about in the trees: then suddenly they hushed into an eerie silence, yet the light wind continued to make them dance. The lights that turned on and off inside the house, the way that it somehow beckoned him.

"Wayne?" Laura said, obviously concerned at my quietness.

Wayne snapped himself back to reality. The clouds were on top of them now. His heart pounded in his chest. A sudden wave of anxiety came over him. He turned to Laura.

"I think it would be a good idea if we left," he said calmly.

"All right," Laura said, curious about my odd behavior, "but aren't you going to tell me what you heard?"

"It's not what I heard," Wayne said. "It's what I didn't hear."

"What you didn't hear?" Laura asked him.

"I will explain everything later," Wayne said with a little more assertiveness. "Now can we please just get the—"

A massive boom filled the air. Laura screamed and covered her ears. They ducked away from the windows and Wayne sheltered her upper body with his. His ears rang in protest and he was certain Laura's were ringing as well. His mind raced. Whatever exploded – if anything did – sounded as though it were very close by. Wayne prayed nothing would crash down on them.

As the seconds ticked by, nothing happened. The rain began its inevitable descent.

Wayne was still unable to hear anything, but he felt the cold drops as they showered his lower back. He sat up and scanned the surrounding area slowly from left to right. Nothing appeared to be destroyed but he stopped once he got to his window. He did not look outside. Instead, he lowered his eyes to the window handle and rolled it up.

"Is everything okay?" Laura asked as she sat up.

"Seems to be," he said.

Wayne was confident with that answer until he finally looked out his window. Of the three pine trees that stood so proudly, only two now remained. He looked at what was left of the missing tree. The trunk still lightly smoked. He adjusted his mirror to view the ground and noticed the tree. It rested across the road and seemed only inches away from the bumper.

"We were lucky," Wayne said. "If we would have stopped just a few feet back that way – it would have come down on us."

Laura looked in her rear-view mirror and found the tree. She gasped.

"Gees, you're right," she said with a concerned tone. "It's time to get the hell out of here. Someone up there is looking out for us."

Laura started the car and put it in gear but stepped on the gas much harder than she intended to – the tires spun and the car lunged forward.

A look of surprise formed on Wayne's face as he was yanked back in his seat.

It was not raining hard at that time, but the wind was picking up. Wayne looked up at the sky through the windshield. The clouds now covered three quarters of the sky.

"Honey, do you really think it's safe to drive this fast?" he said.

Personally, Wayne did not mind storms, but being on the road while one was in progress was a different story. It tended to make the roads slick and dangerous.

"It's not so bad," Laura said.

"Not yet it isn't," Wayne said, "but this storm is probably just moments away from getting much worse."

"Would you stop worrying? We're going to be just fine."

Wayne looked out his window and concentrated on the trees and sky. The ominous clouds zigzagged with the wind as if they were unsure where to go. He hoped they were not about to confront a tornado. He had seen documentaries on tornados and the skies looked a lot like they did then: foreboding and uncertain. In real life, he never witnessed such a phenomenon. He turned on the radio and it came to life. The sports personality announced its conclusion and that the weather was next. He wondered if they were going to mention anything on the storm.

"Thank you, Fred," a man's voice said. "Well folks, we went from a beautiful sunny day to—"

The voice of the weatherman cut off and replaced by static. Wayne and Laura glanced at each other. He tried to adjust the tuner to get a better frequency, but the static persisted. He then tried other stations, only to receive the same result.

"Too much interference from the storm I guess," Laura said.

"Damn," Wayne grumbled as he leaned back in his seat.

"I'll turn it off."

Laura kept her eyes on the road and leaned forward. Her index finger was a millisecond away from the power button when a faint voice distracted her.

Wayne, on the other hand, had not heard the voice and curiously watched as she stayed still.

"Laura?"

"Shush," she said as a look of deep concentration formed on her face. "Listen."

Wayne listened closely and heard nothing but the static. He looked from Laura to the radio. Finally, the static dissipated and he heard it. It was very faint, but definitely female. The static returned briefly and disappeared again. The mysterious voice quickly returned and appeared to be communicating with them. Wayne understood the words '*save*' and '*free.*' Finally, the static cleared and the female voice spoke much more clearly:

"1 – I was once there but have been lost for countless years. 9 – Tied to the air, I suffered through my screams and tears. Encased in metal – five x four, with a soul of orange brown, 5 – Proof of my existence will be no more, for in twenty-four hours they will crush my crown. Surrounded by a rainbow of colors, old yet true. 1 – Save me, or to my capture I will bring you."

Wayne played the words around in his mind and suddenly, the words *'tied to the air'* reminded him of Emily's story.

"Emily was right," he said, though more to himself.

"What are you talking about?" Laura asked.

"She was telling the truth," Wayne added more clearly. "The riddle refers to..."

At that moment, a blanket of water covered the windshield, blinding Wayne and Laura. It sounded as though they were driving through a car wash with the blasters on. The shocked looks on their faces suggested they had never seen it rain so hard.

Thinking quickly, Laura put the windshield-wipers at full speed but it was useless. Visibility was still zero. She slowed down and looked out her window. To her amazement, the opposite side of the street was barely visible.

What the hell are we driving into? Laura wondered.

Foolishly not noticing she was going forty kilometers an hour, Laura carefully began to pull over. Wayne knew she was unable to see so he guided her through his window. Yet once they were safely on the shoulder, the front tires hit something…something deep yet narrow. To Wayne it felt like an old-fashioned sidewalk. Laura slammed the brakes and the car came to a rapid halt. Stunned by the minor accident, they stayed still for a moment. Wayne's left hand rested on the dashboard while his other hand clutched his stomach. He looked over to Laura. She was slumped over the steering wheel.

"Are you okay?" he asked.

Laura was silent.

"Hey, are you okay," Wayne asked again as he placed a hand on her shoulder.

"I think so," she finally answered as she began to stir. "You?"

"Yes, for the most part," Wayne replied.

"For the most part?" she said. "Why? What's wrong?"

"I think my heart just transplanted itself into my kidneys," Wayne replied.

"I know what you mean," she said.

"I'm going to go see if any damage was done."

"Be careful," Laura said.

Wayne opened the door and the rain soaked his arm. He looked down and was glad to see they were still on the shoulder. He got out and closed the door. The wind howled through his ears and the rain soaked through his clothes in mere seconds.

Why did this have to happen? he wondered. Was it because of the third spirit and the riddle she gave us, or was it just coincidence? Was it God's way of saving us from certain disaster, or was it Nathan Christopher hoping for one?

Wayne shook his head as no answer to any of those questions appealed to him. He looked to the front of the car and made his way to it. To his surprise, there appeared to be no damage. A look of deep curiosity formed on his face. He knew they hit something. It was only a question of what. Sheltering his eyes, he looked along the driver's side of the car and all appeared to be in order. Growing frustrated, he went back to the passenger-side and searched the shoulder. Carefully, he made his way to the rear of the vehicle. As he approached the rear tire, the answer finally revealed itself. The lower half of the tire was in a deep but not so narrow rut. To Wayne, it looked like one of those gutters from a bowling alley: except, it was twice as deep and twice as wide. He crouched down and looked past the tire. The opposite tire was in the same rut. He then scanned the undercarriage for damage. Visually, he was unable to see any. Mentally, he did not really know all that much about cars. Like any average

Joe, he only recognized obvious damage. Standing, he reached for his door to open it. Just as his hand touched it, the storm grew abruptly worse. It caught him off guard and he almost fell, but somehow kept his footing. With a little bit of muscle, Wayne managed to open his door. He got in and closed it behind him.

"Where did you disappear to?" Laura asked, concerned. "You had me worried."

"Sorry." Wayne said.

"Did you find any damage?"

"Not from what I can tell but the back tires are caught in a deep rut," Wayne said.

"A rut?" Laura said curiously.

"Yes, something like a narrow trench," Wayne replied.

"Will we be able to get out?" Laura asked.

"Don't worry," Wayne said. "We'll be back on the road in no time – even if I have to get out and push."

Laura looked at Wayne with both surprise and admiration. No one else she knew would have ever offered with such a nasty chore. She found his courage quite refreshing. She tried to peek through the windshield to see if the storm had let up any. To her disappointment, there was no change.

"I guess we should wait until this storm blows over," she said.

"You're right," Wayne agreed. "The motel can wait."

At that moment, the car wobbled under the fierce winds. Laura's hand rose to her mouth as a tiny scream escaped her lips.

"It's okay. It's only a storm," Wayne commented softly.

"That's easy for you to say," Laura said. "I have never been caught in a storm like this."

"Neither have I if it's any consolation," Wayne said. "The last time I saw anything like this was on television," Wayne said.

"What type of storm is this?" Laura asked.

"My first guess would be a monsoon, or maybe a tornado," Wayne replied.

"My goodness," Laura said.

"Don't worry. We'll be fine," Wayne assured. "Maybe if we concentrate on something else it will take our minds off the storm."

"Such as?" Laura asked as the car continued to wobble from the wind.

"For example, the voice on the radio," Wayne said.

At first, Laura thought Wayne was referring to the weatherman. She opened her mouth to ask why but stopped when she remembered the other voice.

"Oh yes. I almost forgot about her," Laura said. "Do you remember what she said?"

Wayne nodded. "Most of it," he said.

"Encased in metal, 5 x 4 with a soul of orange brown, proof of my existence will be no more, for in twenty-four hours they will crush my crown. She also said something about being surrounded by a rainbow of colors – and the numbers one, nine, five and one."

"How can you remember all of that?" Laura said, both surprised and impressed.

"I am not sure," Wayne replied. "I guess I just work well under pressure."

"I see," Laura said. "Oh yes! You said Emily was right. What did you mean?"

"The riddle refers to her mother," Wayne replied.

"How can you be sure?" Laura asked.

"Okay. Let's go over this one thing at a time," Wayne continued. "Emily was told they found her mother on a sacrificial machine of sorts at that house."

"Right," Laura agreed.

"The riddle had the words 'tied to the air' in it. Therefore, that means Emily's mother really was there."

Laura nodded, agreeing that the story fit the riddle. Yet she wondered if it was merely a simple coincidence. Nevertheless, it was still another victim.

"Now," Wayne continued. "What metal objects do you know have the measurements five by six?"

"Rock bands use large cases for their equipment," Laura replied. "I wouldn't know if they are metal though. Magicians also use all kinds of trunks."

"Yes, they do," Wayne agreed. "On the other hand, none of those things have a crown to crush."

The car wobbled from the wind again.

Wayne could tell that Laura was still frightened, but she appeared to remain calm.

"That's the main question," she continued. "What type of trunk has a crown?"

Wayne played the question through his mind, but had no idea what the answer was. He shook his head, stumped.

"I don't know either," Laura said.

Wayne stared at the dashboard thoughtfully. "The answer is probably right under..."

"What?" Laura said as she watched him.

Wayne suddenly remembered that most guys referred to their vehicles as machines with feelings. If they would not start or if the engine sounded odd, they would try to talk to them.

"Cars," he said. "It's the trunk of a car!"

"Are you serious?" Laura asked.

"Absolutely," Wayne replied.

"How can you be sure?" she added.

"I've seen so many guys look and talk to their vehicles like they are alive," Wayne said, "as if they have a soul. And the trunk of a car could be as big as five feet by four feet."

"Okay. For argument sake, let's say you are right. What type of vehicle has a crown?"

Wayne thought about that for a moment.

"A taxi," he said.

Laura was shocked. She was beginning to think he was right.

"You're pretty good at this," she said.

"Well, I'm not saying I am right," Wayne said. "This is just a guess."

"I see. So what do we do now?"

"When this storm clears up, we should try a junkyard," Wayne suggested.

"All right detective, why a junkyard?" Laura asked.

"With a soul of orange brown," Wayne said, quoting from the riddle. "So, either the car is really old, or really ugly. Nevertheless, the only place I can think we would find a car like that – is a junkyard."

"What if it's just ugly?" Laura asked.

"Would you ever own such an ugly car?" Wayne asked.

Laura opened her mouth to reply but stopped. She was distracted as a sudden silence fell over the car. Keeping her eyes on Wayne, she watched as he made facial expressions of curiosity.

"Is it over," Laura asked.

"Sounds like it," Wayne said. "Maybe now would be a good time to try to find a junkyard: while we still have time."

"Yes, and before the storm decides to come back," she added.

Laura started the car and carefully rocked it out of the rut. She turned back onto the road and this time, drove at a more normal speed-rate.

"See," Wayne said. "That wasn't so bad."

"That was one hell of a storm," Laura commented. "Look at all the loose branches on the road."

"Yes," Wayne agreed.

In a short time, Wayne spotted a billboard in the near distance. As they drew closer, he read what was on the sign out loud.

"Need to get rid of your old car? Bring it to Jeff's Junkyard, at 22 Bentley Way."

"Huh?" Laura said.

"That is what the billboard says," Wayne said. "We will try that one first."

Chapter Twenty-Six
A Puzzle of Junk

Before long, Wayne and Laura turned onto Bentley Way. They were roughly three miles from where they were when the storm hit. Slowing down, they approached the address they were looking for and turned into it. It was a long, pitchfork shaped lane way. They stayed in middle lane and stopped in front of a house. It was an average looking home. It had a black shingled roof with white siding and a gray concrete base. There were no front steps to the front door. It was level to the ground and a single gray patio stone rested in front of it. A seven-foot high fence adjoined both sides of the house. One side had a wide gate and the other had a narrow one.

"I know what the big door is for," Laura said, "but why the smaller one?"

Wayne shrugged. "Anything small I guess like toasters, microwaves and such."

At that moment, the front door to the house opened. A young man opened the door. He was slim, stood roughly six feet, and looked as though he was in his mid-twenties. He wore a plain black shirt, dark blue jeans and white running shoes.

"Good day," the young man said. "How may I help you?"

"Hi," Wayne said. "We are looking for a rusty 1951 orange Crown Taxi."

A puzzled look appeared on the young man's face. He scratched his head, apparently uncertain if such a car even existed. He knew there were many types of old cars in the yard but he did not know of any old taxicabs. He held up his hand as if to say wait here and went back in the house. A moment later, he reappeared with a large ring of keys.

"To be honest, I'm not sure we have any brand of taxi at all," he said. "My father would know, but he's not here right now. My name is Maynard. I am his son."

Maynard unlocked the wide gate and they went inside. To Wayne and Laura, the junkyard seemed small on the outside. To their surprise, the inside was much larger. There were vehicles to the left and to the right. They walked through several wide snaking turns and noticed many rusty vehicles. Some of them had large dents while others had only a few small ones. Some appeared as though they were in horrific accidents.

Shortly, they reached the end of the yard. To Wayne and Laura's disappointment, there were no taxis of any kind.

"Sorry," Maynard said. "I guess we don't have any."

"Just out of curiosity," Wayne said. "Is there a special place you bring vehicles to be crushed?"

"Actually yes," Maynard replied. "We bring them to a crushing plant. The one we deal with is not far from here. Why do you ask?"

"Well," Laura said. "You could say we are—"

"Collectors," Wayne interjected.

Laura slowly turned to Wayne with a look of curiosity.

"You two are collectors?" Maynard asked, somewhat surprised. "I don't mean to pry but why would you want to buy such a worthless clunker? I mean, I've never seen it but it can't be in good condition if it's in the crush-yard."

Laura knew Wayne was about to do or say something foolish. Her look of curiosity grew more profound and she folded her arms across her chest.

This I have to hear, she thought.

"It's okay, honey. We can trust this young fellow," Wayne said with the sudden air of a businessman.

Laura turned to Maynard and smiled gently.

"I am sure we can," she said, quickly deciding it was best to go along with Wayne's plan.

"Now, what we are about to tell you cannot leave this area," Wayne said with a look of warning.

"I understand," Maynard quickly replied.

"We have a client whose uncle used to drive a taxi. He informed us he received a letter from a law firm two weeks ago. It stated that something very valuable was inside in the trunk of that vehicle. When our client called us, I asked him if he knew what the item was and he did not. He only knew it was some form of inheritance, as stated in the letter he showed us."

Laura was doing her best to keep the shock out of her face, and hoped Maynard did not notice it. She never thought Wayne was able to lie so easily. It was not something she liked but deep down she knew he meant no harm.

"We have been looking for the car since that time," Wayne concluded.

"Oh, I see," Maynard said. "So you do not want the car itself. You just want what may or may not be in the trunk?"

"Precisely," Wayne said.

"Well, why didn't you say so in the first place?" Maynard said. "Once we get back to the house, I will call them to see if they have it."

"Thank you," Wayne said. "That would be so kind of you."

"Not a problem," Maynard replied.

They started walking back to the house. Wayne and Laura were a foot or so behind Maynard. Wayne turned to her and noticed that she seemed a little upset. He wondered why but was unable to think of a reason.

Roughly halfway to the gate, Wayne noticed a rusty black Crown Victoria. The passenger doors were dented in. It appeared worthless, but somehow kept his attention. He stopped for a moment and stared at it. The riddle before the massive storm flashed through his memory.

"Hey!" Laura said, snapping Wayne back to reality. "You coming?"

"Right behind you," Wayne replied and waved off the old car.

Wayne took one last look at the old car before turning to catch up with the others.

Laura and Maynard waited for Wayne to catch up. Laura spoke.

"Something interesting about that old car?" she said.

"Nah," Wayne replied as they continued walking. "Just thought it looked familiar, but I was wrong."

After locking the gate behind him, Maynard went back into the house to call the crushing plant. He walked into his father's office and found a list of phone numbers by the telephone. In just seconds, he found the contact. Pointing to it, he picked up the receiver and dialed. On the fourth ring, a mature female voice answered.

"Hello?"

"Hi. This is Maynard calling from Jeff's Junkyard."

"Well, hello Maynard. This is Mrs. Tackleworth. How is your father doing?"

"He's fine ma'am, thank you."

"Good. Now, what can I do for you?" Mrs. Tackleworth asked.

"To be honest, I'm not sure if you can really help me," Maynard said. "There are two people here looking for a 1951 Crown Taxi. They don't want to buy it but would like to get a look inside the trunk." At Mrs. Tackleworth's silence, Maynard knew it must have sounded weird. "I know it sounds funky but they are looking for something important. Would you happen to know if your husband has one of those?"

Mrs. Tackleworth tried to recall if her other-half mentioned anything about receiving an old taxi. She had no idea what one even looked like from that year. She shook her head.

"I'm sorry Maynard. I have no idea. Let me get Ted on the radio and I will ask him. He is in the yard right now."

"Okay," Maynard said.

While Maynard waited for Mrs. Tackleworth to return, he plucked some dead skin from his fingers. It was one of his very few bad habits. A habit he tried to stop for the last three years: ever since the wart appeared on the right side of his thumb six months ago. His father kept telling him that would happen one day but he never listened. It was gone now but it took three trips to the clinic to finally burn it off.

You would think I would have learned by now, he thought.

"Maynard?" Mrs. Tackleworth said.

"I'm here."

"Ted said that we do have one but by noon tomorrow it will be crushed. He also said your guests are more than welcome to come over and look at it."

"Thank you so much. I will let them know immediately."

"You're welcome Maynard. Bye for now."

"Bye."

Wayne and Laura were waiting patiently by the locked gate. As Maynard opened the door and stepped out, they turned to him.

"Good news," Maynard said. "They have one and say you are welcome to go over and see it. I also told them you were looking for something important but that is all I said. I hope that's alright."

"Yes, that's fine," Wayne said.

"Did they mention a time we could go?" Laura asked.

"Well, the time would have to be either now or in the early morning," Maynard said. "The vehicle is set to be crushed at twelve noon. Here is the address and the telephone number in case you get lost." He handed Wayne a piece of paper with the information.

"Thank you, my young friend," Wayne said.

"No problem," Maynard replied.

Wayne and Laura got back in their car with high hopes they would find the car they were looking for. Laura started the car and they were on their way once again. If it was not, that meant they had very little time to find a needle in a haystack.

"Should we call Detective Wilson?" Laura said.

"Why? Let's find what we're looking for first," Wayne said. "I'm sure the good detective has more important things do than go on wild goose chases. Besides, if it is not the car we are looking for, then we have very little time left before mud hits the fan."

Before they knew it, they arrived at the address Maynard gave them. They were expecting to see a crush yard but it was only a house. It was slightly smaller than the one at the junk yard. There were no fences or gates and the driveway continued past the house to the right.

"That must lead to the crush yard," Laura said.

"Probably, but I wonder if anyone is home," Wayne said. "I don't see any vehicles unless they don't drive and I doubt we can just drive in. I'll go knock on the door."

Wayne was only a few feet from the door when it swung open. A woman in her mid-forties appeared.

"Hello," Mrs. Tackleworth said. "May I help you?"

The woman was wearing a bright pink blouse with black slacks and pink high-heeled shoes. Not one strand of her blond hair seemed out of place. To Wayne, she appeared as though she were about to go out. She looked from Wayne to the car and spotted Laura.

"Oh! You must be the folks young Maynard spoke of," she added cheerfully.

"Yes ma'am," Wayne replied. "We are here to see the taxi."

"My husband is expecting you. Just follow the lane way down to the crushyard. You can park in the employee parking area. I'll radio him and announce your arrival."

"Thank you so kindly," Wayne said.

"You are welcome. Have a pleasant day now."

"You too," Wayne said and turned to head back to the car.

"So?" Laura said when Wayne sat down and closed the door.

"Onward," Wayne said. "She said to drive down and park in the employee parking. The man of the house is expecting us."

The driveway led them through a massive backyard. In the middle of the plush green lawn was a white gazebo with a black-shingled roof. There were four comfortable looking chairs around the square table. There were two cars were parked in a distant corner. To Wayne they seemed quite new. One was a gold colored Toyota Camry and the other was a forest green Ford Escort. Beyond all of that was a row of tall evergreens, hiding whatever was on the other side.

This is cozy, Wayne thought.

Just passed the backyard was a gravel parking area. There were seven vehicles parked. It was not a large parking area but there was space enough for a dozen cars.

They parked and got out.

A man wearing light blue coveralls approached them. When he was close enough, he wiped his hands on a rag.

"Hi," the man said. "My name is Ted. Follow me. I will show you to that taxi."

Ted was a tall man with pepper-gray hair. He stood roughly six foot three with a husky build.

"Thank you," Wayne said.

Ted turned and walked forward. Wayne and Laura followed him. As they walked, a handful of people bustled about. Some were removing small engine parts while others appeared to be taking inventory.

"So," Mr. Tackleworth said, "you came all this way just to get a look in the trunk, huh?"

"It's a long story," Wayne said.

"Well I hope you find what you're looking for."

"So do we," Laura said.

"How long have you had this taxi, sir?" Wayne asked.

"Please call me Ted. I've had it for about two weeks."

"Would you happen to know how long the junkyard had it?" Wayne asked.

Laura eyed Wayne proudly. She knew he hated politics but for one reason or another, she thought he would have made a fine politician. He had a real way with people and was able to connect with just about anyone he wanted to.

"Fifty years I think," Ted replied. "Give or take a year or two."

"Wow. That's a very long time," Wayne said.

"Yes. Some would say too long," Mr. Tackleworth said. "There is a little story behind that though. The owner – Willy Kemper – died about ten years ago and passed the torch onto his son. I know that family very well. Willy always said he wanted no one but Jeffery to run the business. Jeffery is his son, but he never told Jeffery about taking over until he was on his deathbed. At first, the boy had no interest in it so he denied his father's wish. An hour later, Willy died. From what I remember, it took Jeffery about three hours to relent. He has been running the junkyard from that day on. The funny thing is he never knew this taxi existed until a month ago. He had no idea how long it was there or why his father kept it."

The trio approached two long separate rows of vehicles. Each one parked directly in front of the other on either side of the road. The rows were wide enough that more vehicles would easily pass through them. On the opposite side of each row was a wasteland of wrecked vehicles.

Wayne followed the rows with his eyes until he noticed the huge crushing machine. It was something he had never seen in real life before. It was blue in color and its maw was wide enough to crush at least five vehicles at a time.

"Look at the size of that thing," Laura commented. "It almost looks like something out of a horror movie."

"Massive," Wayne agreed.

"Here we are," Ted said.

The taxi must have been in a nasty crash. The front end was virtually non-existent and the driver's door was dented in. To Wayne, it seemed as if someone took a sledgehammer to it. The vehicle had large and small patches of rust but still had patches of orange in it.

Wayne and Laura watched in anticipation as Ted opened the trunk. The rusty hinges creaked noisily in protest. To their disappointment, there was no dead body. From what they were able to see, there was mainly garbage: a tire-iron, a few empty cans of soda pop, some newspaper and a baseball glove.

"Here you go," Ted said. "I will be over there by the crusher. Just give a yell when you're finished."

"Okay," Wayne said as Ted turned and walked away.

They pretended to sift through the trunk. After a brief moment, Wayne peeked around the corner to make sure they were alone. They were.

"Great. Now what do we do?" Wayne said. "There is no dead body here."

"Maybe there is another clue somewhere in there," Laura commented.

"Well," Wayne said. "It's worth a shot."

He leaned into the trunk and grabbed the tire-iron. Slowly, he poked through the trash. When he turned over the newspapers, several creepy-crawlies stirred from their slumber. He did not know what they were, nor did he care. All he wanted was to find something significant to their cause.

The seconds ticked by and they were finding nothing but insects. Discouraged and about to give up, Wayne's eyes shot to the baseball glove. He eyed it curiously.

What possible secrets might you be holding? he wondered.

Wayne poked at the glove, checking to see if anything would craw out of it. Nothing did. He pried it open with the tire-iron. To his surprise, there was something inside it.

"What's that?" Laura asked.

"I'm not sure but it looks like an old Polaroid," Wayne replied.

He pulled the glove to him and plucked out the Polaroid. He showed Laura and they looked at it closely.

The black and white photo depicted a young woman standing beside a car. She did not appear to be happy. To Wayne, the car looked like an old Crown Victoria. On the ground – to the left of the rear tire – was a can of paint. The word green was on it. Laura spoke.

"Do you think she is the one we're looking for?"

"I'm not sure," Wayne replied. "For all we know, it may be nothing but a useless photograph. There is nothing else we can do here, let's go find Ted."

They did not have to look far. Ted was already approaching them.

"Find what you are looking for?" he asked.

Wayne nodded. "Yes, we did. Thank you for your time and patience."

Mr. Tackleworth waved the words away with a motion of his hand.

"Think nothing of it," he replied.

"Actually," Wayne added, "there is one more thing you may be able to help us with."

"What's that?"

Wayne showed him the old photograph.

"Just to be certain," Wayne said, "Would you be able to tell us what type of car this is?"

Ted studied it.

"Oh, that's easy," he said. "It's a 1948 Crown Victoria."

Wayne immediately remembered the black Crown Victoria at the first junkyard.

Nah, it cannot be that one, he thought. *It is not the same color, but it must have been a clue.*

"Would you happen to know where we might find one?" Laura asked.

"Well, let me see," Ted said thoughtfully. "I've been to many junkyards and antique car shows over the years. Only two places had a car like that. Taylor's Junkyard and a place called Tommy's. Taylor's is at 1215 Hepburn Street and Tommy's is 102 Plaza Place."

"Are they far from here?" Wayne asked.

"Taylor's is only a few miles from here and Tommy's is about an hour drive across town." At the looks on Wayne and Laura's faces, Ted knew they had no idea where those places were. "Tell you what," Ted added. "I'll contact my wife and have her print out the easiest routes for you."

"Thank you so much," Wayne said. "That would be greatly appreciated."

"You're welcome," Ted said, "and best of luck."

Wayne and Laura turned and made their way back to the parking lot.

As they pulled up to the side of the house, Mrs. Tackleworth was waiting for them with the maps. Laura rolled down her window.

"Hello," Mrs. Tackleworth said cheerfully and handed Laura the map. "Ted asked me to give you these. It leads to both junkyards."

"Thank you so much," Laura said.

"Yes, thank you indeed," Wayne added.

"You are welcome," Mrs. Tackleworth said. "Take care and drive safely."

Wayne and Laura continued down the lane way and turned left onto the road.

Suddenly Laura became confused and turned to Wayne.

"Wait a minute," she said. "I thought we were looking for a 1951 orange crown taxi? Now, all of a sudden, we are looking for a 1948 Crown Victoria?"

"I know," Wayne replied as he concentrated on the road. "It crossed my mind too but we should check it out anyway. Am I turning anywhere soon?"

Laura studied the map.

"Continue down this road and turn left on Hepburn," she said.

Not much was happening as the scenery passed them by. No one was walking their dog or jogging, looking after their lawns. In fact, they barely saw anyone at all. Wayne found it a little disquieting but thought nothing of it.

"Must be a really quiet town," Wayne commented.

"Maybe it's supper time," Laura said.

Wayne slowed down and turned onto Hepburn Street. The first address he saw was 235.

"Must be way up the road," he said. "We're in the two-hundreds."

"Ted did say it was a few miles," Laura said.

They watched the numbers pass and made small talk. To their surprise, Hepburn was just as quiet and uneventful as the last street.

Before long, they approached the address they were looking for. They turned into the driveway and parked behind a red tow truck. They got out.

"To coin a phrase," Wayne said. "May fortune favor the foolish."

"Amen," Laura said. "Let's go."

They walked past the tow truck. The gravel crunched under their feet. Almost immediately, the grace of the property took them by surprise. The grounds were immaculate. A beautiful flowerbed rested in the center of the front lawn. The house was two stories in itself. To Wayne and Laura, it appeared more like a luxury home. It had brilliant white paneling with a red brick base. It also had a chimney surrounded with red brick. The porch was made of wood and seemed well maintained.

"Holy cow," Wayne said. "This is a junk yard? It looks more like a sanctuary."

"Maybe Mr. and Mrs. Tackleworth made a mistake," Laura said.

"I doubt it," Wayne said. "The address he gave is here, and since we are here we may as well check it out."

They walked up the steps and Wayne rang the doorbell. A faint musical sound chimed throughout the house. A man who appeared to be in his late thirties answered the door. He stood roughly five foot six and was slightly stout. He was wearing dark blue coveralls with old-fashioned steel-toe boots. His demeanor was not stern, but did seem as though he was not expecting anyone.

"Beg your pardon good sir," Wayne said. "Would this be Taylor's Junkyard?"

"Yes," the man replied with an Irish accent. "I am Taylor. May I help you?"

"We sure hope so," Wayne said as he withdrew the old photograph from his coat pocket. "We are looking for this car."

The man looked at it and was surprised.

"A 1948 Crown Victoria," he said. "That's a very rare vehicle. You are in luck son. I have one in the yard. It is not in the best condition, but it is certainly not in the worst condition. Just let me get my keys and I will be right with you."

After only a few seconds, the man joined Wayne and Laura outside. They went around the house to the back. To Wayne and Laura's surprise, there were no fences or gates of any kind: only a dirt road that led to the junkyard through a small clump of trees. They walked through it and entered the junkyard. A look of curiosity formed on Wayne's face.

Why does it seem like every junkyard owner try to hide what they do? he wondered. *It makes no sense.*

They continued walking until Taylor stopped. He looked from left to right with his hands raised to his shoulders.

"Is something wrong?" Wayne asked. "You look somewhat confused."

"The Crown Victoria," Taylor replied. "It was parked right here."

They joined Taylor's efforts to find the missing vehicle, but to no avail. It was as if the antique simply vanished. Moreover, Taylor also noticed none of his employees around. This made no sense to him.

A sudden bad feeling overcame Wayne. He wondered if it were possible that the car was already crushed. At the same time, he tried to remain optimistic. He spoke to Taylor.

"Not to sound like you don't know what goes on around here, but maybe it was moved and you just forgot."

"No," Taylor replied. "It was right here just this morning. I parked it here myself."

Laura glanced at Wayne. The look on his face told her he was concerned. She attempted to give him a reassuring look, but deep down knew it was not good enough.

Even as a young boy, Taylor was very perceptive. He knew when people around him were annoyed, worried or sad without the use of facial expressions. He learned over time by studying their body language. In the past, some of his relatives and friends thought he was psychic but he always denied it. He would wave their comments away with a laugh and say 'nonsense.' In Wayne's case, it was too easy for Taylor to tell he was worried. For a brief moment, he wondered why but quickly thought nothing of it. He wondered if Wayne was actually right and the car was moved without his knowledge.

"Just out of curiosity," Taylor said, "let's go have a look at the crusher. If it is in there – God help the bastard who did it."

They all walked somewhat briskly through the maze of vehicles until they spotted the crusher. The massive machine stood silent. Taylor noticed a car in its deadly maw. To his dismay, it looked a lot like his missing antique.

"There it is!" he said angrily, turning to his guests and pointing.

Wayne and Laura quickly spotted the antique. Wayne was surprised to see the color of the car was green.

That must have been what the green paint in the photograph was for, he thought.

The three of them trotted toward the trapped car. Taylor looked from left to right but saw nobody around. The look on his face was not one of happiness.

"Where the hell is everyone?" he shouted. "Since when does everybody take their break at the same time?"

They were roughly twenty feet away from the crusher when its loud engine roared to life. They all watched in awe as the top arm slowly descended. Taylor looked at the cockpit where the controls were. He was shocked to see no one operating it.

"What the hell is going on?" Taylor shouted over the noise.

Stricken with panic and unable to stand by any longer, Wayne charged toward the crusher. Taylor and Laura watched with concern as Wayne climbed into the cockpit. He raised his hands to turn the machine off, but merely stared at the controls.

"Does he know what he's doing?" Taylor shouted over the noise.

"Not a clue," Laura answered honestly, yet sympathetically with a shake of her head.

Taylor ran to join Wayne and watched him fumble with the controls.

The massive arm continued its descent. It was now less than a foot to the hood of the car.

"Hey fella!" Taylor yelled as loud as he could.

Wayne heard him and turned.

"How do you stop this thing?" Wayne shouted.

"You have to hit the blue button on the far left of the controls!" Taylor said.

Wayne turned and saw it. He punched it as fast as he could and the crushing arm came to a halt just a few inches above the hood. As soon as he saw the arm stop, he breathed a huge sigh of relief.

Taylor stared at his brave guest as he climbed down off the crusher. On one hand, he was glad to see his antique saved. On the other hand, he was slightly upset but tried not to show it. He knew that by all legal rights if Wayne somehow got hurt on the machine, he was completely liable.

"Thanks," Taylor said.

"Please, call me Wayne, and this is my girlfriend Laura. I must apologize for that, but if I would have told you why I was doing it you may have stopped me."

A confused look formed on Taylor's face.

"Why would you say that?" he asked.

"We will tell you everything you need to know, but right now we should move the vehicle to safety."

Taylor agreed with him and quickly moved in to move the vehicle. Carefully he drove it out of the crusher's deadly maw and parked it beside them. He got out and re-joined them.

"Now, what is it you would like to tell me.?" Taylor said.

"Taylor," Wayne said. "We are not really sure how to tell you this, but there might be a dead body in the trunk of that car."

Taylor could not help but laugh.

"You can't be serious?" Taylor said.

Wayne and Laura remained quiet.

The smile on Taylor's face dissipated. He went around to the trunk and opened it. He quickly turned away, shocked by what he saw.

"Sweet mother of Mary!" he voiced in awe.

Wayne and Laura joined him. They stared at the skeleton that remained of the dead body. In one way, they were happy that their search was over but at the same time, they also felt sorry for Taylor.

"You do realize I will have to call the police, don't you?" Taylor said in a somber tone.

"Of course," Wayne said. He reached into the back pocket of his jeans and pulled out a business card. He handed it to Taylor. "This is the man you want to speak to."

"What do I tell him?" Taylor asked.

"Just tell him Wayne Saunders and Laura Barns found another body," Wayne said. "He will know what to do."

"Would you like to wait here, or come with me to the house?"

"If it's all the same to you," Wayne replied, "we'll wait here."

"Okay. But you stay here," Taylor said as he carefully closed the trunk.

"You have our word," Laura said. "We are not going anywhere."

Taylor eyed them briefly before turning to walk away.

Wayne and Laura glanced at each other as they watched him leave. They knew Detective Wilson would not be pleased with them. He wanted to be in the loop and they neglected to do that.

"What do we do now?" Laura said.

Wayne turned back to look at the skeleton in the trunk of the antique car again.

"Nothing we can do but tell the truth, and wait."

Chapter Twenty-Seven
Unwanted News

Taylor walked into the house and deep bark sounded through the hall. His pet dog Sammy – a male bloodhound – wagged his tail and approached him. He was dark brown in color. He barked again as if to say hello and looked up at Taylor with big sad brown eyes. Taylor reached down and gave his head a quick rub.

"Hey Sammy boy," Taylor said.

Taylor sat at his desk by the telephone and Sammy happily followed him. He wondered how he would explain the dead body. In all his thirty-nine years, the only place he ever saw a dead body was on television. To see one now in real life shocked him as it would anyone else. Moreover, he had no idea where Wayne and Laura came from, or how they knew where the body was. He picked up the receiver and dialed Detective Wilson's number.

The detective was sitting in his chair in his office reviewing files when his telephone rang. Without moving his head, he looked at it as if to say 'What do you want?' He answered it on the fourth ring.

"Wilson."

"Yes. My name is Taylor Washburry of Taylor's Junkyard. I have a bit of a situation down here. A dead body was found in the trunk of one of my antique cars."

The detective closed his eyes and bowed his head into his hand. He already had a hunch on who found the body but thought it best to play dumb. Ever since he met Wayne and Laura, all they have ever done was find dead bodies. He still did not know how they did it or why. They told him they would be haunted if they did nothing, but he believed there was more to that story.

"Is that right?" Wilson said in a not surprised tone.

"Yes sir," Taylor said.

"When and where exactly was the body found?" Wilson asked.

"About fifteen minutes ago in the trunk of a 1948 Crown Victoria," Taylor replied. He was about to add that the car was almost crushed by an unseen force, but thought better of it. "I was told to contact you personally."

The line went silent for a moment. A look of frustration formed on the detective's face and he shook his head slowly. He had told Wayne and Laura to keep him in the loop and they neglected to do that. He turned his attention to the ceiling above his head.

Why me, God? he wondered. *What did I ever do to deserve this?*

Taylor began to wonder if the detective had hung up. He pulled the receiver away from his ear and looked at it curiously before listening into it again.

"Detective," he said, "are you there?"

"Yes Mr. Washburry. Sorry. I um…just had someone in my office. May I ask who told you to contact me?" Wilson asked, even though he already knew the answer. "And what is your address?"

"A Wayne Saunders and Laura Barns told me to contact you. They said you would know what to do. My address is 1215 Hepburn Street. Please, hurry."

"Thank you, Mr. Washburry. I am on my way."

"Detective?" Taylor added.

"Yes?"

"I swear, I have no idea where those two came from. They just came to my door and told me they were looking for an old car."

"I understand. Don't worry, I know those two well enough to know they mean no harm. They just do not know enough to stay out of trouble. Hang tight. We will be right over."

"Thank you," Taylor said.

Taylor hung up and sat back in his chair. He was relieved to know the senior officer knew Wayne and Laura. He stood up and made his way outside to wait for the detective. Sammy followed him out into the hallway and watched his master go out the door. As Taylor closed the door, he wondered what type of impact the discovery would have on his business. No one ever found a dead body in any of his vehicles before, and he hoped no one ever would again. Moreover, he feared that if the news got into the tabloids, regular and potentially new clients would avoid his junkyard.

Taylor sat in a folding chair at the side of the house and waited for the detective. He also kept an eye out for Wayne and Laura, just in case they decided to leave. If they did try, he would do all he could to stop them. Yet somehow, he knew they were still in the yard, waiting for him to return with the authorities. That was what his gut feeling told him. He could not help but wonder what their story would be, and if it would be true or not.

Chapter Twenty-Eight
Uneasy Anticipation

The minutes felt like hours as Wayne and Laura waited for the detective. They were sitting on the rear bumper of the antique car. They knew they were in trouble, yet knowing they were not going to jail gave them some peace of mind. Wayne studied the old photograph once again, hoping the name of the woman would pop into his mind.

Laura watched him with interest. She wondered why he still had interest in it, especially since they found the body.

"A penny for your thoughts," Laura said.

"I still can't figure out who she is," Wayne replied. "I cannot even be sure it is Emily's mother since we do not know her last name."

Laura shook her head, surprised at his tenacity.

"Why don't you give your brain a rest? Let the authorities handle it. It's what they do for a living," she said.

"Maybe you are right," Wayne said, nodding.

At that moment – as if by coincidence – a police cruiser and a tow truck approached them. As they drew closer, they immediately recognized Detective Wilson and Taylor. They were sitting in the front seats. Two other officers were sitting in the back, but neither Wayne nor Laura recognized them.

"Speaking of which," Laura added as she stood up.

Wayne stood beside her. He could not help but notice the daggers in the detective's eyes.

They parked about ten feet away and got out. The highly ranked officer glared at Wayne and Laura. He was angry that they neglected to call him.

"I told you two to keep me informed," he said in a huff as he approached them.

"We were going to," Wayne replied, "but we wanted to be sure it was not a wild goose chase."

"Nevertheless, you should have contacted me. Is this where the body is?"

"Yes," Taylor answered. He withdrew his keys and opened the trunk. "See?"

Everyone stood in silence, staring at the off-white skeleton. The looks on each of their faces appeared to pose different questions. What happened? Who would do such a horrible thing? Why didn't I stay home in bed?

Wayne knew it was the work of Nathan Christopher. The shackles were in the same manner as found in the sewer. The right wrist and ankle were at the bottom of the trunk and the left wrist and ankle were at the top.

Detective Wilson remembered the body in the sewer. Memories of it flashed through his mind. He too noticed how the body in the antique car was similar to the one in the sewer. To him, they appeared identical. Suddenly, he remembered the name Nathan Christopher. He glanced at Wayne and then back at the body. Without turning his head, he spoke.

"This is what we are going to do." Wilson waved a signal to the two men in the cruiser behind his. They got out and approached him. "These two men will take care of the body. You two," he added, pointing at Wayne and Laura with his index and middle fingers. "Step into my office."

The detective stepped away from the body and Wayne and Laura followed him. When they were out of earshot, he continued.

"I suppose you are going to tell me this is another one of Nathan Christopher's victims?"

"Yes sir," Wayne replied. He reached into his back pocket and pulled out the photograph. "This is what led us here."

The detective studied it closely. At first, it did not make much sense to him but then he slowly began to put the pieces together. The old Crown Victoria, the woman beside it – but he did not understand the can of paint.

"Any idea who she is?" he asked in a puzzled tone.

"No," Wayne replied, but then decided to go with his earlier hunch. "Well, maybe. I think she was the mother of a librarian at the National Library. Only thing is, we do not know her last name."

"Do you know her first name?" Wilson asked.

Laura nodded. "Emily," she said.

"What does she look like?" Wilson asked.

"She is about five-foot six," Wayne said, "slim, salt and pepper hair."

"And what makes you think this could be her mother?"

"It is a long story," Laura said.

"Shorten it for me," Wilson said.

Laura continued. "We told her we were doing some research on the haunted house on Birchcroft Drive She knew the one we were discussing and tried to warn us away from it."

"Smart lady," Wilson said with a nod.

"She also told us that her mother was found dead at that house," Wayne added.

The detective grinned halfheartedly. "For a short time there, I was actually beginning to think you two were psychic. I guess I was wrong."

Wayne and Laura glanced at each other.

"Ah, think nothing of it. Two out of three ain't bad," the detective added in a more serious – yet seemingly teasing – tone.

Wayne and Laura eyed the detective with mild curiosity. Even though they barely knew him, they still found his behavior a bit odd. To them, this was a man who never smiled or joked about anything.

"How many more bodies do you intend to find?" the detective added, back to his normal self.

"Hopefully none," Wayne said, "but we may have to find Nathan's. We are not sure yet."

The frustrated detective eyed them curiously.

"If you do have to find him, you had better call me. Understand?"

"Yes detective," Laura said. "We hear you."

"Good, because if I have to find out the way I did about this one; I will not be a happy camper."

"Understood," Wayne agreed.

The detective turned and was about to walk away but stopped.

"Oh," he added as he turned back to face them. "I also wanted to let you know you were right,"

Wayne and Laura glanced at each other curiously.

"We were?" Wayne said.

"Yes. The body in that sewer belonged to Norman Henderson. I do not know how you are finding these bodies. I really do not, but so far, this is the third cold case you have solved. Congratulations."

Wayne and Laura were surprised. They were not expecting a compliment.

"Thank you," Wayne said.

Laura nodded her agreement.

The detective nodded his approval but still had a look of curiosity.

"Do either of you have any idea who this one is?" Wilson asked.

"No," Wayne replied. Once again, he removed the photograph from his pocket. "But we did find this."

The detective studied it. He found the can of paint particularly interesting.

"Where did you find this?" he asked.

"In the trunk of a 1951 taxi cab," Laura said.

"Here?" the detective said curiously.

"No, at another junkyard," Wayne said.

The detective was fascinated. He was beginning to wonder if Wayne and Laura were private investigators in a past life.

"And you think this is the victim?" he said.

"Yes sir," Wayne said.

The three of them turned to watch the officers carefully lower the skeleton into a body bag. Another man led them to a white station wagon marked Coroner.

"Okay boys, let's get this wrapped up," the detective said. "Bring the tow truck in so we can get this car to the lab."

One of the officers flagged in the tow truck.

Everyone watched the driver back up to the front bumper of the antique car. In just a few minutes he had it hooked up and ready to go. The driver waved at Detective Wilson to signal he was ready to go. Wilson nodded his approval and watched as the driver slowly left the scene. He looked at Taylor.

"Taylor?" Wilson said.

"Yes?"

"How long have you had that car?"

"About two weeks," Taylor replied. "Why?"

"Just out of curiosity," Wilson said. "Who supplied it to you?"

"Am I in trouble?" Taylor asked.

"Not at all," Wilson said with a wave of his hand. "But this is obviously a homicide, so I have to ask these questions as standard procedure."

"Ah! Well, it came from Jeff's Junkyard," Taylor replied.

Wayne and Laura glanced at each other curiously. That was the first junkyard they went to in their search for the old taxi. Then suddenly, Wayne put two and two together and realized who Jeffery was.

So that's it! Wayne thought, nodding his head slowly.

Detective Wilson noticed the exchange.

"Do you two know this junkyard?" he asked.

"Yes," Laura said.

"It was the very first junkyard we looked for the old taxi," Wayne added. "The address is 43 Turnpike Lane."

"Okay. We will start there then," Wilson said and looked at his watch. "It is only six-thirty so they should be there. May we contact you if we have any more questions Taylor?"

"Of course," Taylor said. "Anything I can do to help."

"Thank you," Wilson said, "and we apologize for the inconvenience."

Taylor nodded, turned and walked back into the junkyard toward his house.

"Detective?" Wayne said.

"Yes Mr. Saunders?"

"I am not sure if the owner of Jeff's Junkyard is there. When we were there, his son said he was away on business."

"Thank you. Should I ask where you two will be if we need you?" Wilson asked.

Wayne and Laura glanced at each other. One waited for the other to make a suggestion, but there were none.

"Wherever we end up we will surely let you know," Wayne said.

Wilson nodded and joined his fellow officers. They got into the cruiser and drove away.

Wayne and Laura started to head back to their car. He turned to her.

"It's going to be dark soon. Would you be up to dinner and a movie?"

"Sure," Laura said. "Do I get to choose the movie?"

"Anything your heart desires," Wayne said.

Laura thought about it for a brief moment.

"Pirates of the Deepea?" she suggested.

"Sounds good," Wayne agreed. "I had no idea you were into pirate movies."

"Aye, I love a good swashbuckler," Laura replied in a fake pirate's tone.

Wayne laughed and wrapped his arm around her. He loved her sense of humor.

"Say. Would you ever make me walk the plank?" Wayne asked.

"Only if you really piss me off," Laura replied with a smirk.

Wayne smiled and nodded his understanding.

Chapter Twenty-Nine
Sniffing for Clues

Detective Wilson and his men pulled into Jeff's Junkyard. They parked in front of the house and got out. They walked up to the front door and knocked. A young man in his early to mid-twenties answered the door.

This must be the owner's son, Wilson thought.

"Yes?" Maynard said.

"Good evening young man. I am Detective James Wilson. These are my associates, Sergeant Mason and Corporal Jones. We are with the Edmundston Police Department. Is your father home? We need to ask him a few questions."

"Actually, he just got home. My name is Maynard. I am his son. Come in. I will go get him."

The officers walked in and closed the door behind them.

"Much obliged," Wilson said.

Maynard disappeared around a corner. A moment later an older man appeared and approached the officers.

"Hello," the man said. "My name is Jeffery. I own the junkyard. How may I help you gentlemen?"

"My name is Wilson – Detective James Wilson. This is Sergeant Mason and Corporal Jones." The officers revealed their badges. "We just have a few questions."

"Ask away," Jeffery said.

Detective Wilson withdrew the old Polaroid and showed it to him.

"Do you recall having this car in your possession?" he asked.

Jeffery looked at it and nodded. "Yes, I do, but I sent it to Taylor's Junkyard for crushing about two weeks ago."

"How long did you have it for?" Wilson asked.

"Fifty years or so," Jeffery said.

The detective nodded thoughtfully. He did not know much about junkyards, but wondered why one would keep a car so long.

"Were you the original owner?" he enquired.

"No sir," Jeffery replied.

Wilson eyed him curiously but believed him. In all his years in law enforcement, he met more than his fair share of cons and murderers. He was a good judge of character and somehow always knew when someone was guilty or lying.

"So why did you send an antique to be crushed?" Wilson asked.

"Well, for starters," Jeffery said, "no one was ever interested in buying it: probably because it needed a lot of work. The few people that did take an interest decided they did not have the patience or finances to do it. It was an antique, but certainly not a showpiece. Why do you ask?"

"Not long ago, a dead body was found in the trunk of that car," Wilson said.

A look of shock formed on Jeffery's face. He had no idea. In all of the years he had the car, he never once thought of peeking in the trunk.

"Oh my God," he said.

"Sir," Wilson said. "We need to know who – or what company – supplied the car to you."

"Oh my," Jeffery said. "That was ages ago."

Jeffery had a very good memory, but was not sure if he would be able to remember something that happened fifty years ago. He thought back to that day long ago. To his surprise, he recalled a red tow truck turning into his laneway.

"The tow truck was red," Jeffery said. Then he closed his eyes, hoping he would see the truck better. At first, he saw nothing but then it suddenly hit him. "Timothy's Towing."

"Are you sure?" Wilson asked.

"Positive," Jeffery replied.

"Good. Thank you. I think that is everything."

"My pleasure," Jeffery said. "Well gentlemen, if you would excuse me—"

"Of course," the detective said. "Oh! I do have one small favor to ask of you."

"Yes?" Jeffery said.

"Would you have a telephone I could use? It is police business."

"Certainly," Jeffery replied and pointed to an open door. "There is a telephone in my office."

"Thank you," Wilson said. "I will only be a moment."

Wilson went into the office and looked for a telephone book. Finding it, he picked it up and looked for the number for the National Library. He found it quickly and dialed it. On the third ring, a female voice answered.

"Hello, this is the National Library. May I help you?"

"Yes ma'am, my name is James Wilson. I am a detective of the Edmundston Police Department. I am looking for one of your employees, but I only have a first name."

"Oh my," the female voice said. "Is this person in trouble?"

"No ma'am, not at all. I only have a few questions for her," Wilson replied.

"Do you know her name?" the voice asked.

"Yes. Emily."

"Ah yes, Emily is our head librarian. She is right beside me. One moment please."

"Thank you kindly," Wilson said.

"Hello Detective Wilson, how may I help you?" Emily asked.

"Hello Emily. I apologize for disturbing you at work, but I have some important questions to ask you."

"Go on," Emily said.

"Emily, what I am about to tell you will be disturbing. I only ask for your cooperation."

"I understand."

"Good," Wilson said. "Earlier today we discovered a body in the trunk of a car at a junkyard."

"Oh my," Emily said.

"Two of the people who found the body, claim that they have been to see you about a haunted house."

"Yes, that is correct."

"They said you tried to warn them away from the house. Is that also right?" Wilson asked.

"Yes. I knew of the house they referred to and tried to warn them," Emily replied.

"Now this next question is a little more personal," Wilson said.

"Continue," Emily said, undaunted.

"Did you tell them that your mother was found dead in this house?"

The line went quiet, but only for a second or two.

"Yes, I did," Emily replied.

"I am deeply sorry for your loss," Wilson said sympathetically. "Would you be able to identify her body?" Again, the line went quiet, but this time for a few seconds longer.

"Emily?" Wilson said, wondering if she had hung up.

"I am here," Emily replied. "To answer your question, I doubt I would be able to. You see, she died when I was only a few months old."

"I see. Do you remember her name?" Wilson asked gently.

"My father told me her name was Victoria Green."

"Thank you, Emily. You have been huge help to us."

"You are welcome," Emily said with a shaky voice.

"We will inform you of our findings," Wilson said. "Thank you for your time."

"Thank you for calling detective," Emily said and gently hung up.

Wilson stood there quietly for a moment. He hated making those types of telephone calls, but it was part of his job. He then stepped out of the office and joined the others.

"Thank you again," Wilson said.

"If you have any other questions, please do not hesitate to call," Jeffery said politely as he opened the door for the officers.

The detective and his men walked back to their cruiser and got in. He picked up the c.b. and spoke into it.

"Wilson to base?"

"Base here," a deep masculine voice said. "Go ahead sir."

"We need an address for Timothy's Towing Company."

"Ten four," the voice replied. "Stand by."

Corporal Jones spoke from the back seat.

"Who is to say they will have any record of the old Crown Victoria?"

"Before I got into law enforcement, I used to work for a towing company," Wilson said. "As I recall, they kept track of every pick up they made."

Mason was skeptical. "Yeah, but for fifty years?" he said.

"Do you have any better ideas?" Wilson asked.

Mason was about to add something when the radio sounded.

"Ten four, Detective. The address is 42 Kemp Road. Over?"

"Good, it is close by," Wilson said before he replied into the radio. "Copy that."

Placing the c.b. back in its holster, they headed in the direction of the towing company.

Wilson and his men approached their destination. The building was a fair size with three wide garage doors. At first, it appeared closed. The lights were off in the building and in the parking lot. That made it even more difficult to see what they looked like. They were about to drive on when a faint light inside the main office caught Sergeant Mason's attention.

"Wait," Mason said and pointed. "Look. Someone might be in there."

Wilson and Jones looked in the direction of Mason's finger.

"It could be just a light they keep on after business hours," Jones commented.

"Nevertheless," Wilson said, "we should still check it out."

They all got out of the cruiser and headed for the office door. As they approached, they noticed a man in the office. He was sitting behind a desk doing paper work. To the detective, he appeared no older than thirty-five. The man wore a dark blue mechanics uniform. The officers readied their badges and the detective knocked on the door. They watched as the man looked up at the door and then at his watch. Then he looked at the window and a confused look formed on his face. He stood up and walked to the door. The detective was not sure if he spotted them or not. A bright light popped on above their heads and they squinted at it.

"Yes?" the man said and then noticed the badges of the law. "Oh my."

"Good evening," the detective said. "We are looking for information on a 1948 Crown Victoria. A witness said it was towed to his junkyard by this company roughly fifty years ago."

Curious, the man stood aside. "By all means, come in."

"Thank you, Mr.?"

"Gibbons, Jason Gibbons. I own this company."

A somewhat amused look formed on the detective's face.

"My apologies," Wilson said with sincerity. "I did not know owners dressed as mechanics."

"I normally wear a suit and tie," Jason said casually, "but two of our mechanics called in sick, so I had to fill in."

"I see."

"So, how may I help you?" Jason asked.

"Mr. Gibbons, we are investigating a homicide. Less than an hour ago, a dead body was found in the trunk of the vehicle we are inquiring about."

A confused look formed on Jason's face.

Apparently, not everyone knows the meaning of the term homicide, Wilson thought with a not-so-surprised look.

"Oh my God!" Jason said as he suddenly understood what the detective meant. "This is a murder investigation?"

"Yes, I am afraid so," Wilson said. "So, we need to know when and where the vehicle was picked up, who picked it up, and the owner if possible."

"Well, let's see what I can find out for you," Jason said. He walked over to a black file cabinet behind his desk and opened the bottom drawer. "Anything that happened that long ago should be in here somewhere."

The detective wondered if the lab had any information on the antique car and the body that was in it. He hoped it would all lead to Nathan Christopher. If it did, then it would solve three cold cases. He wanted to believe Wayne and Laura. He truly did, but without solid evidence, it was difficult to point the finger. From the beginning of his career, he used nothing but facts and honesty.

That was how he worked his way up to detective. It took years of hard work, but he did it.

"Ah! Here it is," Jason said, drawing Wilson's attention.

He sat down at his desk and opened the file. Wilson waited patiently.

"According to this," Jason said, "it was found abandoned on a narrow path in the woods fifty-one years ago. It was reported by, Sandra and Brian Corbs. The driver's name was Wilson Savard, but the owner of the vehicle is not listed here."

The detective frowned, but only for a brief moment.

Damn.

"Well," Wilson said. "It was a shot in the dark anyway."

Corporal Jones spoke up. "Wait. If it was found in the woods, how did the tow truck get in there to retrieve it?"

"That's a good question," Wilson said.

"I agree," Jason said and looked at the file again. At the bottom of the driver's report, he noticed a small scribble that read; *see page two*. He picked the second page and found a rough sketch. "Oh! Here it is. It says it took him one hour to work his way in and out of the woods. He even mapped it out from Bridgewater Way." He handed it to the detective.

"I know where that is," Mason said.

"So do I," Wilson said.

"Should we check it out?" Jones asked.

Wilson shook his head.

"No point," he replied. "The case is older than we are. If there was any evidence, it is probably long since gone. We would have to dig up that whole area."

"That could take weeks," Mason said.

"Exactly," Wilson agreed and handed the sheet back to Jason. "Thank you for your help Mr. Gibbons."

"My pleasure," Jason said. "Good night."

"Good night," Wilson said.

The officers walked out the door and closed it behind them. They made their way back to the cruiser.

"I'll drop you guys off at the station," Wilson said. "I want to pay a visit to the Coroner and see if he came up with anything."

The detective pulled into the Coroner's parking lot and got out. It was a blue two-story building with two main entrances and two emergency exits. The parking lot was big enough to support twenty vehicles. He noticed the Coroner's car and two others, not including his own. He walked into the building and made his way to the morgue. The lights were on in the hallways but most of the offices were dark. He found the Coroner and another man hunched over a skeleton. As he walked into the morgue, the Coroner heard the approaching footsteps and looked up.

"James?" he said. "What brings you to my parlor this time of night?"

"Hello Tom. I was just wondering if you had any information for me."

Tom McQueen was a British man in his late-forties. He was Coroner for the past twenty years. That alone should have been enough for a full head of gray hair, but it always stayed dark brown. Many people he met commented on how young he looked. Some – considering Tom's career – even went so far as to ask where his gray hair was. He always replied with the phrase *'I always eat my greens.'*

"We know she was in her late mid to late twenties," Tom said.

"Do you know who she is yet?" Wilson asked.

"Not yet," the other man said, "but we're working on it as fast as we can."

"This is Daniel," Tom said, "a pathologist. I have asked for his assistance in examining the body."

The detective grinned and raised his hands, as if a child had a toy gun pointed at his back.

"No need to justify to me Tom," Wilson said. "How about the antique, do you have anything on that yet?"

"I gave it a good comb-over," the pathologist said. "Found a few articles of hair, but we have nothing on them yet."

"I see," Wilson said. He was very eager to get answers but kept his patience in check. "Please let me know as soon as you find out. You know the number. I'm going to head home."

"We will James," Tom said. "Sleep well."

The detective nodded and walked out of the morgue. As he made his way to the parking lot, he wondered what the fabric and hair would reveal.

Chapter Thirty
A Night to Remember

Wayne and Laura had just finished eating their meal. They decided on Chinese food and enjoyed it quite nicely. Wayne found the service somewhat slow, but the restaurant was quite full. He looked at his watch.

"What time does the show start?" he asked.

"Nine," Laura replied. "We still have an hour to kill."

The waiter approached their table.

"Will there be anything else this evening?" the waiter asked.

The waiter was Chinese, but communicated in English very well.

"No thank you," Wayne said, "just the check please."

The waiter bowed his head with a simple nod and walked away.

While they waited, Wayne took the opportunity to get a better look at the establishment. It was quaintly decorated with colorfully designed hand-held fans made of bamboo. He noticed several beautiful paintings of Chinese landmarks. The walls were a light shade of tan and the floor had brown ceramic tiles. Each table had a red tablecloth with white napkins and appeared as though set for royalty.

"Wow," Wayne said. "This is really a nice place."

"Yes. It is," Laura said. "Wayne?"

"Yes?"

"I have been meaning to ask you something."

"Ask away my dear," Wayne said.

"Now that we found the last body – if we found the last body – is this thing finally over?"

Wayne grew quiet for a moment. He hoped it really was over, but knowing Nathan Christopher was still in the house he had no idea.

"We saved the three trapped souls," Wayne replied, "but now I have to somehow get rid of Nathan."

Laura paled at the mere words.

"You can't be serious," she said. "You saw what happened to Officer Malloy."

"Don't remind me," Wayne said.

"I have to," Laura added in a firm whisper. "I do not want that happening to you or anyone else, but you did what you were supposed to do. You freed the trapped souls."

"I know, but Nathan has to be stopped. Before other souls become trapped." He took a sip of his tea, and then continued. "Look, let's forget about all that tonight. The movie will start soon. Now if we could only get the—"

"Check? Here we are," the waiter said as he placed the bill on the table.

"Thank you," Wayne said.

"You are welcome. Good night," the waiter said and walked away.

They finished their tea and then got up to leave. Wayne paid the check and left a five-dollar tip for their waiter. He held the door open for Laura and they walked out.

Hand in hand, they walked into the Cinemas Theatre. It was full house. Dozens of people waited in line for tickets, popcorn and snacks. Children played at the mini arcade laughing and yelling.

Wayne looked at Laura and was happy to see her smiling. Wayne gave her hand a gentle tug and she turned to him.

"Why don't you go sit down," Wayne suggested. "It might take a while for me to get our tickets."

"All right," she said and spotted a bench right away. "I will be over there."

"Did you want anything to eat or drink?" Wayne asked.

"No, thank you." Laura replied.

"Okay then," Wayne said and let go of her hand.

He stood in line and waited his turn. The line must have been about thirty feet, but it seemed to move along quickly.

Wayne was surprised. It was only a matter of a few minutes before he paid for their tickets. He found Laura sitting exactly where she said she would be. She was all smiles as she watched people walk around. When she was happy, he was happy and he smiled warmly.

"Are you ready for some sword fighting and swashbuckling?" Wayne asked as he sat down beside her.

Laura turned to him and grinned.

"Aye me foolish landlubber!" she replied excitedly.

Wayne laughed hard.

"Well, come on then, you crazy pirate," he said.

Laura laughed too and they went into the theatre. They found the perfect seats near the back middle and sat down. They were dead center to the screen.

The theatre filled up in just a few short minutes, but Wayne and Laura lucked out. There were people sitting near them, but not directly beside them. They actually preferred it that way. It made them feel like they were not being crowded.

Finally, the big red curtain rose up and the movie started. Wayne wrapped his arm around Laura and she snuggled into him.

Chapter Thirty-One
A Cause for Concern

One hour after they went to bed, Wayne jolted awake out of breath and in a sweat. He had a horrible nightmare but not like any he had before. To Wayne it felt much more like a warning instead of a nasty dream. He remembered a deep voice whispering to him in tongues and a torturous contraption of sorts. It was on four steel legs and roughly three feet from the floor. Connected to it was a steel drum, covered with thick silver metal mesh. The drum looked like a medium-sized trash can. It was one foot higher on one side of the structure and a thin steel pole stuck out from both ends. Hundreds of extremely sharp, short and thin needle-like pins protruded through the mesh. There were four shackles on the structure – one on each side of the drum for the hands and two at the opposite end for the ankles. The dream became even more disturbing every time the drum moved. It only moved occasionally but when it did, a loud clunk would ring out. Immediately, Wayne knew what the device was used for. The victim would be tortured slowly and eventually bent into a "j" type shape. He did not know what part of the body would be against the needles but he supposed it could have been the stomach or the back.

Careful not to disturb Laura, he rolled out of bed and made his way in the dark to the bathroom. He closed the door softly behind him and covered his eyes before turning on the light. As his eyes slowly grew accustomed to the light, he placed his hands on the edge of the sink. He bowed his head.

This cannot go on forever, he thought. *I will not let it. I have to find a way to stop it. The only question, is how?*

Now used to the light, he lifted his head to look in the mirror. Immediately, he noticed the small bags under his eyes. He leaned in closer and stared into his pupils. He always believed the eyes were mirrors of sorts. Windows to alternate worlds even. That if he concentrated hard enough, he would be able to see anything he wanted. Of course, all he ever saw were images of himself and his own memories. This time, all he wanted to see were clues. Things or ideas that would help him end Nathan Christopher's demonic rule. Instead, he saw the rotted corpses of the three victims he and Laura helped find. Frustrated, he turned away from the mirror. He placed his hand on the light switch to turn it off when suddenly an idea occurred to him. He looked back into the mirror and an almost devilish grin formed on his face. He turned off the light and slowly opened the door. Carefully he made his way through the darkness to the chair where his clothes were and scooped them up. Then turned and went back into the bathroom and got dressed.

Once again, he emerged from the bathroom in darkness and cautiously made his way to the long dresser where Laura's car keys were. Ever so quietly, he picked them up and turned to her as if waiting for her to wake up. He knew she was a light sleeper and would have to think quickly if she asked him where he was going. A part of him wanted to warn her about what he was about to do, but he knew she would never let him go through with it. In fact, he was certain she would do everything she could to stop him. Deciding not to tell her, he made his way to the door. He opened it as quietly as he could and slipped out. He dashed toward Laura's car, unlocked the door and got in. As quietly as he could he closed the door. Once Wayne heard the small click, he briefly watched his motel room door as if expecting Laura to be standing there. Yet as the seconds ticked by, the door remained closed. He started the car and slowly drove off.

I cannot believe I am about to do this, he thought, *but I see no other choice. I just hope the attic is not a mess like those places usually are.*

After only one block, Wayne noticed two tiny beams of light on both sides of the windshield. While keeping his eyes on the road, he watched as they appeared to lead the car forward. He smiled. It reminded him of when he was a little boy. While his parents were in the front seat, he was in the back playing Spider-Man. That was his favorite super hero. He pretended to hang onto the beams and swing from post to post.

He turned onto Lepine Street. As he drew closer to the house, an uneasy feeling burned in the pit of his stomach. He knew he was making a serious mistake going back but he knew one day that he would have to go back and face Nathan.

I guess tonight is that night, he thought.

He turned onto Birchcroft Drive Once again, it was in complete darkness but it hardly surprises him anymore. He pulled over in front of the house and got out. For a moment, he stared at it, as if to let Nathan know he was there. Under the pale moonlight it almost seemed intimidating – yet at the same time – inviting to him. He popped open the trunk and grabbed the flashlight. Not to wake the neighbors, he closed it gently. He put his hand over the bulb and made sure it still worked. Wasting no more time, he walked up to the front door. Like clockwork, the door slowly creaked open. He turned on the flashlight and cautiously went inside. The familiar musty scent of old carpet and mildew filled his nose. Without thinking, he went for the stairs. As soon as he placed a foot on the first step, the door slammed shut loudly behind him. He turned slowly to look at it. A low evil chuckle sounded through the house.

Laura stirred from a sound sleep. She turned over to put her arm on Wayne's chest. It took her a moment to realize that her arm was resting against the mattress. Thinking her mind was playing tricks on her, she moved her hand over his side of the bed. To her surprise, it was empty. Her eyes fluttered open and she lifter her head. She looked around the room but saw nothing but darkness.

"Wayne?" she said. "Are you okay?"

There was no reply.

She turned on the lamp on the night table and rolled out of bed. Her eyes blinked a few times but quickly grew accustomed to the light. Curious, she looked in the direction of the bathroom. She stood up and walked toward the closed door. Her white nightshirt covered her body to her knees. Instead of knocking, she placed her ear against the door and listened intently. She heard nothing but silence.

"Wayne?" she said through the door.

Still no answer came.

In a slight panic, she removed her ear from the door. She wondered if it was possible that he suffered the same disaster she did with the mirror. The vivid memory of the ugly distorted face she saw before it exploded flashed through her mind as if it were only moments ago. Her right hand moved up to her face and gently moved her fingers over the small scars. Snapping herself back to reality, she shook her head to ward off the vision.

No, I cannot think like that, she thought. *I am sure it is nothing serious.*

She placed her hand on the doorknob and turned it slowly.

"Honey?" she said. "I'm coming in."

Cautiously, she opened the door. The lights were off and the bathroom was empty. She breathed a sigh of relief, at least glad he was not standing there with a face-full of glass. Then her look of relief quickly turned into one of deep concern. Her right hand lightly brushed through her long hair.

So then, where is he? she wondered.

Laura walked past the bed to the window and looked outside before opening the door. There was no one around and all was quiet. The only source of light came from three street lamps in the parking lot. She opened the door and looked up and down the walkways that lead to the other rooms and then scanned the parking lot. There was no sign of Wayne and her car was gone.

She angrily shook her head in disbelief and went back inside. She paced back and forth in front of the bed.

How could he just get up and leave like that without leaving some type of note? she wondered. *What was he thinking? Wayne should know I hate that by now! I hope he is okay. I really do. Because when he gets back, I'll kill him!*

She plopped herself down on the edge of the bed. All she could do was wait for him to return.

Wayne tried to ignore the evil laugh and continued to climb the stairs. The uneasy feeling in his stomach grew a little worse with every step he took. In a very short time, he felt nauseated, as if he had not eaten for days. He hoped it was just his nerves playing tricks on him. Nevertheless, he knew being in that house – and with Nathan Christopher inside it – anything was possible.

As he reached the top of the stairs, the laughing stopped. A chill rushed up his spine as if Nathan wanted him to know he was watching. Undaunted, Wayne flashed the light along the ceiling to look for the trap door to the attic but he found none.

Maybe it is in one of the bedrooms, he thought, confused.

Cautiously, he stepped into the first bedroom and searched the ceiling. Again, there was no trap door. He then proceeded to the second bedroom. He was disappointed with the same result yet again. That surprised him a little. Just then, he had a thought on where the attic door possibly was. Slowly he turned back into the hall and shown the light on the third bedroom door. His heart pounded in his chest. He was warned numerous times to stay away from the third bedroom. Nevertheless, deep down he knew he had little choice but to explore it.

Where else could the attic door be – if there is one, Wayne wondered. nervously as he inhaled a deep breath and exhaled it.

Ever so slowly, he cautiously moved toward the infamous closed door. With every step he took, no sound arose from the old wooden floor. Anxiety ignited his heart to beat harder as a deaf silence filled his ears. Wayne detested that sound. That made him even more nervous. He felt beads of sweat drip from his forehead and down his back. It reminded of the night of his first encounter with the house he was in at that moment. The wind rustled the leaves yet the leaves made no sound at all. Now in arms reach of the door he paused. Apprehensively he reached out his hand to grasp the doorknob but paused once again. He felt something horrible was about to happen and waited. His breath caught in his throat. A faint sound behind him suddenly caught his attention. Wayne turned to face the sound quickly but nothing was there. A rapid breath of relief escaped his lips. He turned around again to reach for the doorknob but the door was wide open. Startling him, he gasped and his whole body twitched in fear. He expected something or someone to jump out at him so he took one-step back, yet all was quiet. Without stepping into the room, he slowly moved the flashlight from corner to corner. It appeared safe, although he knew it was far from that. There were dozens of old photographs on the wall in front of the bed. It was virtually covered with them. From where he stood, he was unable to tell what was on them but had a feeling they were not portraying blissful gardens. The bed was messed and had patches of brown stains on it. The stains were worse on the thin pillow.

Probably because it is so old, he thought.

Gaining more courage, he stepped into the room and moved toward the photographs. He looked at them. As he suspected, they were disturbing images of human sacrifice, torture and brutal murders. Disgusted, he turned away and faced the bed. Something caught his eye on the ceiling. At first, he thought it was just a piece of square plastic covering a hole. Then he realized it was the trap door to the attic. He looked from the bed to the ceiling. The bed was a standard size. It had a one-person mattress with a standard box spring.

I might be able to reach that door, he thought.

Carefully, Wayne stepped onto one side of the bed. It creaked loudly in protest. He knew no matter how old the bed was the strongest part of it was the frame. Keeping his balance, he placed his other foot on the opposite side of the frame. He steadied himself and waddled up to the trap door. To his surprise, he was closer to it than he thought. Leaving the flashlight on, he shoved it into his back pocket. As he reached up to place his hands on it, a vague creaking sound caught his attention. He turned to notice the bedroom door slowly closing. A sudden sense of urgency overtook him. He pounded on the trap door forcefully until it finally nudged open. Dust fell into his eyes and stung them but he did not care. He jumped up and grabbed onto the attic floor with his hands and forearms. Wasting no time, he pulled himself up.

Standing, he dusted himself off. He reached for his back pocket and pulled out the flashlight. He pointed it toward the back of the attic and moved it over the floor. It was not nearly as cluttered as he expected. He actually found it quite bare. Something in the back caught his attention. At first, he thought it was some form of bench. Curious, he drew closer to it. As he swept the light over the object he realized it was not a bench at all. It was the torturous con-traption from his dream. In awe, he slowly moved toward it and his heart sank into his stomach.

Oh God, it is true! he thought. *Maybe I really am psychic. I wonder. Maybe this is what Cathy Saint-Pierre meant when she did not know if it was a dream or a vision.*

The torturous device was exactly as he dreamt. He stared at the rusty old drum. When he was much closer, he noted patches of darker rust. It took him a few seconds to realize the darker patches were not rust. It was dry blood. For one reason or another, he was not surprised. He recalled a quote from the riddle he and Laura received in the car during the storm:

Tied to the air, I suffered through my screams and tears.

At that moment, Wayne knew what happened to her. His eyes widened. He tried to turn away from the contraption but was unable to. To him, it was as if something held him there, forcing him to watch what was about to happen. Unwilling to cooperate he slammed his eyes shut but it made no difference. The trembling female victim stared up at him. Her eyes wide with fear. She was tied and bound to the device. A man wearing only black jeans stood slightly to her side. He was holding a long sharp blade. Though Wayne was unable to see his face, he knew who it was. Every time she squirmed to free herself, the tiny needles would dig deeper into her flesh. Every movement brought screams of agony and tears. The man reached for a lever on the contraption and pulled it. The drum slowly turned and the clunk sounds came every few seconds. Her deafening screams filled Wayne's ears as the pins slowly shredded her skin.

"God make it stop!" Wayne pleaded as his hands covered his ears. "I have seen enough!"

As if Nathan heard him, he grabbed the woman by the hair and shoved her head back into the pins. She gasped in horror. For a brief moment, Nathan stood back and watched her suffer. She tried to speak but was incapable as blood seeped from her gaping mouth. Apparently bored, Nathan finished the job and viciously stabbed her three times in the chest and slit her throat. Her final breath was a simple yet sickening gurgle.

The images of Nathan and the woman vanished and Wayne's eyes snapped open. Darkness surrounded him and he was uncertain of his bearings. The flashlight was no longer in his hand. Carefully, he went down on all fours and felt around for it. He found it by his left foot and fumbled to turn it on. The light revealed a bare wooden wall. In a way he was glad that was the first thing he saw. The last thing he wanted to see was that demonic contraption. He shuddered at the memory of what he just witnessed. Deep down, he knew it was something he would never forget. Standing, he slowly turned to get his bearings. He knew he was still in the general area of the contraption. As the drum emerged from the darkness, he stopped and stared in disbelief. The dry blood was gone and the words *'recite the right verse'* were written in fresh blood. Sensing he was no longer alone, he backed away slowly.

I am going to end up in a loony bin, he thought.

Another icy chill ripped through his spine and the hair on the back of his neck rose. He gasped at the shock of how much it stung. To him, it felt like hundreds of small needles. He pointed the flashlight toward the ceiling from just below his chin and exhaled deeply. His breath was as visible as a full moon. He slowly turned toward the trap door. As he neared it, a very pale light appeared in his peripheral vision. His eyes swung to it and suddenly they widened with horror. Nathan Christopher stood in his way, blocking the attic's only exit. His dead black eyes stared at him as a twisted grin formed on his lips. Wayne tried to back away but fear kept him in place. He summoned the courage to speak but his voice was shaky.

"It's over Nathan. Your prisoners are all free. Now it's your turn."

Nathan laughed.

"Pathetic human pig!" the demon grumbled. "You cannot kill me. I am already dead."

"M-m-m-maybe, but I will find the way to send you back to hell."

The demon laughed again and vanished.

Wayne stood there, alone and uncertain about what to think or do. Obviously concerned, he frantically swept the flashlight over the attic but there was no sign of Nathan. He had a bad feeling something was about to happen. Yet as the seconds passed, all remained quiet. He pointed the light back at the torturous contraption to take one final look at it. The disgusted look returned to his face and he turned away from it. Just as he turned to face the attic trap door, he felt a sudden hard shove and flew backward against the far wall. He cried out in surprise. His body thudded sickeningly and fell hard to the dust-ridden floor. Gritting his teeth through the pain, he wanted to scream out but did not want to give Nathan the satisfaction.

With powerful God-like strength, Nathan hauled Wayne roughly to his feet and he stared into Nathan's dead black eyes.

"What, are you going to kill me now Nathan?"

Without answering, Nathan flung Wayne as if he weighed nothing back into the same wall. Stunned by the hard blow, Wayne once again slumped to the floor and lost consciousness.

Chapter Thirty-Two
The Time to Act

Laura paced the motel room worriedly. She had no idea where Wayne was or if he was okay. She glanced at the clock on the night table. To her surprise, it had been four hours since she woke up. With everything they went through that week, the last thing she wanted was for Wayne to go off and get himself into trouble, or wind up hurt or dead for that matter. Once again, she went to the window and looked outside. There was still no sign of him. Unable to stand it any longer, she walked over to the telephone and picked up the receiver. She dialed the police station. A man answered after only two rings.

"Edmundston Police Department, Lieutenant Jennings speaking."

Laura spoke in a state of panic.

"Yes, I don't know if you remember me, Lieutenant, but my name is Laura Barns. I went to your station to report that body my boyfriend and I found in the old barn. But now—"

"Yes," the lieutenant replied, "I remember you but you will have to slow down a little. What is the matter?"

"He's missing," Laura said.

"Who is missing? You're boyfriend?"

"Yes," Laura replied in a slightly calmer tone.

"Okay. Here is what I need you to do," the lieutenant said calmly. "Start by taking a few deep breaths."

Laura obeyed and paused. She took her deep breaths and then continued.

"I woke up four hours ago and since then he has been gone. My car is gone as well, but I don't know if Wayne took it – or if someone took him."

"Was there any sign of a struggle at all?" Jennings asked.

"No," Laura replied.

"Good," the lieutenant said. "Is it possible that he just went for a drive?"

"No," Laura replied. "He does not just leave like that without telling me."

"Did you have an argument at all?"

"No," Laura replied.

The lieutenant grew thoughtful. He wondered if it was possible that Mr. Saunders went back to the haunted house on Birchcroft Drive He hoped not. He remembered what happened to Officer Malloy.

"Lieutenant?" Laura said.

"Yes, I'm here. Sorry I was distracted for a moment. Would you mind terribly if I put you on hold for a moment?" the lieutenant said. "My other line is ringing."

"Not at all," Laura said.

He hated lying to the young woman, but he was well aware of Detective Wilson's orders. The lieutenant dialed the number of the detective's home. After the third ring, a husky male voice answered.

"Whoever this is, it had better be very important," Detective Wilson grumbled.

"It's Phil Jennings sir. I have Miss Laura Barns on the line. She says her boyfriend is missing."

"Her boyfriend?" Wilson said groggily.

"Yes sir. Mr. Wayne Saunders," Jennings said.

The detective's eyes snapped open. He sat up and turned on his night table lamp. His eyes slammed shut at the bright glare.

"He's missing?" Wilson said.

"Ms. Barns said she was awake for a few hours and there has been no sign of him. Her car is also missing," Jennings replied.

"Wait a minute. He has only been missing for a few hours?" Wilson said as his eyes slowly blinked open and adapted to the light. "Maybe he just went for a drive."

"That's what I thought," Jennings said, "but she says it's not his way to simply leave without saying anything."

A hunch suddenly occurred to the detective. He hoped he was wrong – but recalling his few run-ins with Wayne and Laura – he knew anything was possible. If his hunch was right, Wayne Sanders was in serious danger.

"Find out where Ms. Barns is staying and get her room number."

"Sir?" Jennings said in a puzzled tone.

"He may have gone back to that place on Birchcroft Drive You remember the one, don't you? I'll meet you at the station in ten minutes," the detective said and hung up.

Jennings knew the exact house to which the detective was referring. A perplexed look formed on his face. He vividly remembered what happened to Officer Malloy and wondered why anyone would ever want to go back there. Anyone in his or her right mind anyway. Without further delay, he pressed the button to go back Laura.

"Sorry about that Ms. Barns," he said. "I was just on the phone with Detective Wilson. I do not want to alarm you, but it is possible that Mr. Saunders went back to the haunted house on Birchcroft Drive."

Laura froze as a look of shock formed on her face. Her left hand slowly rose to the base of her throat. That possibility had not occurred to her. At worst, she thought he just went for a midnight drive. The look of shock turned into one of anger. The receiver creaked softly as her hand squeezed it firmly.

"Ms. Barns?"

"If that's true then you better hope you find him before I do," she said somewhat coldly with a blank stare.

"Where are you exactly? The detective and I will meet you there."

"Why do you need me?" Laura curiously asked.

"Because," Jennings replied, "if he did go back to that god forsaken place you might be the only one who could talk some sense into him."

Relaxing a little, Laura thought about that briefly. She wanted to help Wayne in every possible way she could. At the same time, however, she was furious because he left without even leaving a note. She rolled her eyes and shook her head as if to say, why me?

"The address is 223 Mayfield Street, room 8."

"Okay. Sit tight. We will not be long," Jennings said and hung up.

Laura slammed the receiver down and sat on the edge of the bed. She hoped the authorities were wrong as to Wayne's whereabouts. Everything she read about that place and witnessed there made her dread going back. Not to mention, everything that happened to her in the last few days. She remembered Wayne telling her – on two separate occasions – that she had been temporarily possessed. First by Wendy Saint-Pierre at the barn where they found her body, and then by Nathan Christopher at his home. She also remembered neither experience and was very grateful for that.

Well, I guess I had better get ready, she thought. I cannot go out looking like this.

Standing, she grabbed some clothes and went into the bathroom. She dressed and brushed her hair and teeth, and then went back to sit on the bed to wait for the police.

Just as Laura sat down, the lights went out and darkness engulfed the room. A frightened gasp escaped her lips. Deep down, she hoped it was just a loss of power, but her instincts told her otherwise. A sudden chill shot up her spine and the hair on the back of her neck rose. A glowing white figure of a little girl appeared in her peripheral vision. Laura's heart pounded in her chest. Slowly, she turned, expecting to be horrified yet again but was surprised to see Wendy

Saint-Pierre. The many scars that once covered body her were no longer there, but she did not appear happy. She appeared concerned.

"You must hurry to him," Wendy said. Her small voice almost seemed to echo through the small room. "Go now."

"Go to whom?" Laura asked.

"To the other savior whom freed us," Wendy replied.

"Wayne?" Laura said.

"Yes, he is in great danger."

"Is he where I think he is?" Laura asked.

"Yes," Wendy said, "above the top floor."

"Above the top floor," Laura repeated, obviously confused. "What do you mean above the top floor?"

A gentle knock came to the door and Wendy Saint-Pierre slowly began to vanish. She reached out her hand to Laura.

"Hurry," Wendy added in a panic-stricken whisper before vanishing completely.

The lights turned back on and Laura went to the window and peeked outside. A police car was parked in front of her room and two men stood at her door. She recognized them right away and opened the door.

"Just let me grab my keys," she said.

Laura quickly scooped up her keys from the dresser, shut the lights off and followed the officers outside.

Lieutenant Jennings allowed Laura to sit in the front seat as they piled into the cruiser. They drove off.

"We need to get there as fast as possible," Laura claimed. "I have a very bad feeling."

Without saying a word, Wilson turned on the sirens and stepped on the gas.

Laura thought about what Wendy said. The words played back in her mind repeatedly: Above the top floor… Above the top floor. What could it mean? Unless…the attic. That's it!

"I know where he is," Laura said excitedly. "He is in the attic."

"How can you be sure?" Wilson asked.

"Trust me," Laura said. "That is where he is."

Chapter Thirty-Three
Bound for Trouble

Groaning softly from the pain in his head and torso, Wayne slowly began to stir. The last thing he remembered was slamming into the wall and hitting the floor. He opened his eyes and once again found complete darkness. He attempted to move his arms, but was unable to. Curious, he tried to move his legs but it was no use; the result was the same. Finally, he realized he was restrained and no longer on the floor.

"What the hell?" he mumbled.

Very carefully, he tried once again to free himself and again was unsuccessful. At that point, he realized where he was and what was happening. Utter fear struck him like a ton of bricks. He squirmed harder, but as he did so many very sharp objects pressed into his back. He gasped in pain at the mere sensation of it. To Wayne, it felt like tiny shards of glass piercing into his back. Finally, realizing resistance was futile he stopped moving. He closed his eyes and bowed his head in defeat. Laura's face popped into his mind and he wondered what would happen to her. Scattered memories of their journey of mysteries flashed before his mind: the barn where they found Wendy Saint-Pierre's body and the sewer where they found Norman Henderson. Laura's face covered in blood at Reggie's motel and the mausoleum where they found the note. The loud pounding from inside the old refrigerator at Nathan's home, the rats in the kitchen and Laura hanging upside-down against the wall of the second bedroom. Hearing screams and seeing images of mutilation in the mirror at the clinic, the disfigured face of Nathan Christopher and insects crawling up the mirror. A car crusher that turned on by itself to destroy the remains of a dead body found in an old Crown Victoria.

Father, he prayed, if this is my time then let it be my time. When my suffering is through and this is finally over – if I do not survive – take me, so that Laura can move on with her life and live in happiness. She is suffering also. I ask forgiveness for my sins through Jesus, your son and my lord and…

A deep yet barely audible giggle broke Wayne's concentration. His eyes snapped open and it stopped abruptly. His breath caught in his throat, fearful of what might happen next. He scanned the attic for any sign of Nathan, yet found nothing but complete darkness. He knew it sounded like Nathan's laugh, but wondered if his mind was playing tricks on him. Keening his ears, he listened intently for any type of sound. All was quiet.

Closing his eyes, he bowed his head once again. He was just about to continue praying when he heard the laugh again. Only this time, slightly louder. Before he opened his eyes, he wondered if he should or should not waste his time.

There was nothing there before, he thought. *Why would something be there now?*

The eerie laugh grew a little louder with each passing second. Unable to help himself he lifted his head and opened his eyes yet again, and again nothing was there. His frustration mounted. He knew Nathan was up to his old tricks.

"Nathan!" Wayne shouted.

Nathan popped into view just inches away from Wayne's face. His fiery dark red eyes glared.

Startled, Wayne inhaled a quick gasp at Nathan's unbearable ugliness and his body jerked in fear. The needles ripped into the weak flesh of his back and poked into his spine and shoulder blades. He instantly screamed in agony and the muscles in his back tightened. Yet somehow, miraculously, his neck and skull avoided injury.

Nathan laughed wickedly. His blackish-yellow teeth appeared to gleam in delight. Then his smile quickly faded. He grabbed Wayne by the hair and brought his face as close to Wayne's as possible. At the same time, he held Wayne's head exceptionally close to the needles.

"You pitiful excuse for a human," Nathan said. "I will truly enjoy killing you."

The foul stench of the demon's breath filled Wayne's nostrils and he gaggled. He sensed the needles threatening his neck and skull but waved it off. He was too busy concentrating on the needles in his back. Every time he tried to breathe, the pain grew worse. yet he glared into Nathan's dead eyes with defiance.

"Then what are you waiting for?" Wayne growled hoarsely, gritting his teeth through the pain. "Finish me!"

Nathan giggled again. "No," he said. "This will not be over so easily. I am going to torture you so slowly that you will beg for death!"

Wayne closed his eyes, as if already praying for death. He had no idea what would happen next, but knew whatever it was would be most unpleasant. In one sense, he did hope it would be over quickly, but he did not want to die. He wanted to live and spend the rest of his life with Laura. Nevertheless, he could not help but feel a sense of doom. He was certain the grim reaper would soon be coming for him. Suddenly, Wayne realized how quiet it was. He opened his eyes and realized Nathan was gone. He exhaled a slow breath of relief. At last, he had an opportunity to try to relax his back muscles and ease the needles out. It was a slow and painful process. Several beads of sweat dripped down his face.

Once his back was free of the tiny needles, he let his body drop limply. He took several deep breaths and rested for a moment. His efforts took more energy than he had anticipated. In only a few seconds, he felt something warm drip down the sides of his ribs. Without even looking, he knew it was blood.

"Recite the right verse," a female voice whispered.

Wayne heard the voice and wondered where it came from. To his surprise, it sounded like Wendy Saint-Pierre.

But that's not possible, he thought. *I freed her from this prison.*

He listened closely and waited to see if she would speak again. Unfortunately, the only sound he heard was that of his breathing.

Come on, Wayne thought frustratedly. *If that is you, Wendy – I need your help. Say it again!*

Silence remained.

Wayne bowed his head again. He was about to continue praying when he heard something. It was a faint sound, distant and barely audible. To him, it sounded like a footstep, but he could not be sure unless it happened again. He lifted his head and looked for any signs of Nathan – or anyone else – but found none. Then he heard it again, this time a little closer and heavier; then again. Now he was certain someone was approaching. His heart beat faster as the heat of anxiety mounted from the pit of his stomach to his face. Even though he was blind from the darkness, he focused on the ominous sounds of the footsteps. He had a bad feeling that he knew who it was.

"I knew you would be back Nathan," Wayne said.

The footsteps continued at a relatively slow pace, drawing closer and closer to Wayne. They stopped right beside the contraption. Unbeknownst to Wayne, it was the side where the lever was that operated the contraption.

Wayne's fear doubled instantly. He began shaking uncontrollably. He had no idea what was about to happen but felt that he was about to find out.

A deep yet slow eerie moan filled Wayne's ears, followed by a loud '*clank.*'

The contraption creaked to life and the rusty barrel slowly began to turn.

Wayne immediately knew what was happening and arched his back to keep it away from the needles.

"You son of a bitch!" he screamed.

Nathan laughed wickedly in reply.

What Wayne did not know, was that his wrists were also turning. He was so worried about his back that he paid no mind to his wrists. It took a few seconds, but he finally realized it when he felt a pull in the pectoral muscles of his chest. At that point, he knew time was a luxury he no longer had. Suddenly, he remembered what the female voice said about reciting the right verse. He could not believe it took him that long to get it. He wanted to lash out at himself for his lack of vision but had no more time to waste. The pain in his chest was growing and his back was getting closer to the needles. Every passing second he wasted, brought him closer to death. He quickly recalled the verse and recited it:

"I call upon the dark lord, Satan," Wayne spat through the pain. "Keep thy word and punish this – your failed servant. He deserves not to dwell in this house above your world."

"No!" Nathan shouted. "Be silent!"

Another loud *'clank'* resounded through the attic and the needled barrel went a little faster.

Wayne wanted to scream out in agony but refused to give Nathan the pleasure. He continued the verse.

"Chain him to your fiery gates…"

"No!" Nathan howled and appeared in front of Wayne. He grabbed Wayne by the hair and glared into his determined eyes. "He will never let me out again!"

Wayne stared back into Nathan's eyes with fierce defiance. Warm tears dripped from his eyes but he quickly blinked them away.

"And allow him no escape. I beg of thee! I beg of thee! I beg of thee!"

Nathan released his grip on Wayne's hair and took three big steps back. The look on his face was that of disbelief. He crumpled to his knees and stared at the only man who challenged and beat him.

"Do you know what you have done?" Nathan asked.

He looked at Wayne and his eyes turned black as night.

Wayne's arms felt as though they were about to snap and the needles began to nip at his flesh, but he no longer cared about that. He succumbed to the fact that he was about to be torn to shreds and die. In his last remaining moments, all he wanted was to see Nathan vanquished back to hell. He continued to stare Nathan down.

"Yes," Wayne replied in a husky growl through gritted teeth. "So, fuck you!"

As if by a miracle of God, the barrel stopped moving. Wayne never took his eyes off Nathan, but he could not help but wonder what happened.

Nathan howled loudly and looked up at the ceiling as flames engulfed him. He vanished in only a few seconds.

Wayne stared into the darkness, glad it was finally over. Now all he wanted to do was fall sleep. He closed his eyes but found he was in too much pain to sleep.

'Clank, clank'

Wayne expected the barrel to start moving again, but to his amazement, it did not. This time, the pole his wrists were cuffed to was all that moved. It slowly lowered him away from the needles. A sense of relief overcame him before he passed out from exhaustion.

Chapter Thirty-Four
Two Days Later

Sitting in a chair at his bedside, Laura hoped Wayne would be okay. The sound of the heart monitor and drops from the intravenous were all she heard. The nurses walked back and forth in the hallway and communicated their tasks, but she paid no attention. She wondered why Wayne had to be so stupid and brave and go back to that house. She recalled Wilson and Jennings going up into the attic, insisting she wait there in the bedroom. She watched their flashlights move until they stopped. One of them said, *'over here.'* After that, there was nothing but silence. The suspense was eating her up inside. All she wanted to hear was that he was okay. Then she heard a voice from the attic but was unable to make out most of what it said. She heard the words, *'emergency, cutters'* and *'now.'* Panic struck her like a wall of bricks and she climbed up into the attic. They tried to stop her from seeing him in that condition, but she insisted. When her eyes gazed down at him, her heart dropped and she screamed. She was stunned and dumbfounded. His body was limp and attached to a device she could only define as evil. There was blood all over his back and on the floor.

A gentle knock came to the door. Laura turned to see a female doctor standing there. She seemed young. Laura assumed she was roughly her age, perhaps early-thirties. The doctor motioned Laura to join her in the hallway.

Not knowing if he was alive or dead, Wayne began to hear a slow faint beeping sound. His eyes remained closed and he wondered where he was. He felt as though he was flat on his back, and somehow sensed he was no longer on the torturous device. Yet he did not know if he was still at the haunted house. He was afraid that if he opened his eyes, Nathan would be in front of him.

"Your friend was very lucky," he heard a distant female voice say.

Wayne did not recognize the voice and wondered who it was. He only knew it did not sound like Laura.

"Any longer and he could have died," the same voice added.

Where am I? Wayne wondered.

Trying to stir, his breath caught in his throat from the pain. It was the type of pain that made him feel as though he was ran over by a moving vehicle. Finally, his eyes slowly opened and without moving his head, he scanned the room. He was glad to see he was no longer at Nathan's home. A brief smile formed on his face as he realized he was in a hospital.

I think I am okay, he thought. *Let me try moving my fingers.*

He wiggled his fingers and felt a tiny poke on his right hand. Curious, he lifted his right forearm and discovered an Intravenous in his wrist. He frowned.

Or maybe not.

"Well, look who is finally awake," a familiar voice said.

Wayne slowly cocked his head to the left and found Laura looking at him from the doorway. She was speaking to a woman wearing a white jacket and a stethoscope around her neck.

Well, that answers my question, he thought with a low-sounding grunt.

Wayne closed his eyes for what seemed like only a split second. When he opened them again, Laura was standing by his bedside. A smile beamed across her face. Not quite getting it, he wondered why she was so happy.

"There is my man," she said. "You must be starving. The doctor says you can start eating right away."

"Am I?" Wayne asked weakly. He did not feel hungry at all. "Should I be?"

Laura nodded. "Yes, you should be," she said. "You have been sleeping for two days now."

At first, Wayne did not quite comprehend what she had just said. It took a few seconds to register in his mind. Suddenly, his eyes snapped open.

"Two days?" he grumbled and tried to sit up again.

Laura quickly tried to warn him to stay still, but he was too stubborn to listen. Immediately he growled in pain and laid back down.

"Let that be a lesson to you," another familiar voice said as the sound of his footsteps entered the room.

Laura turned to see Detective Wilson and watched as he walked to the foot of Wayne's bed.

"You just lay there and listen to this young lady," Wilson added. "If it was not for her, you would be dead now."

Wayne thought about that for a moment before he replied. "Yes, I know." He reached for Laura's hand and gently squeezed it. "Thank you."

"I am not the only one he should thank though," Laura said as she glanced at the detective and then back at Wayne. "The ambulance crew were the ones got you out of that…that nightmarish—" She paused and looked away, as if she heard something behind her. She did not want Wayne to see that she was crying. Wiping the tears away with the back of her hand, she took a deep breath and turned back to Wayne. "The detective and Lieutenant Jennings helped too. When I saw your limp body dangling from that thing, I honestly thought you were dead. Don't you ever run off like that again. So help me. If you do – next time you had better be dead. Because if I catch you, I will give you even more pain than you have now." Laura paused again and pointed her index finger warningly. "I mean it."

Detective Wilson bowed his head to hide a smile. He was married once and he too learned a few lessons. He knew when a woman spoke that way, she was being very serious.

Tread lightly son, he thought. *You are swimming in dangerous waters.*

"Honey," Wayne said. "I promise you, and God as my witness, my mystery solving days are over."

"No more paranormal mysteries?" Laura said.

Wayne raised his right hand. "No more haunting mysteries."

Detective Wilson patted Wayne on the shoulder and smiled.

"You have no idea how glad I am to hear that," he said. "By the way, this is for the both of you," he added, removing a small orange envelope from his tunic.

Laura accepted it. "What is it?" she asked.

"Just a little token from the Edmundston Police Department," the detective said with sincerity.

"Oh, thank you but…" Laura said and tried to hand the envelope back.

"Nonsense," Wilson said. "Listen to me. You two did something that we were never able to do." He paused and looked around to make sure no one was nearby. "Even if you did have help from the great beyond, you still solved three cold-cases. You both deserve that," he concluded, nodding at the envelope. "Enjoy it. Well folks, you take care now."

"Thank you," Laura said.

"You too," Wayne added.

The detective turned and headed for the door. As he neared it, the telephone on Wayne's night table rang. He stopped and turned to look at it. For all he knew, it could have been for him.

Laura looked at it curiously. She had not ordered any telephone service since Wayne's arrival. She picked up the receiver and put it to her ear.

"Hello?" she said.

A masculine voice spoke. "I beg your pardon, Miss, but would this be the room of Mr. Wayne Saunders?"

"Yes," Laura answered slowly. "Whom shall I say is asking?"

"My name is Gregory Hanson. I am a dispatcher with the Edmundston Police Department. I am looking for Detective James Wilson. Would he still be around by chance?"

Laura looked to the senior officer and nodded at him.

"Actually, yes he is still here," Laura acknowledged. "One moment please."

Wilson approached her and she handed the receiver to him.

"Wilson here," he said.

"Corporal Hanson here sir," said the dispatcher. "The lab just called and requested I contact you immediately. They said they have the results you have been waiting for."

"Excellent! Thank you Corporal," Wilson said in a business-like tone.

The detective hung up and dialed the morgue right away. On the second ring, Tom McQueen answered.

"Edmundston Morgue?"

"Hey Tom," Wilson said. "I understand you have some news for me."

"Hello James," Tom said. "Her name was Victoria Green."

"Are you sure?" Wilson asked.

"Quite sure," Tom replied casually.

"Damn, you are good," Wilson commented with a smirk. "I must admit, I actually anticipated your answer. I will inform her family personally."

"Thank you," Tom said. "It's a gift you know."

Wilson chuckled, thanked Tom again and hung up. He turned to Wayne and Laura.

"I just found out who your last victim was," he said.

"Yes? Please, do tell," Wayne said.

Wilson looked down at Wayne. He remembered how Wayne had trouble with the name at the junkyard. Now, Wilson knew he was on the right track.

"You're going to kick yourself," Wilson said.

Wayne smiled and rolled his eyes. "I am already kicking myself for going back to that house," he said.

"Her name was Victoria Green," Wilson said. "She was also Emily the librarian's mother."

I knew it, said the look on Wayne's face.

Laura giggled softly. She remembered how hard Wayne tried to uncover the woman's name. Still, she was a little surprised he managed to get the others.

"I knew you would kick yourself," Wilson said with a grin. "Well, I hate to cut this short but I have to get back to the office."

"Thank you again detective," Wayne said.

"You two take care now," Wilson added and turned to head for the door once again.

This time, he made it through the door.

Wayne and Laura listened to his heavy footsteps vanish. Their eyes then turned to the mysterious orange envelope. They could not help but be curious as to what was inside it.

"Shall I open this?" Laura asked.

"Later," Wayne replied. "By the way. Did the doctor tell you what was wrong with me?"

"Which one? Ben the shrink or the one that told me you were lucky to be alive?"

"Yeah him," Wayne said. "The one who called me lucky."

"Well, let's see," Laura said as she recalled what the doctor said. "Both your pectoral muscles were torn, your left triceps muscle had been ripped while the right one was strained, and your back needed five hundred stitches."

The look on Wayne's face said he was sorry he asked.

"Oh, and something about a torn ACL," Laura added in a confused tone.

Wayne noticed her puzzled look. "The ACL is the Anterior Cruciate Ligament. It's a ligament in the knee."

"Oh." Laura said.

"So it's pretty bad, huh?" Wayne said.

"Yeah, but it's nothing that a lot of painkillers and time cannot heal," Laura replied and smiled.

Wayne felt a low growl in his stomach. He glanced down at it curiously. Only moments ago, he was certain he was not hungry. Apparently, he was wrong.

"Laura?"

"Yes dear?"

"I guess I really am hungry."

Laura nodded and smiled. "Yes, I know. I heard it from here. I will be back shortly."

Laura left the room and Wayne turned to look out the window. The bright light made his eyes squint a little. It appeared to be a beautiful day. The sun was shining and the blue sky never looked bluer. At least, from where he was laying, there was not a cloud in sight. A smile broke into his face again and his eyes grew heavy. He closed them and drifted off into sleep.

www.ingramcontent.com/pod-product-compliance
Lightning Source LLC
Chambersburg PA
CBHW061504050726
47593CB00002B/439